Margaret Muir emigrated from England to Australia to raise her family. After a career in diagnostic cytology she completed a writing degree and is now a full-time author. Like her previous novels, *Sea Dust* and *The Twisting Vine*, this book draws on her love of Yorkshire and in particular the moors and villages around Leeds where she grew up.

You can visit her website at:
www.margaretmuirauthor.com

THE BLACK THREAD

1895. Amy's father left home before she was born, but fifteen years later Amos Dodd, a sadistic killer recently released from Armley jail, appears on the doorstep. When her mother dies, Amy escapes her father's clutches, and on the towpath of the Leeds and Liverpool canal encounters a bargee and his wife who take her to Saltaire. There she meets a young engineer from the mill and makes a shocking discovery. Determined to uncover the truth about the man she hates and unravel the mystery surrounding her birth, Amy returns to Leeds — only to step back into the lion's den . . .

Books by Margaret Muir
Published by The House of Ulverscroft:

SEA DUST
THE TWISTING VINE

MARGARET MUIR

◆

THE BLACK THREAD

Complete and Unabridged

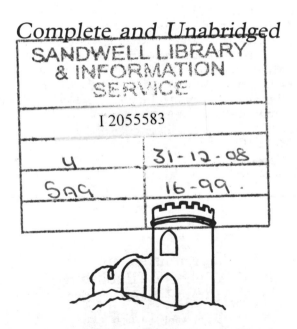

ULVERSCROFT
Leicester

First published in Great Britain in 2007 by
Robert Hale Limited
London

First Large Print Edition
published 2009
by arrangement with
Robert Hale Limited
London

British Library CIP Data

Muir, Margaret 1943 –
    The black thread.—Large print ed.—
Ulverscroft large print series: crime
1. Fathers and daughters—Fiction
2. Murderers—Fiction 3. Engineers—Fiction
4. Leeds and Liverpool Canal (England)—Fiction
5. England, Northern—Fiction 6. Detective and
mystery stories 7. Large type books
I. Title
823.9'2 [F]

ISBN 978–1–84782–517–9

Published by
F. A. Thorpe (Publishing)
Anstey, Leicestershire

Set by Words & Graphics Ltd.
Anstey, Leicestershire
Printed and bound in Great Britain by
T. J. International Ltd., Padstow, Cornwall

This book is printed on acid-free paper

I dedicate this book to a fellow Yorkshireman, a friend, and an inspirational work colleague, Dr Darrel Whitaker. Darrel's tireless work in the field of diagnostic cytology, cancer research and teaching, particularly in the area of asbestos-related diseases, was acknowledged worldwide. Darrel died on 23 April 2007 following his personal battle with cancer.

By the margin, willow veiled
Slide the heavy barges trailed
By slow horses; and unhailed
The shallop flitteth silken-sailed
   Skimming down to Camelot:
 But who hath seen her wave her hand?
 Or at the casement seen her stand?
 Or is she known in all the land,
   The Lady of Shalott?

Alfred Lord Tennyson

Acknowledgements

To my editor Gill Jackson and all the staff at Robert Hale Limited for their expert help and guidance in the production of my books, I thank you.

1

Leeds, 1895

The Homecoming

Whenever she heard her mother crying, Amy always remembered the day her father came home.

Though she was almost fifteen, she had never met her father before that wet Saturday when he stepped over the doorstep and entered her life. Up to that time, the name Amos Dodd had hardly ever been spoken of.

What she did remember was nattering her mother with questions about him. Why had he gone away? Where had he gone to? When was he coming back?

'You'll find out, one day,' was the most Lisbeth Dodd would say, leaving Amy to draw her own conclusions. All she ever learnt was that he had left home shortly before she was born. As he'd never returned, she presumed he'd gone abroad to seek his fortune. But sometimes, she wasn't sure.

Most of the men in the street worked at Fanshaw's Mill. They returned home regular

1

as clockwork every night. A few worked away on the railways, but they always came home on Sundays. One or two went away and never came back. They'd sailed to America in search of gold. But they'd taken their wives and children with them, and everything they owned.

Unlike those men, her father had gone away leaving a wife and unborn child, and to her knowledge, not once, since he'd left, had he written. It was possible, she thought, that he couldn't read or write, as there were never any messages from him. No word at all. Then she wondered why her mother hadn't followed him, perhaps tried to join him wherever he was. She was puzzled why her mother wouldn't answer questions about him. Didn't she know where he was or didn't she want to say? Perhaps she knew he was successful and felt jealous or guilty?

Despite not knowing, Amy longed for that day when he'd return. She'd convinced herself her father would be rich and knew exactly how that special event would unfold — a scene she'd imagined thousands of times. It'd be like the reception Mr Medley got every night, only a hundred times better.

Since she'd been old enough to climb the cellar steps, Amy had sat on the top one, gazed out through the iron railings and watched their neighbour trudging home from the mill. Though his dark hair and whiskers were always speckled with balls of fluff, his eyes would glint when he saw her and he would wave. Everyone in the street knew when Moses Medley was heading home. He was always whistling and it was always the same merry tune.

As soon as Mrs Medley heard him, she'd open the door, and the two youngest would scamper down the pavement to meet him. When the pair was within arms' reach, he'd squat down on the cobbles, put his hand in his pocket and pull out a sweet for each of them. Returning the boys' infectious smiles, he'd ruffle their hair, then swing the bigger lad on to his shoulders. With the little one cupped in the crook of his arm, the gentle-giant of a man would continue up the street to deposit the pair at his wife's feet.

'Inside, you two! Wash your 'ands,' Mrs Medley would say. 'Tea'll be ready in two ticks.' It was always the same. Never changed. And as the boys ran inside, Mr Medley would lean forward and peck his wife on the cheek, and she would grin back at him and tap him playfully on the leg. Then he'd wink and follow her inside, closing the door quietly behind him.

With that homecoming fixed in her mind

firm as any gutter grate, Amy knew, when her father returned, it would be a memorable event. Amos Dodd would swagger up the street, bold as brass, dressed in his Sunday best, but he'd not be whistling, he'd be shouting, calling her name at the top of his voice. 'Amy Dodd! Amy Dodd! Where are you?'

He wouldn't care what people thought, and she wouldn't care either. And when she heard him, she'd run up the steps from the cellar, and gaze up at his kindly face through the iron railings, his soft hair outlined against the sky.

She was sure he'd be a fine figure of a man, and he'd bend down and kiss her through the bars. Then he'd pull his hand from his pocket, but in place of sweets, there'd be coins — gold coins and lots of them. And in his other hand he'd have a box tied up with fancy ribbon which he'd present to Lisbeth, his wife. Then he'd hug her and she'd invite him in. But he'd say he wasn't going to live in that dingy cellar, that he'd come back to take them with him to a new life in a country far away . . .

It was a long-time dream!

And it was so very wrong.

How stupid she had been!

In all those years, she never knew that her

father had been living not more than a mile from the two-roomed cellar which she and her mother called home. Lisbeth had never said that her husband, Amos Dodd, had spent the last fifteen years staring at the sky through iron bars but that those bars were on the ugly round tower which dominated the Leeds skyline — Armley Jail.

★   ★   ★

The thirteenth of April 1895 was a Saturday. And it was wet. The rain hadn't stopped since early morning and when it poured like that, the water on the street overflowed the gutters, washed over the pavement and cascaded down the cellar steps into their tiny yard. Puddles formed quickly and continued filling until the whole yard was a reservoir several inches deep. With nowhere else to go, it slid over the doorstep, poking its broad wet tongue through the gap under the door. Once inside, it slithered and squirmed until it found the grooves between the slabs, branching into fingers and trickling silently along the narrow channels. As a child, Amy loved watching the water, wondering which stream would win in the race to the other side of the kitchen.

Thinking back to 13 April, her mother

5

must have known her husband was returning. For several days there was awkwardness about her, a distance which had never existed before. It was during that week that the sunshine disappeared from her eyes.

From the day Amos Dodd returned, Amy never heard her mother laugh. But she certainly heard her cry.

He never knocked when he arrived, just flung the door open and stood on the doorstep, dripping wet, allowing the wind and rain to blow across the room. At the table, Amy glanced at her mother, expecting her to speak, but Lisbeth said nothing. Then she looked at her father and her dream of his homecoming died. It fizzled like the flame of a snuffed candle.

Amos Dodd was far from the father she'd envisioned. He was short. The same height as her mother and perhaps only an inch taller than her. His coat was wet, smelled wet, and was pitted with holes where the moths had chewed through it. The sleeves were too short and, though he was thin, the buttons hardly met across the chest. He certainly wasn't a rich man.

Needless to say, there was no parcel with ribbons under his arm, only a sodden bundle of old clothing tied up with twine. The only foreign thing he brought into the house was the smell of a smoky alehouse.

'Bloody rain!' he said, dropping the bundle and throwing his wet hat on to the horsehair chair in the corner. Though the fire reflected a glow on his wet face, it didn't disguise the pallor of his skin.

She'd imagined he'd have a mop of yellow hair, just like her own, but his hair was short cropped and black as chimney soot. Bristling straight back from his temples, it was divided in half by a cap of crusty skin from which erupted one ugly black cauliflower wart and three single hairs. She stared.

'That's it, is it?' he said bluntly.

For a moment, Amy thought he was looking at something behind her, then she realized he was looking at her.

Lisbeth nodded. 'Say hello to your father.'

Was this really her father? she asked herself.

When her mother nudged her, she mumbled the word, 'Hello.'

'Huh!' he said, casting his eyes over the frugal furnishings. Amy held her mother's hand as he moved about the room, sniffing and pawing things like a wild-eyed feral cat. He opened a drawer, shuffled the contents noisily, then slammed it shut. Peered into the iron pot. Dipped his finger in the stew and sucked it clean. Then he reached for the metal vase and rattled its contents before tipping them out on the mantelshelf. Running his fingers through the assortment of pins, buttons, needles and hooks, he ignored the ones that fell off and dropped to the hearth.

With a smirk on his face, he stepped through to the small room where the bed was. As far as Amy could remember, there had never been a door hanging in that gap. Only the remnants of one rotted upright remained fixed to the wall. After rubbing his back across it, her father unfastened his coat and let it drop on the floor.

'Come here,' he said.

She felt her mother's hand tighten on hers.

'Come here, woman, I said!'

Amy suddenly felt afraid. Lisbeth Dodd had never responded to anyone like that before. She'd been a self-sufficient woman, regarded as quietly confident and hardworking. Though she usually kept herself to herself, she was praised on the street for having raised a daughter with no man to support her.

'Can it wait till later, Amos?' she said quietly. 'How about I get you a nice cup of tea?'

The cutlery jumped on the table as his fist thumped down. 'No, it can't bloody wait. I've waited fifteen bloody years. You get in there right now, or I'll bloody well drag you in!'

Lisbeth didn't move. Her grip tightened. Amy could sense her mother's heart was racing.

'It's either you or the brat! Take your choice. I'm not fussy.'

As he spoke he slid the braces from his shoulders and began unfastening the buttons on his trousers.

'Go to Mrs Medley's, Amy, tell her . . . '

'You stay right where you are, girl. You don't move one step outside this door!'

With his pale eyes fixed on her, Amy froze.

He didn't tell Lisbeth again, just grabbed her by the wrist and dragged her through the opening in the wall and pushed her towards the bed. She offered little resistance.

Whatever happened after that, Amy didn't see, though she heard the sounds well enough. She thought they would never stop. The beat of the iron bed-frame drumming against the wall till it rose to a crescendo. Her mother's pleadings: 'No, Amos. Don't, Amos. Please stop, you're hurting me.' Then a muffled, painful cry — and his breathing, fast and laboured, like a man running from a pack of wild dogs.

Almost as abruptly as the noise had

started, it stopped, save for the sound of her mother sobbing.

Edging slowly to the entrance of the windowless room, Amy peered at the bed. She could barely see her mother on it. Her face and arms were buried under her cotton petticoat; only her long red hair was visible on the pillow. She was pinned beneath her father, who was spreadeagled over her. Amos Dodd lay motionless, eyes closed, his trousers bunched around his boots.

It was the first time she'd seen a man's bare bottom. It was the same colour as the petticoat — greyish-white. The soles of his boots glistened even in that dull light. They were thick with mud and still wet. She was thankful her mother couldn't see her, though she wanted to touch her, hold her. After watching and waiting for a moment, she stepped slowly back. The only sound she could hear were her mother's sobs. She was crying in a way she had never heard her cry before.

★　★　★

The fact he found no money hidden in the house incensed Amos. After turning everything upside-down, he eventually had to accept that the pair had nothing put aside.

10

'It's past time she had a proper job,' he said, hardly looking at Amy. 'Waste of time doing people's odd jobs and errands. What does she make? A farthing here or a bag of scones there. With a proper job, a girl her age would bring home near ten shillings a week.'

He'd have sent Lisbeth out to work too, but she argued the jobs she did for the landlord provided them with the cellar rent free. They couldn't afford to live anywhere else unless Amos went out and got a job. As for Amy returning to school, Lisbeth took the brunt of his anger.

'What good's learning to a girl,' he said. 'Don't need to figure numbers to produce a dozen kids. She should've been working when she were eleven. The younger the better, I say.'

$\star \quad \star \quad \star$

The following day, Lisbeth took her daughter to the main office at Fanshaw's Mill.

The man perched behind the tall desk only spoke to Amy once. 'What's your name, lass?' he said.

'Amy Dodd,' she answered timidly.

After that he directed all the questions to her mother. He wanted to know how old she was. If she was healthy. Asked if she had bugs in her hair. Did she cough at night? Did her ankles swell? Had she ever run away from home?

'We don't tolerate cheek or misbehaving,' he said.

'My Amy's a good girl.'

He made a note in his book. 'All right,' he said, after checking her fingers. 'She looks healthy enough. She can start tomorrow. Come here to this office in the morning at six o'clock sharp. Do you understand, lass?'

Having no choice, Amy nodded.

'And get her a cap, missus. I don't want chunks of her hair getting caught up in the machines! A young lass had her scalp ripped off a few months back. Bad for production, it was!'

★   ★   ★

It was still dark when she arrived the next morning though the mill windows glowed from the light of hundreds of gas lamps. Climbing the seventy stone steps to the spinning floor made her legs ache. It was something she would have to get used to. It was the same with the din. She'd never heard so much noise — or witnessed so many objects moving at one time. Hundreds of bobbins were constantly turning and filling, while girls, younger than herself, moved up and down the gait between the machines removing the full ones, winding threads on to empty ones, or deftly joining loose ends of broken yarn. Though she tried hard to concentrate on what the manageress was saying, she could hear little for the whirring of spindles and clatter of machinery. She was relieved when a man tapped her on the shoulder and indicated for her to follow him. He said she looked fit and strong and that they needed someone to work at the carding machine. He also said, if she did well, she'd get more money working down there.

By seven o'clock, she'd been shown how to feed greasy wool into the mouth of the machine and left on her own. One of the few instructions she was given was to make sure her sleeves didn't get caught on the hooks as they tore at the tangle of matted fibres.

The carding machine was the ugliest piece of machinery Amy had ever seen — not that she'd seen much machinery before. It roared with every rotation and resembled a giant rolling pin with dozens of sharp hooks sticking out of it. The looms and bobbins and their webs of dyed wools were pretty by comparison, and the women who worked them didn't look unhappy as they worked. Some even smiled.

During her first few weeks, Amy went home each evening totally exhausted, but at night slept poorly on her makeshift bed on the kitchen floor. For several nights, she woke with the same troubled dream. A huge mouth, set with sharp teeth, was threatening to devour her. Lying awake, she'd long to go to her mother, but she knew she couldn't because her father was there.

On the nights when the dreams didn't wake her, it was the sound of the bed frame that did. Or her mother's pleading cries, 'No, Amos, let me be.' Then as the banging continued, she'd visualize her father — not his face, but his bare white bottom and his trousers bunched up below his knees. And every night when she woke, she'd pray he'd go away.

In the mornings, she'd hear her mother get up quietly and tiptoe around, thinking she was still asleep. Amy would watch as she lit the lamp, then set the fire. Lying on the hard floor, she'd listen to her mother sighing or sobbing, but never humming or singing the songs she used to sing. They'd speak little over breakfast, and only when it was time for Amy to leave for the mill would her mother fold her arms around her. Sometimes it seemed she held her so tightly it was as though she didn't ever want to let her go.

Lisbeth never once spoke the words 'good-bye', and she never smiled.

From the day her father came home, Amy never saw her mother smile properly again.

$$\star \quad \star \quad \star$$

Nothing changed much over the next three years. At first Amos Dodd hardly ever left the cellar, except for a visit to the Hungry Crow. He never got a job, so at times it was hard to know where his money came from, but neither Amy nor her mother dare ask. On a few occasions he worked for a few days, but he always complained about it. Said he hated the overseers and managers. He hated the navvies. Amos Dodd seemed to hate everyone and everything. He disliked the neighbours, and didn't like Lisbeth even speaking with them. He hated the cellar they lived in. Amy hated it too, though she remembered at one time it had been a cosy home.

Over those years, Amy learned never to answer back; in fact she spoke as little as possible. She learned new words from her father, words she didn't know the meaning of but knew they were utterances no god-fearing girl should ever let pass through her lips.

During that time, Amy watched her mother fade from a poor but proud woman to a timid wife who lived in fear of the man she had married. Though Amy never saw him hit her, she did see the bruises on her mother's face. The rest of her body, Lisbeth always kept covered.

The lifestyle Amy and her mother had enjoyed quickly disappeared. It melted like snowflakes on water. From the day her father returned, nothing was ever the same between them. They couldn't talk freely with him around. Couldn't share jokes or laugh. And they hardly ever hugged.

Amy missed her mother's touch and the closeness they had shared through the long winter nights in the only bed. How protective her arms had felt, wrapped around her whenever she'd been hurt. How warm the embrace that comforted her when she'd been sick. How secure her mother's lap when she'd laid her head against it and fallen asleep in front of the fire. Now there was neither coal nor money to buy any. Alone and rejected, Amy resented her father for returning and demanding her mother's attention. How she hated the man who had come between them.

The only thing that puzzled her was that her father never tried to have his way with her. Perhaps her mother had threatened him, or perhaps it was because she allowed him to use her whenever he wanted. There were times, however, when his pale stare fixed her in a way that made her shudder.

Because she woke early, Amy liked to light the fire and have the kettle boiling before her mother got up. That gave them a little time together. Sharing whispered words, they'd eat porridge and talk about everyday things: work and the weather and the folk on the street. The man sleeping noisily in the other room was never mentioned.

It was when they talked together privately that Amy sensed there were things her mother wanted to say, and there were questions she needed to ask. Yet they never dare chance those conversations in the house. Their only time to talk intimately was on Sunday. Twice a month they would walk to the chapel, arm in arm, never hurrying. It didn't matter if the congregation were already singing the first hymn when they arrived because they never went in. Lisbeth wouldn't step foot inside the place, but she wouldn't say why.

'What is it, Mum?' Amy asked.

'Nothing, love.'

'But there is something, I know there is. Why won't you tell me?'

'Not now,' Lisbeth said wearily. 'But one day, I promise, I will.'

'Why don't you leave Father?' Amy asked. 'Why don't we both leave and run away?'

'I can't.'

'Why not? If we both worked, we could go far away, live somewhere else. We'd be better off without having him to feed.'

She sighed heavily. 'You don't know him like I do. He'd follow us and find us. He'd never let me leave him. He'd see me dead first.'

'Did he kill someone? Is that why you are afraid of him? Is that why he went to jail?'

Tears welled in her mother's eyes but she stared straight ahead without blinking.

'He swore it were an accident, that he had nothing to do with it.'

'But they sent him to jail.'

'And he still said he didn't do it.'

'Who did he kill, Mum?'

Lisbeth paused and put her hand across her mouth, muffling her words. 'He killed my sister, Rose. She was five years younger than you are now. She was only thirteen.'

2

Fanshaw's Mill

1898

Harold Lister's first visit to Fanshaw's Mill was in June, about a month after the accident which claimed young Sally Plunket's life. It was the sleeve of her cardigan which had got caught in the carding machine and before the power could be stopped it had dragged her arm and half her chest into its teeth. Word was passed around that the stained wool went right through to the next batch of cloth but Amy knew for a fact that wasn't the case because she, and two other girls, had the job of stripping the machine and sending the fibre back to be scoured.

It was Mr Fanshaw himself who first showed the gentleman through the mill. Though not a word was spoken out loud, the message was quickly mouthed across every floor in the mill that the good-looking young man, who walked with a slight limp, was an engineer. That he was unmarried and that his leg had been broken when he was run over by a coach when he was a boy. And that he was working on a new shuttle which would fly faster than the shuttles used in most Yorkshire mills, and when it was finished he would be taking it to America where his ultimate wish was to build a bridge. It amazed Amy how the women got their information and how fast it travelled in the mill, where the noise from the looms was such that you could hardly hear yourself think.

When Harold Lister visited Fanshaw's, it wasn't to introduce a new machine but to examine the old ones and find ways to make them safer.

Seeing his soft hands, it was obvious he didn't work hard for a living. His face was soft too, with a fine fuzz of ginger hair matted loosely along the sides of his jaw. The top of his head bore a thatch of auburn curls.

Amy was surprised and a little concerned when the overlooker pulled her from her machine and told her she'd to run downstairs and report to the office. Girls off the floor never got asked into the office. When she was told the engineer wanted to ask her about the machines, she was puzzled. What could she tell him about machines?

* * *

'It's Amy Dodd, is that correct?' the young gentleman said, putting down his pen.

Glancing across to the table, Amy recognized her name in his journal. The ink was still wet.

'Yes, sir.'

'Tell me, Amy, I hear you used to work on the carding machine.'

'Aye,' she said, 'but that was two or three years ago.'

'Have you been on it recently?'

'Aye, these past four weeks since . . . '

'Yes,' he said. 'And I gather you are doing well. You're a mender now?'

'I'm a learner. But I'm told I'm doing all right and I'll be a mender before long. I don't miss anything.'

'Then you must have good eyes.' He took out a pocket book and made a note in it in pencil. 'Tell me. Amy, what do you think about when you're feeding the carding machine?'

Amy laughed. 'Don't rightly know,' she said. 'Anything that comes into me head, I suppose.'

'Do you think about the wool or the machine?'

Amy shook her head and, glancing over his shoulder, gazed out through the window. At the other side of the river, the brickworks boasted one of the tallest chimneys around and the pall of smoke spewing from it rose higher than those from the surrounding factories. Bent like stalks of wheat in a wind, the grey columns leaned towards the city, trailing their soot and ash over the rooftops.

'Out with it, lass,' the overlooker said. 'Mr Lister ain't got all day.'

Amy took a deep breath. 'I think about getting as far away from this place as possible.'

The overlooker gave her a sour look. Mr Lister allowed a smile to curl in the corners of his lips before turning his face away.

'Have you been measured before?' the engineer asked.

'No, sir,' she said, not knowing rightly what he meant. She soon found out, as he took a yard-long ruler and laid it across her arms. Then he measured her height against the wall and recorded the figures. After that he asked some strange questions, like what clothes she wore when she worked on the machine in summer, also in winter. Every answer she gave, he marked down in his notebook.

'Thank you, Amy,' he said, closing his book, then before he had chance to add anything further, the overlooker bustled her from the office. Once outside, she was told to get back to work and make sure she made up the time that had been wasted. The girls on the nearby looms gave her questioning looks. Usually a call to the office meant bad news. But as Amy trotted up the stone steps, she felt elated. All she could think about was the young gentleman with the wispy whiskers. Fancy him asking to speak to her! He even called her by her name. And when he touched her accidentally, she'd felt a flutter in her tummy. Then she reminded herself he was only talking to her because of what happened to Sally Plunket and that there'd be no possibility he'd speak to the likes of her outside the mill.

She was wrong. Not that he actually spoke, but he almost did. It happened as she was leaving that same evening. She was chatting with a group of women as they came out of the yard. It was always the same at finishing-off time; no one wanted to hang around, but three of the women who lived on the same street were asking about her mother, saying they hadn't seen much of her lately.

As they passed under the stone archway at Fanshaw's main gate, Amy spotted Mr Lister on the pavement by the lamppost. He was speaking with another well-dressed gentleman. Wearing her mother's old coat, which didn't fit properly, and with a scarf tied around her head, she felt dowdy and kept her head down. But she couldn't resist a quick glance as she walked by. She caught his eye and though he never stopped talking, he smiled broadly, his eyes following her as she passed.

It was true he didn't actually say anything, but she reckoned if he'd been on his own, and she'd been on her own, he'd have spoken. He'd have said, 'Good evening, Amy,' and doffed his hat. She never mentioned it to the other girls. If she had, they'd have told her she was daft, but she was sure it wasn't her imagination playing tricks.

The next day Mr Lister returned to her floor. He was checking the combs and the drum carder. Because he wasn't wearing a coat and his sleeves were rolled up, he looked more like one of the workers. This time he didn't have his pocket book or journal or measuring stick.

'Good morning,' he shouted as he came up the stairs. 'It's Amy Dodd, isn't it?'

She nodded, gave him a smile and continued what she was doing.

Around her, machines rumbled and churned. Further along the floor, looms clicked and clacked, belts slapped and a thousand spindles spun endlessly, but Amy was glad of the noise. Silence was always more embarrassing. Sneaking an occasional peep from the corner of her eye, she could see the young gent was watching her every move, but she didn't turn her face his way. It was a funny feeling having his eyes on her. Nice, but it made her nervous and brought the blood to her cheeks.

Just when she'd plucked up courage to smile at him, he grabbed one of the empty bins and pulled it close to where she was working. Without saying a word, he touched her lightly on the arm and indicated for her to stand aside. Stepping into her spot, he started feeding the fibre into the bin — the job she'd been doing.

Then it dawned on her, he hadn't been watching her at all! He'd been watching the roving which was streaming from the hole in the machine like matter oozing out of a ripe carbuncle.

After filling one bin, he dragged another across and directed the flow of wool into it. When his fourth bin was full, he nodded for her to come back and continue what she had been doing.

Though she read the words he mouthed, 'Thank you, Amy,' she couldn't smile or reply. She was angry with herself for thinking stupid thoughts. Angry with him too for making her feel the way she did. And jealous. She envied him for what he was and what he had compared with her and her mother, which was virtually nothing. Then she thought of her father, who would be waiting outside the mill gate on payday to take her hard-earned wage, before it even had time to get warm in her hand. And the publican at the Hungry Crow who'd reap the profits from her week's labour. The fact she was destined to a lifetime in the confines of the mill made her angrier still.

★   ★   ★

It was half past six in the evening when she climbed down the stone steps and found her mother asleep, slumped over the kitchen table. She wasn't surprised her father wasn't there when she got home that night. When he first came out of jail, he hardly ever went out — never even poked his nose up the cellar steps. Too used to sitting in a cell all day, every day, she thought. But it wasn't long before that changed and he was out every Friday and Saturday night, then other nights beside. Where he got his money from neither Amy nor her mother knew, but one thing was certain, come Monday morning there was nothing left to put bread on the table.

Closing the door quietly, she tried not to make a noise, but as she brushed a fork from the table with her sleeve, it bounced three times, clanging on the stone floor like the ring of a tinker's hammer. Though the noise startled Lisbeth and she opened her eyes, she seemed drowsy. Even after drinking a cup of tea, she was still half asleep.

'I'm late with the coal buckets,' she said, thinking it was morning. 'But all those stairs . . . '

'Mum,' Amy pleaded. 'You're worn out. You've got to stop, and you and I have got to get away from here.'

'Hush!' she whispered, thinking her husband was in the bedroom. 'It'll be all right, you'll see.'

'But it won't be all right. Not now or ever. Believe me, nothing'll change. It'll get worse. I'm working all day for his grog money and you're working yourself to death. And if you can't keep up with your jobs we could lose this place.'

Amy thought about what she'd said. Perhaps it wouldn't be so bad if they did get thrown out. At least then they'd have to find another place to live and perhaps her father would find someone else to sponge off.

Taking her mother's hand, Amy lifted her chin and gazed deep into her rheumy eyes. How strange, she thought, it's like we've changed places — like I'm the mother and she's my daughter.

'We've got to make a plan,' Amy said. 'I've been thinking about it all this week and I have an idea that'll work.' It had been in her mind for much longer than a week. 'You've got to sneak a bit away each week — hide it somewhere where he can't find it.'

'I couldn't do that. Besides, there ain't enough to go round as it is, let alone any extra.'

'Listen to me; you must make sure there's a little. Buy three ounce of lard instead of four,' she said, 'or five pound of spuds instead of six. He won't weigh what's in the bag, and you and I'll manage on a bit less. And if you get a farthing change — keep it. I'll take a couple of coins from my wage, if he's not waiting for me by the mill gate. And if I can run any errands for anyone or do any jobs after work I will. Then, by next spring, we'll have a few bob saved between us.'

Lisbeth smiled sadly. 'I know you're trying to help, Amy, love, but I know I can't do it. I couldn't look him in the eye — he'd see right through me. And if he asked me point blank if I had any money, I'd have to tell. It'd be written all over me face. And if he found out I was trying to trick him, he'd not think twice about taking his belt to me.'

'Don't worry about it then,' Amy said, squeezing her mother's fingers. 'I'll see what I can manage. You don't need to do anything. Only one thing I ask is, when the time comes to leave and I say we're off, you come with me, because there'll only be one chance.'

Lisbeth Dodd's eyes shone green as wet grass, they fair sparkled — but not for the right reasons. Amy knew her mother was trapped. She wanted to help her, and wished she would at least talk about the things which troubled her. Or talk about something. Anything to take her mind off her present situation.

'Tell me what it was like before I was born. Before you met dad. You said you worked in a big house. You said you had a good job. Life was good for you then, wasn't it?'

Lisbeth closed her eyes and sucked the air through her nose. 'If only he'd never turned up that day. It was those damn rhododendron bushes.'

'Rhododendrons?'

'It doesn't matter,' she said. 'I'll tell you about it one day.'

'Not one day, Mum. Tell me now. Tell me about when you were young, about my grandad and what it was like working in a nice house.' Pulling her chair closer, she took her mother's hands in hers. 'Please.'

Lisbeth closed her eyes. 'When I was fifteen, I was told I was a bonny lass.'

Amy smiled.

'I'd been helping my father until then. There was just him and me and Rose.' She sighed. 'She were three years younger than me, bless her.'

'What did my grandad do?'

'He were a cobbler. Good one at that. Worked in our kitchen at home.' She smiled. 'It were more like a workshop than a living room. When we ate, there were always a row of lasts lined up along the other side of the kitchen table looking at us. But he did all his work on a three-legged stool in front of the fire.

'My job was to deliver the boots and shoes when he'd fixed them. That was apart from keeping house and looking after Rose when she were little. And once a week I'd go down to the local tannery to pick up bits of left-over leather. Always remember the smell of that place. Enough to make you sick. But I'd come back with a sackful — sometimes there were that much I had to drag it home. It made my father happy.

'Anyway, one day I delivered a pair of shoes to the Manse. That was the minister's house. He was the same man who used to preach at our chapel.'

'But you never go to chapel.'

'Not now, I don't, but I used to go regular

as clockwork. We all did — me, your grandad and Rose, every Sunday morning. And I'd take Rose to Sunday school in the afternoon.' She laughed gently. 'Some folk thought Dad were a bit gloomy because he always had his head bowed. But he were just checking on people's feet. If he thought their boots needed mending, he'd tell 'em so. Politely, of course.'

Amy smiled.

'I remember that day well, knocking at the back door of the Manse, with a pair of the reverend's boots in my hands. The cook came to the door, peered at me with a pair of brown beady eyes and asked me what I was up to. Before I had time to explain, Mrs Upton, the reverend's wife, appeared. As soon as she looked at me I knew she weren't really bothered about the boots. It were me she were interested in. I found out later, she'd just got rid of her previous maid. She asked me if I wanted the job, there and then.'

'But you hadn't been in service, had you?'

'Never seen a saucer that matched a cup, before I started there.

'You wouldn't believe how she treated me,' Lisbeth said, her face brightening for a while. 'It was almost like I was her daughter or sister — one of the family. There was no real hard

31

work and I lived-in and still got a few bob besides.'

'But what about Grandad and Rose?'

'I wasn't worried about them because Rose was twelve and big enough to take over the jobs I'd been doing. And I thought it'd be good for the lass to be occupied till she could get a proper job elsewhere.'

'Tell me about the minister's wife.'

Lisbeth took a moment to think before she answered.

'Mrs Upton was nice, poor dear,' she said, shaking her head. 'About thirty, I suppose. Twenty years younger than him. Educated, but real homely. Not what you'd call pretty and a bit old-fashioned in the way she dressed. But she had a head of thick black hair which she used to drape over one shoulder in a loose plait when he wasn't home. I used to brush it for her. My, I could make it shine.'

Amy glanced at the lacklustre look of her mother's red hair.

'Her main failing was that she lacked confidence. She were fine in the house but hopeless whenever she went out. I think some of the chapel ladies said things to her which upset her. She told me she wanted to have a child but somehow that never happened for her. I think that was why she made such a fuss of me.'

'But you were just a maid.'

'I never felt like a servant. I never wore a uniform all the time I worked there. She bought me three velvet dresses, one brown, one navy and one green, and an assortment of lace collars which I changed every day. And she bought me that winter coat you've been wearing for work, and a matching hat. And on Sunday mornings she always insisted I sit alongside her in chapel even though you could hear the murmurs from the congregation. But it didn't bother Mrs Upton, or me for that matter.'

'And what was the best thing about it?'

'Sunday mornings. That's what I loved best. I used to look forward to Sunday all week. Not for going to chapel, or the sermon, or the hymns — though I loved to sing in them days. What I loved most of all was the few minutes after the service, when Mrs Upton stood at the doorway with her husband to chat with the members of the congregation. That gave me chance to nip out and see Rose and my dad. It was the only chance we ever got to talk.'

'What happened to my grandad?'

'He died,' she said. 'While I was at the Manse. I had to sell his tools to pay for his funeral.'

'And Rose?'

Pain tightened Lisbeth's eyes.

Amy reworded her question. 'Where did Rose live after Grandad died?'

'A neighbour took her in, and I paid her board out of my wages. That was until she got my job at the Manse.'

'And what happened then?'

Lisbeth threw her head back then dropped it into her hands. 'It never should have happened. I should never have let her go there. I should have kept her away from Amos. It was my fault.'

'Mum, that's a long time ago. You mustn't blame yourself for the things that happened then.'

'But you don't know what went on in that place.'

'Then tell me.'

'One day I'll tell you. I promise, I'll tell you the whole story,' she said, her voice incredibly weary. 'But not right now, Amy, love. Not right now. You asked me a few minutes ago about running off, saving up and leaving your father. Well, at the moment I don't have the energy to face anything. God only knows what'd become of us if we ran off. Take it from me, it's not that bad here. At least we've got a roof over our heads, and I know Mr Ogilvy, the man who owns this place, won't throw us out. He's a kind man and he's been good to me,' she said. 'Never paid a penny rent in eighteen years. We might have to scratch around to make ends meet, but it's better than being in the workhouse, you mark my words.' Lisbeth shook her head. 'It's more than I could stand knowing your father was chasing after me. I'd never dare open a door again, or close my eyes at night. Don't force me out on to the street, Amy. I'm not strong enough for that.'

There was no point saying any more. Lisbeth hated her husband and she was obviously afraid of what he might do to her. Despite that, she wasn't prepared to leave him. Then Amy thought about Rose. She wished she knew what had happened all those years ago. Had her death really been an accident? She was confused. Could her father have been telling the truth? From what she'd seen and heard, he was a mean and cunning man, and all his actions were calculated and deliberate.

In her opinion, Amos Dodd never did anything by accident.

3

Lisbeth

Amy sensed something was wrong as soon as she opened the door. There was no fire in the grate, no kettle singing on the hob or smell of stew simmering in the pot. The lamp had burned right down. Turning it up, she scraped the wick and re-lit it. From the rug, tiny beads of light reflected like morning sun on dewdrops. She reached down and ran her fingers across the mat, expecting it to be wet, but the scattered specks of lights were the polished faces of mother-of-pearl buttons. The brass jar which had held them was empty and dented. It was lying on the floor under the table where Amy usually put her bed.

Her voice wavered when she called out, hoping that there would be an answer. But there was none. Tiptoeing into the back room, she saw her mother lying on the bed, curled like a sleeping child. When Amy touched her arm and tried to lift her, she knew she was dead.

* * *

36

The Medleys were a tower of strength. Without their help Amy wouldn't have known what to do in those circumstances. Mrs Medley sent her eldest boy to fetch the doctor. He arrived very late. Examined her mother. Asked Amy about the bruises. Were they new? Had she fallen recently? Amy had to tell him she didn't know; tell him her mother bruised easily, and always had some. She didn't tell him about her father. When she told the doctor of her mother's weariness and pains, he said it was likely her heart that had taken her.

It was midnight by the time they laid her mother out.

'You can sleep at our place if you don't mind a chair or the floor,' Mrs Medley said. 'At least till after the funeral.'

Amy thanked her. 'I want to stay with Mum while she's here.' The neighbour never asked after Mr Dodd, and Amy didn't mention him either. She didn't care where he was or what happened to him. She hoped he'd never come home again.

Mr Medley spoke to the minister. Arranged things as best he could. It was embarrassing to admit that she had no money.

Lisbeth Dodd was buried in a pauper's grave. That upset Mrs Medley. For Amy it made little difference where her mother was laid. Soil was soil whether it was in a graveyard or a garden. Only one thing was for certain: when the coffin lid was nailed down, she was never going to see her mother again.

* * *

The evening after the funeral, as Amy sat alone in the cellar, there was a knock on the door. The man standing in the tiny cellar yard looked vaguely familiar — well dressed, but rather weary. An undertaker or preacher? she thought. He was tall and straight, his face gaunt but carrying country colour. His figure was slightly undernourished.

'Is your father in, Amy?'

'No, he's not.'

'Do you know when he'll be back?' he said, a concerned expression etched in the lines of his forehead.

Amy shook her head and said she didn't know.

'I know you don't know me,' he said, 'but your mother did. I should introduce myself. My name is Charles Ogilvy and I'm the owner of this building. It might be best if you invited me in. There are things I need to talk to you about.'

The name, Ogilvy, was familiar but the man meant nothing to her. She thought she had seen him occasionally on the street. And remembered once her mother had pointed to a stranger loitering in the graveyard. It was the same man. He obviously didn't live in the neighbourhood; he spoke and dressed too well for that.

Following Amy inside, Mr Ogilvy took off his hat and cast his eyes around the room.

'Do you want to sit down?' she asked, looking at the armchair's cushion which had shed its stuffing years ago.

The gentleman didn't answer. 'Before I get down to business, let me offer my condolences. I know what it is like to lose someone close to you.'

'I didn't lose my mother,' Amy said. 'She died.'

'Of course,' he said, breathing deeply. 'Let me explain. When I first met your mother, she was in dire need of somewhere to stay. This place,' he said, glancing around, 'is far from ideal, but at the time, when you were born, she had no one to turn to and nowhere to go. I let her have these rooms and I never charged any rent. However, in return she kept the rest of the building clean and tidy for my other tenants: staircases, windows, yards. I am sure you are aware of that.'

Amy nodded.

'And let me add, I never once begrudged her living here.'

'Ta,' Amy said automatically.

'Unfortunately for your mother, when her husband, Mr Dodd, returned three years ago, I was obliged to review the situation. I told her that with a man in the house it would be usual that there would be another wage coming in.'

'But there was no money. He never worked. He never gave her anything. He even took my wages and, with him here, we had less than before he came!'

'I know. Your mother told me, and that is why I allowed you all to stay, though it went against my better judgement. It was only because of the years I had known Lisbeth that I allowed the previous unpaid arrangement to continue for as long as it did. Now, however . . . ' he sighed. 'Circumstances have changed again.

'I'm sorry,' he continued, 'but with your mother dead, the goodwill does not extend to your father. If it were for you alone, Amy, I would be happy for you to stay and continue with the arrangement that I had with your mother. However, under the circumstances, I am not inclined to extend the favour to your father.' He hesitated for a moment as he searched for the right words. 'I have no time for a man who has no respect for women, but I shall say no more on that count. I am truly sorry for your situation, Amy, but I'm afraid that's how it has to be. I understand you have a job at the mill and that you are a good worker. That should provide you with enough funds each week to find yourself a room somewhere. Let me offer you a piece of advice. I feel you would be better on your own, away from the likes of Amos Dodd. As for this place, I have a needy tenant arriving here on Monday. You and your father must be out by Saturday midday, or, I'm sorry to say, I'll be forced to call the bailiff.'

Amy looked at him. What could she say?

As he was leaving, Mr Ogilvy apologetically reminded her that the furniture belonged on the premises. Amy didn't know that her mother had owned nothing.

'Believe me,' he said, as he climbed the stone steps. 'I am truly sorry this is happening to you. But I'll not harbour Amos Dodd under my roof any longer.'

★   ★   ★

Amy didn't know how she managed to work for the next two days. She couldn't even remember walking to the mill. After the funeral, Mrs Medley helped her pack her few possessions, and offered to hold them until she and her father found another place for them. There wasn't much: some threadbare linen, a few pieces of crockery, a pot or two, and little else. Her mother's only personal things were stored in an old shoe box which had been tucked under the bed. She was glad her father hadn't found it, though it didn't contain anything of value: a few letters, some worthless keepsakes wrapped in a yellowed handkerchief, and a pencil sketch which she'd seen her mother looking at when she thought no one was looking. Two trips up the street was all it took to deliver everything to the safekeeping of her neighbour.

'You really must stay with us tonight,' Mrs Medley said. 'And next week I'll have a word with my sister. She knows someone who might have a room that'll suit you. Don't bank on it, though, lass, but I'll not see you walking the street, do you 'ear?' Mrs Medley gave her a hug.

'And you know where to come if you're desperate,' her husband added.

Amy thanked them both. Said she didn't know what she'd have done without their help. Even so, she wanted to go back home while she had one; to be on her own; to get away from the noise of the Medley children

— somehow their happy laughter didn't seem fitting.

Walking back to the cellar, she thought of the young ones; of the fuss their father made of them, of the love he wasn't ashamed to show. Then she compared him with her own father and thought of all those years she'd longed for his return.

Looking down from the street to the greyness of the cellar yard, she stood for a moment watching the swirling leaves as they lifted from the ground and danced in a ghostly circle on the cold slabs. It was a mischievous wind, which often blew down the stone steps and rattled the door. It didn't scare her.

Inside the room the air was still. Stagnant. And damp. She was thankful she had lit the lamp earlier. She hated walking into a dark house.

Though there was no fire, Amy dragged the armchair closer to the hearth and stared into the empty grate. Outside the door, the leaves skittered and scratched on the slabs.

From the corner of her eye, she saw something move.

Amy looked up. Amos Dodd was standing in the doorway, the lamplight reflecting in the yellow of his eyes.

'It's just thee and me now!' he said.

4

The Spider's Web

The front door of the Hungry Crow was closed, yet the unmistakable odour exuding from the building enticed its regulars as surely as a lump of mouldy cheese would attract a pack of hungry rats. To the wives whose housekeeping money was exchanged each week for gallons of the golden fluid, the rancid smell was a reminder of the futility of their existence. A reminder they were unable to ignore, as it was the same smell which drifted from every similar establishment. Always present. Always identical. It were as if the ingredients — smoke, stale ale, sweat and sour breath — were simmered and stirred in some giant mixing pot, and when ripened to maturity, doled out in ample portions to every alehouse, public house and tavern in the town. The odour, as consistent as the scent of fine French perfume, might well have been a patented product.

'I'm not going in there!' Amy shouted.

'Are you not?' Amos said, clapping his

hand firmly around her wrist. 'We'll soon see about that!'

As they crossed the cobbles, Amy glanced up at the sign swinging above the pub's entrance. Written in large gilt letters was the name: Hungry Crow. Beneath it, painted in black on white, the evil bird, its beak latched firmly on an unsuspecting worm, about to devour it whole. Amy knew she was that worm.

'You're hurting!' she yelled, twisting her arm in an attempt to free it, but her father's grip circled her wrist as tight as a hoop on a barrel.

Amos clouted the door with the steel tip on his boot.

Inside, all heads turned and the burble of voices stilled. After the door closed with a dull thud, all that was heard was the sound of the six gas mantles hissing from the walls. Nothing was said.

As her eyes became accustomed to the dim light, Amy looked around. The yellowed teeth, bloodshot eyes and threadbare clothes were uniform around the room. There was not a starched collar in sight.

When her shin hit a wooden stool, she squealed, and a cynical laugh broke the silence, prompting the rumble of conversation to roll on.

'Sit there and don't move!'

Amy rubbed her leg, breathing shallowly in an attempt not to inhale too much of the curling blue air. She heard her father shout his order and looked across at him as he waited. She despised him. How grateful she was he'd been locked away for all her childhood years; at least she'd that to be thankful for. But now her mother was gone and each day she hated him more and more. She was desperate to get away, but the thumping he'd given her the previous day, when he had dragged her from Mrs Medley's, had taught her to be extra cautious. For the moment, at least, she'd do what he said — within reason.

'If you don't fancy 'im, love, I'll give you tuppence if you're nice to me.' A stream of saliva ran down the stranger's beard. His words were slurred. After wiping his ample whiskers with the back of his equally hairy forearm, he poked his outstretched fingers towards Amy's hair. Slapping them away before he could touch, Amy slid herself to the far end of the bench.

'Playful little piece,' the man said. The other drinkers showed no interest.

'You!' Amos called, glaring at the drunk. The man, unconcerned, cocked his head and laughed, but his cockeyed smirk disappeared as the steel blade glinted in the gas light.

Amy hadn't seen the knife before. Didn't know her father carried one. Was instantly afraid of what he might do.

The room was silent. Amos Dodd had the audience's full attention.

Turning his back, the drunk swayed on his seat, mumbled to himself then buried his face in his pot. On her lap, Amy's hands trembled but she sat upright, hoping no one, especially her father, would notice.

'Have a drink!' he ordered, pointing towards his pot with the knife, before slapping it down on to the table.

'I hate beer!'

Picking up his drink, he swallowed half its contents without taking a breath.

'I want to get some water,' she said. 'There's a fountain at the bottom of the street.' She looked at him but he didn't answer. 'I'll wait for you there. I won't go away. I promise.'

'You'd better not!' he threatened. 'Or you know what you'll get!'

Amy nodded and half smiled — not at him, but at the thought of being able to get out of the place. She was surprised he was letting her go so easily. As she slid cautiously off the bench and threaded her way out, the other patrons showed little interest. Pulling the door open, she gulped the evening air, and set off down the hill before he changed his mind.

From the Hungry Crow on Mill Street, Bank Lane ran right down to the canal. In her eagerness, Amy found herself running along the pavement, her feet falling in step with the plaintive notes of a cornet drifting from one of the houses. It was a simple melody, a few bars being repeated over and over. Amy slowed. She loved the sound of brass, especially the mill's band. Hearing them play and seeing the men in their braided uniforms was always a treat. How the yellow brass shone to a mirror shine on a sunny day. And how the tunes had stirred her mother when they'd listened to the band playing in the park on Sundays. There was a special magic in that music; magic which had been able to make them forget their dismal surroundings. Magic which at times made them laugh or cry.

But the notes from the upstairs window were not from a bandsman, more likely from a lad, learning to play; a boy taking lessons from his father. Amy envied him that relationship.

A wire-haired dog defending a doorstep growled, baring its teeth. Amy stepped out of its way as it cocked its leg, sending a yellow stream trickling over the paving slab and into the gutter beside her. She lifted her skirt and stepped on to the cobbles. The dog barked again. A voice shouted from a house. The dog's ears pricked, then it jumped up on to the step and lay down again.

Though it was still reasonably light, the street lamp at the bottom of the hill had already been lit. In a few kitchens, lamps were already burning. Only the houses on Mill Street had gas. Soon it would be dark. Soon the canal and the River Aire beyond it would dissolve into darkness and the area at the bottom of the street would be a place best avoided.

The stone fountain, carved like a giant cockle shell, was set into the wall. After they had witnessed two girls stripped to the waist, washing themselves all over, her mother had warned her daughter not to drink from it. 'Fountains is supposed to be for drinking,' her mother had always said. 'Don't you dare go drinking there!'

Amy never did, but at the time she had wondered what ailed the women and how her mother could tell they carried disease. They were young, not much older than her, and they didn't look sick, or sound it; in fact, she remembered them laughing. They sounded happy. But her mother's advice was enough to deter her. Not that it mattered right now;

her excuse about wanting a drink was only to get away from her father and out of the Hungry Crow. Besides that, she didn't want to be near the place when the men came out buoyed up on a bellyful of booze. No doubt, that would only happen when their money had gone or they became rowdy and were thrown out by the landlord. In any case, she thought it unlikely they would go wandering down to the canal. Most would head for home and bed. Amy thought the fountain seemed a safe place to watch and wait, and hope it wouldn't be long before her father's money ran out.

On the opposite bank of the canal, a group of men were talking. Their voices carried across the water even though they spoke in low tones. They were in a circle around a horse, which was lying on the towing path.

Fifty yards to the right, a woman was standing on the deck of a moored barge. The cabin doors were open and light was streaming from inside. Her hair, drawn back from her face, was the colour of hay. It was plaited and coiled around the back of her head. From her ears swung a pair of yellow rings. Gold was a commodity Amy knew little of. Perhaps the woman was a gypsy. Her eyes were fixed on the men by the river and though the evening was not cold, she had a woollen shawl wrapped around her shoulders. There was no breath of air to ripple the water, no current in the canal to move the barge, but the woman was rocking rhythmically.

'I say we leave it till morning,' one of the men said, lifting his cap and scratching his head. 'Best shift it across a bit. Too late to do owt else right now.'

The nodding of heads sealed the matter and without speaking the men shuffled around the carcase. Dragging it by the legs, the men heaved the ton weight from the towing path and rolled it over into the ditch.

Amy wasn't sure if the animal was dead or alive, as when they hauled it from the path, its head lolled back, flicking the long mane from its dark, wet eyes. They glistened brightly and seemed to stare at her across the canal. Even though she closed her own, she couldn't shut out the horse's gaze. If it wasn't already finished, it soon would be.

With a few final words exchanged, the men shook hands and parted, four of them returning to the line of big barges moored to the left. Two other men headed in the opposite direction and, as they passed the woman on the deck of the short-boat, they touched their caps, spoke for a while and then continued on.

Only an old man and boy remained on the bank. The lad, aged ten or twelve, was kneeling beside the horse, stroking its mane.

'These things happen, lad,' the man said. 'Not a lot you can do about it. But when he's back on his feet, your dad'll find another one just as good, you mark my words.'

Amy saw the boy look up, tears shining on his cheeks. He had probably known the horse all his life, she thought, and walked thousands of miles beside it. Now it was dead and from the expression on his face, it might well have been his mother lying on the ground. When Amy heard him sob, she thought of her own mother curled on the bed, and cried too.

'None of that blubbering now!' the man said, his voice firm but kind, as he touched the boy on the shoulder, coaxing him to his feet. 'Tell your dad, I'll pass the message to the knackers yard. I'll tell 'em to come out here in the morning. Do you understand?'

'Yes, sir.'

'Now, away with you. Get back to your ma. Nowt gained in spending time crying over a dead nag.'

Though it was obvious the boy didn't want to leave, the man placed a hand on his back and shoved him gently in the direction of the boat. Not until he was almost level with it did he turn and look back. Amy wiped her eyes.

Was he hoping it was not dead and that it had risen to its feet? If so, he was disappointed.

When he reached the boat, the woman who'd been watching embraced him briefly, then she ducked her head and disappeared into the cabin. The lad stood for a moment, took off his cap, then followed her inside.

In the ditch beside the towing path, the old man squatted beside the mare. He'd lost a few horses of his own over the years, and he always hated to see them go. A good horse was like one of the family. You lived with it. You worked with it. Day in. Day out. Without it, you didn't make a living. Looking down, he could see the muscles in the legs still twitching. It was as if the dead horse was still wanting to walk on into the darkness. After lingering a few moments, the man got up, rubbed his face on the back of his sleeve and walked slowly down the path leading towards the city.

Amy's eyes played tricks as she stared into the fading light. The black shape appeared to move, seeming to slither like a giant turtle in the ditch. In front of it, the narrow ribbon of water grew blacker. The towing path was empty and apart from the croaking of several frogs, the canal bank was silent.

'Amy Dodd, where are you?' The unmistakable voice echoed down the street.

She'd forgotten about her father. Swivelling around, she lifted her skirt and dashed back to the fountain. As she reached him, his only greeting was a sharp clip across the head.

'You were supposed to wait 'ere!'

'Sorry,' she muttered. But she wasn't sorry. Under her breath she cursed him with the foulest words she'd ever heard in the mill, and the words he had called her mother, though she didn't know their meaning. She was angry with him for what he was. Blamed him for her mother's death. Blamed him for her Aunt Rose's death. And now she wanted to blame him for the fate which had befallen the horse. Perhaps if he had never come out of jail, none of this would have happened.

'Where are we going?' she asked, as he poked her in the back and directed her back up the hill. 'I'm hungry.'

'Shut your trap!' That was the last they spoke.

The boarding house was the same one they had slept in the previous night. It was in a handy location, only a few doors from the Hungry Crow. Amy didn't know if her father had the money to pay for a room for another night. It wouldn't be long before they'd be sleeping in the open.

What would happen when his money ran out, when they had no roof over their heads and no food in their bellies. She knew the only reason he wanted her was for her wages; at least, she hoped that was all. But why couldn't he get a job? She worked, and worked hard. Nine shillings and sixpence for fifty hours of toil each week. And most of that went to the the Hungry Crow. If he wanted a job, there was work to be had. It was obvious Amos Dodd had no intention of working.

If it hadn't been for her father, Mr Ogilvy would have let her stay in the cellar. She could have taken over the jobs her mother was doing — emptying slops buckets and carrying up scuttles of coal for the other tennants. That way, she'd have no rent to pay and with her money from the mill she'd have been able to save.

She was thankful her father hadn't found the box containing her mother's bits and pieces and that he was unaware that she had left things at the Medleys' house. But it upset her that he'd abused Mr Medley for offering to let her stay. Now she worried that her father would return later and harm them. Knowing about the knife made her worry more.

The shadows cast by the candle swayed around the staircase as Amy lumbered up the four flights of stairs with her father following close behind. Though drunk, he could still find his way to his lodgings in the attic of the Mill Street house.

Amy was thankful for the state he was in. It meant he didn't undress or use the pot. He didn't even stop to loosen his bootlaces; just fell on to the bed fully clothed and within minutes was snorting like an angry sow.

With dead moths floating on the water in the china jug, Amy wondered how long it had been sitting there, but she was so thirsty, she didn't care. Scooping the insects aside, she drank her fill. As she hadn't eaten or drunk anything earlier, she didn't need to use the pot either.

It was obvious she couldn't stay with her father. But where could she go with no money for food or board? She'd heard stories about the workhouse when she was a girl. Her mother had told her that their cellar was far preferable. She wasn't sure if her mother was right, but she didn't want to find out.

Pulling the pillow off the bed, Amy stretched herself on the floor between the wall and the bed. It was like being back home in the cellar, only here the floor was wooden.

The sounds from her tummy reminded her of her hunger. She knew in the morning he would take her to the mill to ensure she went to work. But she couldn't work all day on an empty stomach.

Amy wondered what she could do. Tell some of the women at Fanshaw's? They'd say they were sorry, but there'd be little they could do. Many of them were not much better off than her themselves. And if she told the overlooker, he'd likely tell her to go home rather than turning up for work hungry. Wouldn't want her fainting near any of his machines. That might slow production and that would never do.

Perhaps this was the sort of problem Mr Lister should investigate. Why girls fainted. Why they stumbled and fell against the machines. He'd get more answers if he asked the right questions than all his measuring and book entries.

With her head on the lumpy pillow, Amy drew her knees close to her chest and watched a spider shuttling between the bed leg and the wall. It was weaving its way back and forth across the warp of its web. How fine the thread it spun, far finer than the yarn which flew from Fanshaw's spindles.

Mesmerized by it, she thought about the spider. It was hungry, like her. But it appeared neither angry nor frustrated. It went about its task, patiently and methodically, knowing exactly what it had to do — spin its web, set its trap, then sit back and wait for a meal to fall into it.

Amy tried to relate her situation to that of the spider but she couldn't, there was no one she wanted to trap. She just wanted to get away. Away from her father and away from a life in the mill.

Physically tired, she wanted to sleep but she was conscious of the man stretched out only a yard away. Conscious of his smell. His snores. His horrid habits.

'Please God, don't let me ever grow to be like my father,' she whispered. Then her thoughts drifted to Mr Lister, to his eyes, to his soft downy side whiskers and to the few words he had spoken when she had been asked to the office. Like the repetitive bars of the cornet she had heard on the street, her own words played over and over in her head — I want to get as far away from here as I can! She pictured him on the steps, limping slightly on his damaged leg, and forgot about the hard floor beneath her hip. Was his smile real or had she imagined it? She told herself it was real and he had certainly called her by her name.

'Amy,' he had asked. 'What do you think of?'

Maybe she should have answered differently. Told him the truth. Told him just what she thought of standing for long hours at a machine, legs aching, hunger and tiredness welling through her. Yes, she should have told him of the things she thought of; of sleeping each night in a real bed, of drinking from a cup that wasn't cracked, of having a new hat to wear on a Sunday. But most of all to have had a father like Mr Medley. A man who, when she was a child, would have sat her on his knee and read stories to her. Who'd have taken her out on Sundays and stood beside her in the park listening to the band or watching her feed crumbs to the ducks. A father she would have been proud of. A father she would have loved.

Maybe she should have told Mr Lister about her own father. She couldn't help thinking about him; about the way he treated her, about the terrible things he had done, and now the fear he would do the same to her.

How much I hate him, she thought. That is what I should have told the engineer.

But she knew Mr Lister didn't want to hear about those sorts of things, and a young gentleman like him wouldn't understand anyway. There was no ruler long enough to measure her feelings and no words he could write in his book which would express exactly how she felt.

But he did say, 'Thank you, Amy', and he did smile, and his smile and his hobbled gait was what she kept in her mind.

As she rolled over to face the wall, the bed above her creaked. She held her breath, praying her father would not wake. Then the lonely silence returned, save for the voices drifting up the stairwell — a late-night argument over money that went on and on.

The next sound she heard was the pad of the knocker-up man's pole tapping on the windows below. 'Five o'clock. Time to get up,' he called, his sing-song voice almost drowned by the barking of a dozen dogs. The men who worked on the railway would be up by now.

The grimy window, trimmed with a tattered lace curtain, masked the early dawn. Amy rubbed the grit from her lids and looked across to the leg of the bed. The spider and its web were gone. Had she brushed it away in her sleep or had it decided it was time to leave and try somewhere new? She wondered.

Not wanting to stay in the room with her father longer than necessary, she got up as quietly as possible, but the floorboards refused to stay silent. After drinking a handful of water, she splashed a little across her face.

'Where d'you think you're off to?' he growled.

'The mill,' she said, dabbing her face on the hem of her skirt. 'I'll need something to eat.'

Amos grunted, rolled on to his back and scratched at his crotch.

'I can't work with no food in me belly.'

Pushing his hand in his pocket, he pulled out a chunk of dried bread. ''Ere,' he said as he tossed it at her. 'That's all I got.' It bounced on the floor and rolled under the washstand, settling itself in the fringe of matted hair which skirted the room.

'You get paid today?'

'Yes.'

'Then you'll eat tonight.'

Amy picked up the bread, rubbed the hairs off it and dipped it in the jug of water. She only managed one soggy mouthful but knew she'd have to have something inside her.

'I'll be waitin' for thee when t'mill looses. And don't try owt clever cos I'll ring thee bloody neck if thee do!'

Amy didn't answer.

The staircase was dark. There were no windows and she had no candle. When she reached the first-floor landing, a door opened. It was the woman who took the money for the rooms. She was wearing a nightshirt with a stained apron over it. Tied around her neck was a moth-eaten woollen muffler. Rags hung from the ends of her grey hair like long rats' tails. 'Where are you off to,' she said, 'sneaking out this early?'

'Fanshaw's Mill. I work there.'

The woman looked surprised. 'And what about 'im you're with?'

Amy turned her head up towards the attic. 'My father's still asleep.'

'Your father, you say?' Then she laughed.

As she was about to start down the final flight of steps, Amy thought of her stomach and the cunning spider. 'Can you spare a bite to eat?' she asked as nicely as she could manage.

'This ain't no bleeding almshouse.'

'I get me wages today,' Amy said quietly. 'I can pay whatever you ask.'

'You sure you're coming back 'ere tonight?' The woman's face screwed.

'No choice. We ain't got nowhere else to go.'

The woman worked the sums in her head quicker than the clerk in the mill office. Surprising how much arithmetic a woman of no learning can pick up on the streets, Amy thought.

'Wait there,' she said, closing the door behind her. The landing reverted to its habitual darkness.

As Amy waited patiently, her eyes closed. She was tempted to sit on the steps and put her head down but thought if she did she was likely to fall asleep.

'Here,' the woman said, reappearing and thrusting a small bundle into Amy's hands. 'You owe me sixpence. And mind you return the cloth.'

'I will,' said Amy as she hurried down the stairs. She was pleased. My web has caught its first fly, she thought.

5

Where there's smoke . . .

It was too early to go to the mill, so Amy took her breakfast bundle down to the canal. The street was empty.

Of the barges which had been moored along the bank the previous night, only the one with the woman on board remained. Across the canal, the dead horse was still in the ditch beside the towing path. Its belly had swollen up and its legs were now poking towards the rising sun.

Sitting on a broken horse trough, Amy opened her food package and was quite surprised by the contents of the rag: a slice of cake, a lump of cheese and a bruised apple. Though a grub had got under the wrinkled skin, she ate around it and wasted very little.

From her perch, she could see the back of the mill, its brick wall rising five floors perpendicular from the canal bank. More than a hundred windows overlooked the water. At the bottom of Fanshaw's wall was a narrow path running the full length of the building. To the side of the mill was a lane leading into the receiving yard and loading bays. It was used by the wagons which lumbered in and out laden with bales of wool, or bolts of cloth.

As she watched, a wagon drawn by four draught horses clattered down the cobbled street, slowed and turned into the yard. It was loaded with coal. Fanshaw's boilers were already hot and smoke was rising steadily from the tall chimney.

The sound of the mill's whistle started dogs yapping. In half an hour the machines would all be operating. It was time to go. From the streets came the morning noises, the milk wagon, children's voices, doors banging and the clicking of clogs along the pavements. As the trickle of workers grew, Amy joined them, heading along Mill Street to Fanshaw's main entrance. There was little conversation. Most of the girls' heads were bent; their eyes, not fully awake, stared down at the cracks between the cobbles.

How different to the home-time rush when everyone came out together, a mob of girls filling the street, happy to leave the mill's noise and the dust-filled air. Looking forward to spending time at home with their families. To listening to voices they could hear.

As Amy joined them, no one spoke. She didn't want to talk anyway. Having slept all night in her working clothes, she felt ashamed. Her apron was dirty and she hadn't washed, apart from splashing a little water on her face. She thought about the two girls washing in the fountain and envied them.

Nearing the main gates, she looked up to the words fanned out along the top of them: FANSHAW'S MILL. The letters poked up like the stone turrets on Armley Jail. In burnished bronze, beneath the name, was a shield. Engraved on it was a sheep, a goat and a spindle. The sheep was hanging from a hook, its back arched just like the dead horse. Amy thought about her father. Tonight he would be waiting outside those gates and if she didn't hand over her wage, she could end up the same way.

She slowed almost to a stop.

'What's up with thee?' a girl squawked, as she bumped into her. 'Think you're a blooming statue?'

'Sorry,' Amy said, wandering into the yard, her mind still bent on finding some way to escape.

That morning was the longest she could remember. Her head spun like an empty bobbin, with not a single thread of idea on it. As the throb of the machines counted out every second, she watched the hands of the big clock on the mending room wall. The hands reminded her of the spider's web. Reminded her to be patient. To wait until six o'clock.

When the machines eventually rattled to a stop, the girls dusted the wool fibres from their hair and ears, grabbed their shawls or coats and clattered down the stone stairs. There was an air of excitement in the yard. It was always the same on pay day.

The queue at the pay office window was five deep, disorganized but orderly. Anxious to get home, there were shouts for the clerk to hurry. He seemed to delight in making the girls wait before he opened his window. Amy made sure she was not far from the front of the queue but she also hid herself behind several taller women. Across the street from the mill, she could see her father waiting. He was leaning against the wall, hands in pockets, one leg crossed in front of the other.

When the window eventually opened, there was a cheer. By now almost every girl who worked at Fanshaw's was in the yard and Amy could feel herself being jostled forward. As the girls collected their pay, they chatted happily, waited for friends or wandered out through the main gate.

'Amy Dodd,' she said to the man in the gold-rimmed glasses. He ticked her name off the list. She signed, checked the coins, then waited until several more girls had been paid and a mob of lasses were heading towards the gate.

'Fire! Fire!' she suddenly screamed. Those immediately in front of her turned, staring at her as though she was daft, but the ones in the queue who couldn't see her became silent. Faces scanned the mill's windows, the loading bay, the engine room, looking for smoke. The cry sent a chill through the mob. Most had experienced the horrors of fire at some time in their lives. Fire in a mill was devastating.

'Fire!' someone else shouted, then another voice echoed from across the yard. Suddenly, like a bunch of startled rats, the girls took flight, squealing and running helter-skelter for the street. The pay-office window slammed shut and an alarm bell started ringing. From the loading bays and mill office, the clerks and managers came running out, only to be bumped aside by the warehouse men who were heading for safety.

As the girls ran for the main gate, Amy turned back and wove between them, darted across the yard, around a wagon, heading for the mill's side gate. She was running as fast as she could but as she rounded the corner, she slipped and fell headlong, the coins bouncing from her hand along the hard ground. As she struggled to get up, a hand reached out and grabbed her arm.

Her father? If it wasn't him, it was the overlooker. If he knew it was her who had raised the alarm, she would lose her job.

'Amy Dodd, are you all right?'

She recognized the voice but, gathering her coins, the only words she could utter were the ones which were fixed in her head. 'I have to get away, far away,' she said.

Picking up a shilling, Mr Lister pushed it into her hand. 'Be careful,' he called. He could see the fear in her face was far more than that of an imaginary fire.

From the side gate, Amy headed down the street, not daring to look around. It was only a short distance to the canal at the bottom. She knew what would happen when the panic subsided; it would soon become evident the alarm was false. The girls who'd been paid would wonder what the commotion was about. Those empty-handed would be angry, demanding their pay. There'd be women shouting, men yelling orders, horses rearing, no one listening. General confusion. The only thing that was certain — there was no fire.

With the coins clasped tightly in her hand, Amy reckoned it would take ten or fifteen minutes for the ruckus to die — ten minutes at the most before her father discovered she was gone, then he would come looking for her. He'd search the yard and the street and then he'd search the Medleys' house. She felt concerned for Mrs Medley and the children.

He might go back to their old cellar, to the junction where the trams stopped, perhaps to the railway station. One thing was for sure, he wouldn't be satisfied until he found her. In her mind there was only one place which would be fairly safe — the no-man's land between the canal and the river.

She almost fell again as she ran down the lane, her legs getting tangled in her petticoat. By the time she reached the canal bank, she was out of breath. Behind her an alarm bell was ringing and the mill's shrill whistle was blowing regular blasts of steam.

Without looking back, Amy turned beside the mill to the narrow path which ran along it. But it was not a path at all! Not much more than a ledge the width of three or four bricks and there was nothing to hold on to. Laying her chest against the wall, her arms outstretched, she slithered along it. At times her feet slipped from beneath her on the slurry of ooze seeping from between the bricks. Her fingernails broke as she tried to grip them. If she fell into the water fully clothed, she'd not get out. She couldn't swim, and no one would hear her cries above all the noise.

Now there was a second bell ringing and getting louder. The fire brigade was on its way. Her heart was pounding. Her mouth dry. Time was passing quickly and it was taking much longer than she had thought to get clear of Fanshaw's. Ahead was the stretch of open ground — nearly half a mile to the bridge. It was wasteland with not a bush or tree growing on it and it was wide open for anyone to see. She prayed her father was still searching for her at the mill's gate. If he looked in that direction he'd spot her easily.

It was as she neared the bridge that the bells stopped ringing and the whistle died. Glancing back, Amy could see people wandering about but no one was hurrying and, thankfully, no one appeared to be following her.

Ahead, the two bridges, which joined in the middle, were busy with evening traffic: carts, wagons, horse-drawn trams and lots of people. Girls and men on foot, dirty and tired, were returning home from the factories and workshops. Hurrying across the bridge, Amy was confronted by a pack of workmen heading towards her. Leading them was a man Amy recognized — the hairy drunk from the Hungry Crow. Turning her face towards the water, she kept her head down, hoping he wouldn't remember her.

'Well!' he cried, stopping dead in his tracks. 'Look what we have here!' As he spoke, he opened his arms to catch her or prevent her passing. His pals laughed.

Avoiding his grasp, Amy darted to the side, startling a pair of drays as she dashed in front of them. The horses snorted. The driver cursed as he fought to hold them, but Amy kept running through the throng. Midway across, she ducked down the iron stairs which led to the towing path.

As she reached the black land between the two waterways, she caught her breath and looked up.

From the bridge's rail the hairy man leaned over. He smirked as he shouted, 'I'll tell your pa I seen ya, when I see him at the Crow tonight!'

6

The Towing Path

Aware the man had seen her and fearful he might tell her father, Amy hurried back from the towing path, climbed the steps to the bridge, and mingled with the throng of workers streaming home from the mills and factories. With the long daily grind behind them, most were impatient to get home, and Amy found herself jostled to quicken her pace. The unlucky ones heading towards twelve hours of night noise and sweat wore sullen faces. They resisted the urgency to hurry and responded to the elbowing with disgruntled growls.

Moving with the river of bobbing heads, Amy passed the shoddy mill and the new printing shop, the foundry which still echoed with the clang of cold metal, passed the boot makers at the other side of the road and the gates of the tannery whose foul smells often drifted in through Fanshaw's windows. Glancing back, there was no sign of the hairy man from the pub, or of her father. She was grateful to the crowd for swallowing her up, but once the mob reached the rows of houses, the flow began to thin. Workers peeled off, scurrying up the side streets like scared rabbits running for the warren at the first crack of a rifle. The only sounds on the streets were the clicking of steel toe-caps on cobbles and the clatter of wooden clogs. There was little conversation. Some said a polite, 'Good night, see ya in t'morning,' before disappearing into a poorly lit kitchen, but the replies were merely mumbled echoes of the same phrase, or the greeting was ignored, answered only by the slamming of a door.

Amy envied the lucky ones their families and homes; a meal waiting on the stove and the excited cry of children's voices. She felt sorry for the few confronted by the cold comfort of a locked door, the girls left stamping their feet on the stone step, banging on the window, calling out, 'It's me, Mam. For God's sake, open t'bloody door!'

As she walked on, Amy reached into her pocket and ran her fingers around the loose coins. Even before spreading them on her palm she knew she was short. There were three florins, a shilling and a sixpence — a total of only seven shillings and sixpence. She checked both pockets. They were empty. Darn it! She must have lost the other florin when she fell in the yard. It was probably still lying where it fell unless some worker had been lucky enough to see the silver glinting in the sun. What sun? she questioned. There hadn't been any that day and probably the coin was still there. That money would have bought her sufficient rations to last her for a few days, but she couldn't go back now. The thought of food reminded her she hadn't eaten since morning. It had been a long day and she was hungry — and thirsty too.

The grocer, on the next corner, was busy sweeping the pavement outside his shop. No doubt it was his regular ritual this time of the day, though the steel-grey slabs showed little evidence of his effort. Amy studied him as she approached and found herself staring at his hands. They were pink and clean — so different to the other men from the lanes.

'What are you after?' the shopkeeper asked brusquely, leaning the broom against the wall.

Amy blinked. 'Do you have any bread?' she asked, a flush reddening her neck.

'Sorry, love. All gone. Come back in t'morning. I'm closing up right now.'

'Do you have an apple?'

He looked at her quizzically. 'You in trouble, lass?'

She tried to smile. 'Not really. I've got some money, and I'm hungry.'

'Come in 'ere, lass,' he said rubbing his chubby hands down the front of his apron. 'Let's see what we got left over.'

Five minutes later, Amy emerged from the shop, a blot of milk on her chin, a parcel wrapped in newspaper tucked under her arm, and her money only short by the sixpenny piece. She looked satisfied as she stepped out.

'Tek care of yoursen,' he said, reaching for the broom. 'An' if you'll tek my advice, you'd best not hang around these parts after dark.'

Amy nodded, thanked him and turned back. The bridge she'd come from looked a long way off — and the road was almost empty. There were no crowds to lose herself in, only the stragglers wending their way home; the limp and lame, and the elderly with no youngsters to support them. An old lady smiled. For her the day had been extra long, though at her age she was lucky to have a job at all. Perhaps she too should have been grateful for the job at Fanshaw's. But it wasn't the mill she was running away from, though she wasn't sorry to leave.

When she reached the bridge, she felt agitated and angry. She was almost back where she had started from. She was getting nowhere. The thought of her father searching for her made her hurry down the iron steps but as her hand slid along the rusty railing, it

76

scratched her palm. She had to take more care.

Below the bridge, the two channels of water lay like a pair of ungainly twins separated only by a cord of lifeless land. On one side, the River Aire flowed purposefully towards the city, leaving only its putrid smell in its wake. Midstream, its current circled constantly, churning the debris carried on its surface. Along the banks, sticks and litter attracted bubbles of brown scum. A dead rat bobbed as if frolicking in the foamy water.

In contrast, the canal lay as still as a black shroud, its only trim, the hem of a path, tacked along its straight edge. On the twenty-yard strip of land between the two bodies of water, mounds of grey sludge dredged from the canal's bottom provided a habitat for weeds and rodents. The dank atmosphere coveted the unhealthy smell. Not a single tree grew in that part of the city.

From the shop's clock, Amy guessed it was almost eight, but there was still too much daylight to chance walking beside the canal without being seen. Now she must wait until it was fully dark before setting off, and pray that there'd be little or no moon that night.

Settling herself on the pile of rubble under the bridge, Amy faced the river knowing that it was not used by the barges. From the parcel wrapped in paper, she took one slice of brawn and the Eccles cake. After breaking the pastry in half, she carefully wrapped the remains of her food in the rag which had held her breakfast. Tying the four corners, she made the package into a secure bundle.

Gazing along the water through the tall nettles which flourished in the black silt, Amy could see the mill and its tall chimney poking up from the far end of the building. On most days it gushed with clouds of ash, which fell back to the streets for miles around, but for the moment it was dormant. She looked at the building — five storeys high, but unlike Armley Jail, Fanshaw's lines were straight, its angles square. It had no turrets running along the top. Yet, she thought, considering the fretwork of iron bars barricading its smutty windows, it could well have been a prison. Even the windows on the third and fourth floors were crisscrossed with twisted metal. Were the mill owners expecting someone to break in — or were the bars in place to stop the workers getting out? She was glad she had left and swore she was never going back.

When her riverside vigil had begun, a cold sickle-shaped moon had emerged from behind the tall chimney. It looked lifeless and dull at first, but as the evening wore on it rose slowly, the backcloth of sky darkened and the crescent shone as if honed to a fine polish.

Amy stretched her legs and scrambled from her hiding place. Her bottom was cold, her coat damp at the back. Even though it was July, she sensed the coming night would not be warm. Without clouds, the stars were already pricking patterns in the sky, and as she stood and scoured the heavens for the Great Bear, a carriage rumbled over the bridge. She cowered back. After a few seconds it was gone and the bridge was again silent. She waited for a few minutes. Then there were no more carriages or wagons, no pedestrians, no voices and no one to see her.

Over the next two hours, she confirmed her decision to follow the canal and get as far away from her father as she could. But which way to go? If she headed towards the city's centre there'd be trains, carriages, barges, even sailing boats, which could take her to the coast. But by going that way, she'd encounter more people, more drunks and more danger. She'd heard the ports were rough places, teeming with foreigners who couldn't be trusted, men who might rape her or cut her throat for the cost of a glass of ale.

To the west, beyond the sprawl of the woollen mills, lay the Yorkshire moors. If she went in that direction, there'd be fewer people, fewer roads, little traffic and it was less likely her father would follow her far from the town. She'd been told that Lancashire was over the summit. That people there spoke with a different accent and weren't always partial to Yorkshire folk. But she'd also heard there were big towns and lots of cotton mills where good money could be made for an honest day's work. Maybe once she was there, she'd get a job, even if it was in a mill — just for a while. At least it couldn't stink as bad as a woollen mill and cotton must surely be cleaner and lighter to handle than wet wool. If that was the case, she'd find herself some lodgings, work hard and never return to Leeds. It seemed a good plan.

Following the canal couldn't be difficult. It was a long way, but it was summer and even if it rained she could easily cover ten miles a day. No different to being on her feet twelve hours in the mill, and the earth would be much kinder to her feet than a cold stone floor. She had a tongue in her head and a little money in her pocket. She could ask for shelter in a farmhouse; farmers' wives were friendly, she'd been told, and she'd be happy to work along the way for bread and keep. The thought of begging a lift on one of the barges had crossed her mind, but most of the boatmen looked unfriendly and had no time for strangers.

Wandering the streets alone at night was considered foolhardy. Walking by the canal was downright stupid. The towing path was an uninviting place. Amy shivered and hugged the bundle to her chest, treading carefully, conscious of every step, alert to every sound; the whirr of birds or bats' wings round her head, the splash of water as a rat slid over the side, the howl of a stray dog in search of a feed, the yap of a fox. Despite her fears, she pressed on.

The thread of black water had neither pulse nor current but tonight its flat surface mirrored the sliver of moon. Along the corridor of darkness only a single speck of light shone faintly in the distance; though Amy was heading towards it, it hardly grew.

She quickly reached the stretch of canal directly opposite the streets by the mill. A single gas lamp circled the paving slabs in cold yellow light. On Bank Lane pale illumination filtered from the row of kitchen windows. Only some of the houses had gas. Further up the street on the next corner was another lamp. Though Amy couldn't see its mountings, she knew it hung from the wall of the Hungry Crow. Not far from there was the boarding house her father had taken her to. She wondered where he was, if he had any money left, wondered if he was already drunk, or asleep and snoring on the bed in the dusty attic. She thought about the spider and wondered if it was weaving its web. She thought about the hairy man on the bridge and wondered if he had spoken to her father in the pub. She quickened her step.

The towing path beside the canal was broad and flat, wide enough for two horses but worn bare in the centre from the regular use of single boat-horses. The grass along the edges was soft, damp with dew and slippery. Though she felt thirsty, the canal water was far from appetizing — stories of bloated bodies being dragged out of it made Amy decide her thirst could wait.

The sound of raised voices made her stop. She squatted on her haunches. Two men were arguing on the other bank. Amy could see them clearly and it was likely they could see her too but she had nowhere to hide.

Suddenly another voice cut like a knife through the night. 'Amy Dodd! Get out 'ere, right now!' She knew it well. It was distant but distinctive and coming from Bank Lane.

Throwing herself down on the ground, Amy buried her face into the bundle of food. Had he seen her? Did he know she was there? She hardly dared breathe.

'Amy! Amy Dodd!'

The two men near the lamp stopped

arguing and wandered off into the night.

With her heart racing, Amy clutched the earth.

'I'll find you, girl,' her father threatened. 'God's oath, I'll find you if it's the last thing I do!'

Amy shuddered. There was real venom in his tone and he wasn't drunk. Never once as a child, when she'd imagined hearing him calling her name, had she ever expected anything like this. She waited, hardly daring to breathe. Then the calls continued. Obviously, he had not seen her.

Crawling crab-like, she slid into the ditch beside the path, settling on a layer of slime and sludge scooped up from the canal by the dredgers. As she was directly opposite the lane, she dared not lift her head. If her father walked over to the bank, only a few yards of water would separate them. Desperate to get further away, she tried pushing herself along the ditch, inching her way forward by her toes. But her coat and skirt hindered her legs. Her boots were heavy with caked mud and her fingers sore from clawing the ground. Edging forwards, her head hit something in the ditch. It stunk, worse than the Crow.

Unable to control her stomach, she retched loudly then quickly clasped one muddy hand tightly over her mouth. Had the sound carried? Had her father heard the noise? She tried to lay still but fear that he might see her made her shake involuntarily. After what seemed like an age of silence, she lifted her head, blinked, and tried to make sense of the shapes in the darkness. Looming in front of her was the bloated carcase of the dead horse. Her stomach churned as she dragged herself back from it and stared. The horse no longer returned her gaze. Its eye sockets were empty, pecked bare by the crows, the gaping mouth was lipless; the yellow teeth smiled at her in a morbid grin. Amy clamped her eyelids tightly shut.

Plop! Close by came the sound like a stone cast into the water. *Plop! Splash!* Another, then another. Was someone throwing stones at her? She waited, petrified, her heart thumping.

Then a frog croaked. Another answered, and as she lifted her chin only an inch, she saw the water ripple as another frog stretched its slippery legs and leapt in. Though there were no stones and there was no one on the bank, her mind would not stop swimming with imaginary images. She was afraid; afraid of the night, fearful that the rats or foxes attracted to the carcase might bite her, afraid she would wake in the morning to find herself covered in ants, or that she'd be woken by her father dragging her to the edge of the river to throw her headlong into the murky water. If she sank beneath the surface, who would know or even care? But what could she do? For the moment she had little alternative. The cold she could feel was not from the wetness which had soaked through to her chest and belly, but from the deep-seated malignant chill which fear had manufactured in her so efficiently. With her face pressed into her bundle, her feet stuck deep in the dredged waste, she squeezed her eyes tightly closed. She knew she was trapped.

7

Running Away

Harold Lister folded his clothes. He was looking forward to leaving the Leeds mill and returning home. Having packed little more than his nightwear, socks and a shirt for that short visit, his travelling bag was half-empty. After placing his notebooks and drafting equipment neatly on the top, he sat down in the armchair beside the fireplace. Though outside the evening was warm, the hearth was empty. An empty hearth somehow had a feeling of chill about it.

Thinking back over the past few days, he hadn't achieved as much as he would have liked. Despite Mr Fanshaw being livid at the alarm which had been falsely raised, and even angrier at the report which had appeared in the *Yorkshire Post*, the mill's owner had asked him, only that afternoon, to draw up plans for an external staircase to the main mill building. Designing such a fixture would not be a simple assignment and it would necessitate him spending more time in Leeds — more time in the one-room lodging which the mill provided for him, the room he had grown to hate.

But he had no reason to grumble. Mr Fanshaw was a good man to have dealings with — unlike some of the mill owners he had been engaged by. The superintendent of the fire brigade, however, was less amiable, and far less intelligent. Having to consult with him over the evacuation plan irked him. He would have preferred to have drawn up a schedule independent of the brigade's senior officer. However, though the work was not what he would have chosen, it would, no doubt, be a well-paid contract.

Had it not been for the girl's actions, the fire safety standards at Fanshaw's wouldn't have been reviewed and there would have been no necessity for him to return in the following few days.

He smiled to himself, recollecting the event, but his mood changed when he thought of the young worker sprawled out in the mill yard, her hands grazed as she grovelled about for the few coins she had lost. He could still picture the look of desperation etched on her face.

How lucky he had been. He had never experienced such feelings in his life. How terrible that a girl could be driven by fear to go to such lengths — especially the fear of her father. How evil could he be? All he'd heard was that the man in question was a nasty piece of work.

Harold shook his head and picked up the copy of *The Times* from the side table. It had been sitting there for over a week. On the front page were details of the Spanish surrender in Santiago de Cuba, but it was the article on page three about Santiago in Chile which interested him. He read it again.

With the export of nitrates and the mining of copper, silver and other minerals, Chile is not only politically stable, but is experiencing an era of national affluence.

Since the opening of the railway tracks across the country, immigrants from many non-Iberian countries are being attracted to this South American country.

Foreign investors and engineers from the United States and Germany are working together to construct bridges, roads and cable railways. Routes to the north and south are being opened and the construction of a rack railway across the Andes has already been discussed.

With the founding of the Chilean Electric Tramway and Light Company in London recently, German and English investors intend to electrify the tramway system in Santiago, a city with a rapidly growing population.

After reading the advertisement which appeared beneath it, Harold carefully tore it from the paper, folded it and placed it in one of the compartments of his desk alongside several similar newspaper cuttings.

It had always been his wish that one day he would sail to America. One of his few regrets in life was that, apart from visiting Italy to study its architecture, he had never travelled. The articles he had read recently about some of the engineering projects being undertaken in Chile interested him greatly, as did the geography of the country itself — a narrow strip of land, clinging to the west side of the Andes; in the north, pure desert — gilded by a burnished sun; in the south, frozen ice fields — bright white, sliding slowly into the sea.

As he glanced out of the window over the Leeds potted skyline, he considered how very different it would be to the blackened landscape and grime of the industrial north.

★   ★   ★

When Amy next looked around, the sliver of curved moon was high in the sky. The streets were silent. The two men had disappeared and there was no voice calling her name. For a short while, she'd slept.

Chilled to the marrow, she struggled to her knees. The front of her coat, skirt and blouse, even her underwear, were damp. She wasn't sure about her boots as she couldn't feel her feet. She knew she must get up and walk and get the blood moving in her legs.

Scratching the dirt from her hands opened the fine grazes etched along her palms. They stung as she dabbed the blood on her coat. Then she remembered her money; remembered the coins rolling across the yard. She remembered spending sixpence and hoped the remainder of her wages were safe. The pockets of her mother's coat were deep, they had no holes. The coins jangled. But the bundle of food she'd rested her head on was caked in mud. Its contents were damp and possibly ruined.

She had to move on, get away from the dead horse, away from the street opposite and the open towing path. A light still shone up ahead. Was it a boat? Was it the one with the woman on board she'd seen over the last two days?

As she drew closer she could see the outline of a barge, its thin chimney poking up from the cabin's roof, the brass chains glinting in the moonlight. The barge sat low in the water under its heavy cargo. Though she'd heard terrible tales about bargees and had often been warned to keep clear of them, she envied the boat's occupants — dry, safe, well fed. It wasn't until she was almost level that she realized the vessel was moored on the opposite bank. Voices drifted over the water — a man and a woman talking. They were comfortable voices with comfortable silences between the sentences. As she watched the shadowy figures, the woman lifted her skirt and squatted down on the bank. After a moment she stood up, straightened her skirt and followed the man back on board.

Though Amy knew it was neither the barge nor the woman she'd seen before, she was tempted to call them, ask for help and shelter for the night. But that would mean retracing her steps back to the bridge to cross over the canal. It would mean she would be heading back towards Fanshaw's and that would never do. She must stay on the towing path and continue the way she was going.

Unaware if midnight had come or gone, Amy felt tired and struggled to think positively, but there was little to spur her on. Ahead the canal turned slowly and stretched into the darkness. The grey cottages beside the locks looked greyer in the night light. Each bridge she met was different. Each offered shelter, somewhere to hide, but the arches were dark and ominous and when a train rumbled above her head, she felt afraid.

With the fear of stumbling in the dark, she slowed her pace, continuing on the horse path, her eyes glued to the ground. It wasn't long before she stopped. She didn't know where she was. There were no buildings or lights or sounds apart from the croaking of a dozen frogs and the call of the night birds. The ground all around looked marshy. She could smell the damp. A clump of bushes offered shelter. The bundle of spoiled food was her pillow. The coat wrapped round her was her blanket. Amy prayed it wouldn't rain.

Sleep came rapidly but with the same disturbing dreams. Her hands and feet were bound. Her hair was caught on the combs of the machine. Her head was being dragged closer to the ugly teeth. She wanted to scream, drag herself clear, call for help, but her mouth wouldn't utter a sound. With her knotted hair being pulled into the rollers, she woke with a start. A small dog, scratching at the bundle of food beneath her head, was tugging at the tangles in her hair. When she lifted her head, it dropped to the ground and growled. It was broad daylight and she could hear the sound of a man's boots pounding along the path towards her. Was it her father?

'Are you all right, miss?' the man yelled. 'You had me worried. I thought for a minute you was a gonna.'

Amy tried to smile. What a mess she must have looked; her coat-front caked in mud, clay crusted on her hands; her face dirty; her hair dishevelled.

'I tripped,' she said, smoothing her hair. 'I must've knocked my head.'

'So long as there's no damage. Here, give us your hand.'

The man's help was appreciated. She was stiff and sore. 'Is it Saturday?' she asked.

He looked her up and down and nodded. 'Well, I must get along,' he said.

'Yes,' said Amy. 'I should've been at the mill hours ago. I best get home too, the folks'll be wondering what happened to me.'

'I'm sure they wouldn't want you wandering these parts at night in future. Some odd sorts around at times.'

They exchanged glances.

'I'll remember that,' Amy said. 'Thanks.'

The small dog whined as it scratched at a hole. The man touched his cap, whistled and walked on.

Amy looked around. Everything was green. There was no sign of streets or mills, just trees and reeds and ponds and everything moist and lush. On a pond nearby, a goosander swam in circles till a kingfisher dived, disturbing it. A family of moorhens ducked in and out of the reeds, the ducklings cheeping unconcerned. Apart from the birdsong, the place was strangely quiet.

In her pocket, the coins rattled. Some consolation at least. There was dampness in the air and she was grateful for her mother's old coat. When the layer of mud dried, she'd be able to rub it off.

Above, the dark clouds tinged with rusty pink, looked troublesome. It was going to rain. Running away was not working out as well as planned. She should have been further from Fanshaw's by now. Her efforts of the previous night had only carried her a little over a mile and despite her earlier thoughts of travelling in the rain, one spell in a wet ditch had taught her differently. It would be foolish to get soaked right through.

The rain came as expected. Heavy sheeting rain which was impossible to see through let alone walk. Sitting on the towing path as it curved beneath one of the bridges, she waited. A sparrow kept her company. The time passed very slowly. Then, as quickly as it had started, it cleared and the July sun shone warmly, raising a haze of mist across the meadows. Amy continued, this time at a quicker pace.

By midday she'd passed more locks. She heard the sounds of a forge, and smelt the hops from a brewery. Perched on the hills were houses, church spires; mill chimneys poked up from the distant valleys. She was still close to the villages which surrounded Leeds. The woollen coat was cumbersome and heavy, and carrying it made her sweat. She was thankful that most of the walking was along the flat path with only short hills beside the locks. During the morning a couple of coal barges swam quietly by. She stepped off the towing path to let the horses pass, but the boatmen ignored her. Considering her appearance, she wasn't surprised. She satisfied her hunger with a piece of cheese salvaged from her rations, washing it down with water from a spring which bubbled from the bank. Several more barges passed, going in the other direction. This part of the canal was busy, but like the railway beside it, she knew it was heading west and taking her away from Leeds.

With no sign of her father, her thoughts turned to food. As she emerged from the marshlands, a field of untended rhubarb offered some relief. Scrambling from the bank, Amy pulled several stalks, broke off the broad leaves and chewed on the sappy stems. Her face screwed when she swallowed but despite the fact it was sour, she collected a handful of stalks and pushed them into her pocket. Five minutes later, pains rolled across her belly and she had to stop.

From behind her came the chugging of a steam barge. As it rounded the bend, she saw the chimney with smoke puffing from it before the boat emerged. Slowly it caught up to her. It was towing a smaller barge behind it. Amy lifted her hand to wave, but the boatman's only interest was the channel ahead and the dumb-boat he was pulling. Amy watched as they drifted by. The lead boat was a pretty craft with decorations painted on its flat transom. The second boat was dull in comparison. It was heavily laden and had no cabin. Both barges were loaded with sawn timber.

As she walked on, she watched the boats extend their distance till they finally disappeared, but at the next set of locks, she passed them. As she walked up the short hill beside the risers, the man on the gate acknowledged her. But that was the last she saw of the two boats.

In the course of the afternoon, Amy walked on. On the tops, the grey-green fields melded into mauve. The dry-stone walls crisscrossed the hillsides like cracks in an old plate. Roads and bridle tracks didn't linger beside the canal but crossed on swing bridges barely high enough for the barges to swim under. Along the bank blackberry bushes abounded, but it was too early to sample the fruit. Then the showers returned.

The next passing boatman was sociable. He knuckled his forehead and wished Amy 'Afternoon'. A young boy, hardly the height of the horse's withers, strode beside it on the towing path, whistling. Amy smiled and echoed a reply. A dog poked its head from a painted kennel atop the cabin roof and snapped out a greeting. Had the boat not been heading towards Leeds, she would have asked for a lift. She knew there would be other barges heading west and hoped one, at least, would appear friendly.

As the afternoon wore on, Amy's stride shortened. Only one more boat floated by that afternoon — another steam barge. Resting her legs, she perched on a stump beside the towing path and gave the boatman a wearied wave. Though she was sure he had seen her, he showed no response, his eyes not shifting from the waterway ahead. The boat left barely a ripple in its wake but it was enough to attract a flock of swallows which swooped, skimming the water in search of food. A few feet away, a vole crossed the path. It stopped for a moment and studied Amy before sliding into the water. On the other bank, a fox appeared and drank from a puddle. When it saw her it turned and trotted stealthily away.

A line of clouds on the horizon looked ominous. More rain would mean she'd need to shelter somewhere. On the hillside, not fifty yards from the canal, stood an old farm cottage. A track led from it down to a little-used wharf. Now overgrown, it was merely a worn pad where boats could moor to load skins or stock feed, or unload timber. Amy clinked the coins in her pocket. Perhaps she could purchase a cup of milk and a nob of bread.

Rubbing the dried mud from her clothes, Amy raked her fingers through her hair, spat on her hand and tried to wash the dirt from around her mouth. She wandered up the track. Cows lowed in the meadow and the smell of the hay-barn reached her before she got to the farm gate. It leaned open, hanging from one hinge, old grass woven through its wooden slats. It was a long time since it had been shut. From the gate, a path, potted with puddles, led to the house. As Amy started into the yard, a gaggle of geese advanced on her, necks extended, wings flapping, beaks clacking at her alarmingly.

'We don't want none o' your sort round

here!' the farmer cried, as he appeared from the house. 'Be off with you, before I set the dogs on you! We don't want no beggars around 'ere.'

'I want to buy a pot of milk. I've got money. I can pay,' Amy replied, as defiantly as she dare, but her voice only encouraged the din and when the two dogs headed towards her, she turned and ran. The black and white pair stopped when they reached the gate, their tails wagging. Amy stopped and looked back. The dogs appeared friendly but the geese were another matter. As she returned to the canal path, she heard the farmer's piercing whistle. The dogs turned and hared across the yard, scattering the geese as they waddled back to the pond.

In the doorway of the farmhouse, a robust woman shook scraps from a chequered cloth. Within seconds, a scurry of chickens were squawking around her feet, pecking at the morsels.

'What's all the hullabaloo about?'

'Bloody gypsies!' the farmer mumbled, patting his dogs. His wife glanced around then disappeared inside.

Feeling drained and tired, the few yards back to the towing path seemed like a mile. Amy knew there was no real shelter, only weeds and bushes and a hedgerow full of blackberry bushes. If it rained in the night she'd get soaked. Perhaps she should turn back to Leeds and the shelter of the bridges. But she'd no energy or enthusiasm for walking, and those places were dark and dismal even by day. Certainly not the sorts of places to loiter under at night. She'd seen enough of Leeds and the smell of the nearby brewery had reminded her of the Hungry Crow. At the moment, she couldn't go on, but she wouldn't turn back. She'd have to find some other alternative.

8

Milkwort

Sinking to the grass, Amy pulled a stick of rhubarb from her pocket and bit into it. It wasn't ripe and though she tried to chew it, it was too sour. Remembering what had happened the last time she ate a piece, she spat it out.

For quite a while she'd seen no boats or trains. The air was ominously still — no wind, no birds, only gathering clouds which were rolling down from the moors. Already they had shrouded the sun, and dusk was draining all too quickly. Amy hugged her legs and laid her head on her knees. She wanted to sleep, to wake up and find she was somewhere other than on the canal's bank. She knew she had to move on. But where to? Ahead there'd be more bridges to shelter under, she hoped. But how far away were they?

On the far hillside, beyond the trees, smoke rose from several chimney pots. A row of houses? Another village? Maybe. She thought of asking for shelter. Then she looked down at her coat and laughed cynically. Who'd take me in? No one. And she didn't want to be turned away again.

As evening changed quickly into night, the wind, streaked with rain, returned. It gusted down the canal, disturbing the stagnant surface. The sliver of moon she'd watched the previous evening did not appear, and there were no stars. The only visible light was from a downstairs room in the farmhouse. She imagined a kitchen and the table set with a gingham cloth: there'd be the smell of meat roasting in the oven, cabbage cooking in a pot, a kettle singing on the stove and a cat with a litter of kittens sitting by the hearth. She turned the collar up on her coat and huddled forward, the wind against her back.

As she watched, the light in the farmhouse flickered and dimmed. It was as if the lamp's wick was almost spent. Then a moment later, the glow reappeared from the upstairs window, shining more brightly. A figure moved across the room, then within minutes the light was extinguished, leaving the farmhouse as a black silhouette against the hill.

A sheep bleated anxiously from a nearby field. The dogs barked for a while, but the farmer was settled for the night and showed no concern. Soon all was silent on the canal bank, save for the wind rustling through the rushes at the other side.

* ★ *

Using her coat as a blanket, Amy covered her ears to the sound of rain pounding on the slate roof. The pile of hay and manure at the back of the barn exuded warmth and she slept soundly. Sometime during the night, the dogs joined her, though she was unaware of it till morning, when she woke to the drag of a rasping tongue on her cheek. For a moment she thought she was back on the canal path.

In the yard outside, the geese honked. Chickens squawked. It was daylight and the rain had stopped. Clambering from the hay, Amy heard the farmer whistle for his dogs. In an instant, they were off, out of the barn, jumping the puddles in the yard to join the farmer as he headed up over the field.

Amy pulled on her coat.

'You should see yourself!' the farmer's wife said. 'You look like a blinking scarecrow!'

Amy hadn't noticed the woman leaning over the milking bail. There was no hint of a smile on the ruddy face, but there was a twinkle in her brown eyes.

Rubbing her head, Amy pulled the stalks of hay from her hair, but the ears of wheat were hooked firmly between the thin threads of her woollen coat.

'Come 'ere,' she said. 'Turn your body around.'

Following the instruction, Amy let the woman brush the straw from her.

'Now, tell me what you're up to in our barn. You're no gypsy, that's for sure, and I've seen better-looking tramps.'

Amy couldn't lie. The woman had an honest face. 'I'm heading for Lancashire, and I fell in a ditch, but I've got some money and I just wanted to buy something to eat.' Pushing her hand in her pocket, she retrieved the few remaining coins and held them out. 'I can pay.'

'Running away, I bet! Well, that ain't none of my business. But we got milk to spare, and I've pickled more eggs than I care to mention. If you're quick, I'll feed you up and pack you off before my man comes back.'

Amy was grateful. She drank two mugs of tea sweetened with honey and a cup of cream, and ate as fast as she possibly could. The bread was thick and buttered. The apple pie warm from the oven. By the time she'd cleared her plate, there were six eggs ready to slip into her pockets — hard boiled and still hot.

'How much do you want for them?' Amy asked.

'The dogs and pigs eat what we can't

manage. You just get on your way before his nibs comes back.' There was a smile in the woman's eye as she wished Amy good luck. It was like the smile she used to see in her mother's eyes — before her father came home.

'Thank you,' she said.

★　★　★

Mist rose from the canal's bank. The air was dank, the reeds decked with dozens of beaded cobwebs. As the sun shone on the dewdrops, it caught on a few, transforming them into shining gems — brilliant blue, red or green. Amy watched mesmerized. Then the sun disappeared, taking its magic with it.

Aware she was still not far from Leeds, she urged herself to hurry on. She wondered about the canal path stretching out in front of her. Did it ever end or did it wander around England from one corner to the other? She consoled herself with the fact that this morning her hunger had been satisfied and she felt refreshed. She'd been lucky. The farmer's wife had been generous. Others might not be so kind.

During the morning a barge approached. The horse towing it was a black shire. It was handsomely decorated with bright red terrets and a pair of white lace earcaps trimmed with coloured tassels. The polished brasses, hanging from its collar, glinted as they swung. Amy eyed the woman walking alongside it. How strangely she was dressed. Her pleated skirt was wide and short, revealing the tops of her boots. Over her shoulders she had a brightly coloured crocheted scarf, which she crossed over her chest and tucked into her skirt. And on her head was an ample black bonnet whose flounce fell almost to her waist. She wore gold earrings and the bangles on her wrist jangled. The woman acknowledged Amy with a nod and walked on, her eyes fixed on the waterway which was her home. The boatman, his arm resting on the brightly painted tiller, murmured, 'Hello,' but nothing more.

The rain started again mid-morning, the steady drizzle shrouding the hills in mist and making it hard to see far ahead. Not wanting to get any wetter, Amy took shelter in the bushes on the bank and waited for the weather to clear. She ate one of her eggs and threw the shell into the water. A pair of brown ducks squabbled over the broken pieces. A barge carrying coal steamed past heading west. A boat loaded with skins swam east to the tanneries in Leeds. The horse flicked its tail as it walked along, but the boatmen didn't seem to notice that his cargo was alive with flies. The rotten smell lingered long after it had gone by. Though the rain dripped from the brims of the boatmen's caps, they seemed oblivious to it. They were interested in nothing but the navigation ahead.

When the rain finally stopped, the sun emerged, and Amy hurried out along the path. Half a mile ahead, the path rose steeply beside two sets of locks. A boy walked around to the beam of the top gate and waited. He looked familiar. As she got closer, Amy could hear a woman's muffled voice calling from the bottom of one of the chambers. 'You can open the paddles now.'

Amy smiled at the boy and peered down into the lock and the broad barge which almost filled it. The brick walls were much deeper than Amy had imagined. The boatwoman, whose voice she had heard, was poised with her hand on the tiller. As the boy operated the ground paddles, water began pouring into the chamber. Very slowly the level began to rise, lifting the heavily laden short-boat with it. Once the water in the lock was level with that of the canal beyond, the boy leaned his back on the beam, opening first one gate and then the other. Then he returned to the towing path and started pulling on the rope. From the deck of the boat, the woman pushed against the gate behind her with a pole, but the boat didn't move.

'Do you need some help?' Amy asked.

The boy didn't answer, but he handed her the end of the rope. They hauled on it together.

Inch by inch, the barge slid out of the lock and drifted along the canal.

'You can stop pulling now,' the boy said. 'Drop the line! Get out of the way!'

Amy wondered what she had done wrong. The boat was moving. Wasn't that what they wanted? But the boy had stopped hauling and was winding the line around a wooden bollard.

Within minutes, the woman brought the barge up against the bank and her son secured it to a mooring spike. Once the aft line was secured, all that remained was to tidy the lines and close the gates they had just locked through.

'Ta for your help,' the woman called. 'Good to get through to the next pound. More chance of a tow in the morning.'

Amy looked at her, not knowing what to say. It was raining again, little more than a drizzle, but her hair was plastered to her head and water was running down her neck.

'You walking up from Leeds?'

Amy nodded and wiped the drips from her nose.

'We heard you were on the path. News travels on the cut. Want to come aboard and dry yourself?'

Amy was pleased to accept and thanked her. She hoped the stories she had heard of barge folk were not true.

'Careful when you jump on. Wouldn't want you to slip.'

Amy bunched her skirt into one hand and took the woman's outstretched hand with the other. Now she understood why the boat-women's skirts were shorter than usual.

The barge was broad, almost five paces wide, but the strip of deck, where the woman had been standing, was quite narrow. Ahead of the tiller was a cabin, its wooden roof rising little more than four feet from the deck. The sliding hatch, decorated with roses, was open.

'Who's that?' a gruff voice called from the cabin.

Amy jumped.

'That's Joel, my man. He's laid up. Can't get out of bed. Come in and meet him.' She indicated for Amy to go inside. 'Step down and duck your head, and keep it ducked.'

There were two small steps down to the

cabin floor but the roof still wasn't high enough for her to stand upright. The woman pushed a stool towards her. Sitting down, Amy gazed around, wide-eyed. On the right was the bed, broad and solid, running three-quarter the length of the living quarters. Tacked along the edges of the bed was a fringe of hand-crocheted lace. It hid a row of cupboards. At the opposite side of the cabin was a narrow hinged table and bench, and above them a long single shelf also trimmed with white cotton lace. Various ornaments lined the shelves: brass bells and candlesticks, vases and painted plates. On the panelled wall hung at least a dozen horse brasses, all different and all gleaming as if just polished. Narrow drapes hung by the side of the two small leaded windows, and painted roses similar to the ones on the sliding doors were repeated on the panels of the tall cupboard at the far end of the bed. Every piece of woodwork had been varnished but in parts the varnish had bubbled and in others it was peeling. The stove which backed on to the bulkhead was open fronted. It had a hob clipped on the top bars and a shiny brass fireguard stood in front of it. The tiny galley was opposite the bed. The brass scuttle, filled with coal, had a country scene with a cottage painted on it. A square chimney poked up through the cabin roof and around its neck, it too wore a collar of white lace. The large pot rattling on the hob smelt of mutton stew.

Sitting on the bed was a dark-haired man in his mid forties. His legs were covered by a brightly dyed felt rug. The colour of his shirt amazed Amy. It was whiter than any she'd seen on any mill worker, even on a Sunday. His waistcoat, made from hand-woven cloth, was trimmed with plaited braid while around his neck he wore a bottle-green scarf tied neatly in a knot at the front.

The stories she'd been told of dirty bargees had always made her wary of them. Seeing the appearance of the boatman amazed her.

'How long have you been awake?' his wife asked.

'Not long,' Joel said, as he cast his eyes over Amy. 'Off the cut?'

She didn't understand.

'He wants to know if you work on the canal.'

'No, I don't.'

'Then what's she doing here?'

'She helped Ben pull us out of the Dobson Staircase. She's the lass they've been talking about — walking the cut.'

Joel leaned forward and pressed a cushion behind his back. 'Where you off to, lass? Who you fleeing from?'

The boatman's questions surprised her. How did he know she was running away?

'Anything to do with the cut gets passed along from one barge to another. Like the telegraph, but on the water.'

His wife interrupted. 'Take your coat off, lass, you're soaked. You can answer his questions later. I've got stew and dumplings on the stove. Want some?'

'Yes, please.'

'What's your name, lass?' the man said.

'Amy Dodd.'

'That's right,' he said knowingly. 'This here is my missus, Helen. My lad's name's Ben — Big Ben they'll call him when he's full grown, like the clock on the River Thames.' He smiled. 'Ten year ago we used to navigate them waters. Born on them we were. I worked with my pa for thirty years on the Kennet and Avon. But the railway through to Bath took the trade from us. Brought ruin to a lot of the boatmen. So we came up here.'

As he spoke, the boy's footsteps pattered on the deck.

'You got her lashed firm?' Joel called.

'Yes, Pa.'

'Good lad.'

'You all right, Pa?'

'Aye, son.'

As the man spoke, he folded back the rug

that was covering his legs. From his groin to the sole of his foot, his left leg was cased in slats of wood held together with strips of cloth.

'Doctor said I should get a cast put on it,' he said. 'But we didn't have time to waste. I'm not much for hospitals and I told him so. 'You're all alike, you boatmen — too independent for your own good.' That's what he said. But he straightened my leg and boxed it for me. Now I feel like half of me's in a coffin.' He laughed. 'It'll be a long time before you get the rest of me in though.' As he tried to shift his position, his face screwed with pain. 'Doctor said I shouldn't move it for six weeks, but I told him, 'Bugger that! Couple of weeks and it'll be right!''

Helen smiled sympathetically. 'It were bad. Doctor said he'd broken more than one bone, and though he doesn't complain much about the pain, he gave me some powder to give him when it gets bad.'

'It works a treat,' Joel said. 'She puts a dose in me cocoa and I sleep like a sunken log.'

His wife tapped him playfully on the wrist. 'Only way to keep you from climbing out of bed.'

Not knowing how to respond, Amy asked, 'How did it happen?'

He shook his head. 'Bessie, our horse,

broke down. Just like that,' he said, clicking his finger and thumb together. 'Broke down and landed on me and broke me leg in the bargain. I was glad it wasn't Helen or Ben walking with her that day. A thousand pounds of horse flesh is a fair weight! It couldn't have happened at a worse time. We've got a load of alpaca wool overdue at Saltaire. Valuable cargo, it is. It's come all the way from South America. And here's me laid up and no animal to get us there. And beside that, it's raining.'

'Aye,' Helen said, 'but you must admit, the lads on the cut have been good.' She turned her head to Amy. 'We've had a couple of decent tows from steam barges. But they don't want to wait for us through the rises — the locks, that is. You can't expect 'em to either. That's why we get through on our own. We've been lucky a few times when there's been another boat coming the other way. They've helped us through. Boatmen are good like that when they know you're in strife.' She smiled at her husband. 'If we're lucky tomorrow, we'll get a tow from here right up to the mill. It's not far.'

'If there's no other boats, I can help with the pulling,' said Amy. 'I'm strong.'

'Pulling's for horses,' said Helen, shaking her head, 'but Joel can't get out to buy another horse till he's back on his feet. I told him our Ben's a good judge of horse flesh, but he's choosy when it comes to a boat-horse.'

'And rightly so,' he said. 'A good boat deserves a good horse and *Milkwort*'s a good boat. I fitted her out myself,' he said, looking proudly around his cabin. 'You'll not see another one like this on the cut.'

'So how will you manage, without a horse?'

'We've worked it out, so we make the best of a bad thing. When we get this load taken off, we'll live off our docking money and fix the boat up. We can afford not to work for a while.'

'*Milkwort* is ours,' said Helen proudly. 'It doesn't belong to the Leeds and Liverpool Canal Company.'

Joel continued. 'We're what's known on the cut as Number Ones. We do our own trade. Pick up what we want. Go where we want. No one tells us what to do. Not like the short-boats you see carrying coal. You'll see lots of them around Leeds. They've got the L and L company name on the bow. The men on those barges don't own their craft. They pick up a different one with every load.' He looked at his wife. 'What we plan, when we get to Saltaire, is to put *Milkwort* in Jentz's Yard. She's well overdue for caulking and a coat of tar on her bottom.'

'Aye, and a splash of paint and varnish in the cabin too.'

'You're not going to Liverpool then?' said Amy.

'Who knows where we'll go?' Joel said. 'When we leave Jentz's Yard, we'll pick up another load and go wherever we have to — maybe back to Leeds or down the Aire and Calder to the coast. But I can tell you, lass, we'll not be going over the Pennines. I can't walk or even stand at the moment, so I certainly couldn't leg it for a mile through the Foulridge Tunnel. And I can't expect Helen or young Ben to leg us through.'

Helen looked at Amy sympathetically. 'I can see by your face you're disappointed we're not going to Lancashire. Is that where you want to go?'

'I don't know what I want,' said Amy pensively. 'I just know I want to get away from Leeds — as far away as possible!'

★　★　★

That night, Amy slept in the small cabin at the opposite end of the barge to the main cabin. Between the two bulkheads was the short-boat's cargo — the tons of imported fibre packed into dozens of bales and covered with tarpaulins.

116

The forward accommodation was compact. Ben's bunk was built against one wall. It had a curtain around it which could be pulled back when needed, and like the big bed in the main cabin, the area underneath it was made into cupboards. On the opposite wall was a large wooden locker with a flat top. This, with a flock mattress laid along it, was Amy's bed for the night. Against the bulkhead was a fixed cupboard, stretching half the width of the boat. This cabin also had a stove but it was smaller than the one Helen used for cooking. Stacked neatly on the floor was an assortment of items: two sacks of grain, several bags of flour, a barrel of potatoes, containers, buckets, jugs and a wash tub with a sheaf of wheat laying across it. On top was a coil of white cotton rope, and resting on that a well-worn leather horse collar and harness.

As Amy lay gazing out of the tiny window next to her head, Ben pulled back the curtain and asked, 'Can you read?'

'Yes,' she said. 'Can you?'

'Not yet, but I want to learn, and Pa said, if I learn, he'll buy a paper and I can read it to him and the other boat folk on Sundays.'

'What about school?'

'Never been. We never stop long enough in one place. Pa teaches me everything. Says I'll make a good barge man. Says I already know

117

the cut nearly as good as he does.'

'You like living on the canal?'

'Wouldn't want to be anywhere else!' With that, Ben let the curtain fall back. 'G'night,' he said.

The flock mattress was not as soft as the deep litter in the barn, but the cabin was cosy, and Amy felt safe. Lying on her back, her mind drifted to the events of the previous week. She thought about her mother's burial, about Fanshaw's Mill, even about Mr Lister — the way he walked, the way he'd looked at her and the accidental touches when he measured her which had made her heart flutter.

She thought about the boat family she'd met and of the stories she'd been told of dirty bargees. Then she thought of painted decorations and all the ornaments which made the cabin look like Aladdin's Cave. How fortunate she'd been to meet up with *Milkwort*. Most of the other boatmen had ignored her — though from what Joel said, that wasn't the case. She was surprised that word about her had travelled along the canal.

Then her thoughts flashed to her father.

She could still hear his cry echoing in her head: *Amy Dodd! Amy Dodd! Where are you?* And everyone on the streets would have heard him too. By now they'd all know it was

118

Amy Dodd who'd caused the commotion at the mill, and they'd all know that she'd run away.

But what if he found out where she was? What if word got back to him that she'd been seen on the canal? He'd be on the towing path after her. She knew that for sure.

★   ★   ★

In the dim shadows of the Dark Arches, beneath the Leeds railway station, Amos Dodd breathed heavily as he thrust himself jerkily into the girl. He couldn't see her face, but had no desire to. After the final grunt, his knees crumpled. He threw his head back and his whole body shuddered involuntarily.

'That were quick!' the woman said, tugging at her skirt, which was twisted up between them. 'Want some more?' she asked, as she drew herself away from him.

Dodd didn't answer. He fastened his trouser buttons, sucked in the dank air and tightened the belt around his waist. He was pleased with himself. The bit of news he'd gleaned deserved a treat. The day spent hauling baulks of timber from the barges had paid off in more ways than one. He'd satisfied the yapping of his landlady and he'd heard word of a girl sheltering under one of the

Leeds bridges. But that was all he heard. Nothing more, and no amount of threats would jog the boatmen's memories. Even so, Dodd was certain it was Amy. It had to be. Now he had to find out which way she'd gone. Was she heading east for the Humber and Hull, or west on the Leeds and Liverpool towards Lancashire?

As he'd heard the news near the Basin, he thought it more likely she was on the Aire and Calder. He doubted she'd ever step foot near Fanshaw's again, but he intended to make certain.

'You'll burn in hell when I find you, girl!'

A train rumbled overhead.

'What's that you say?' the figure beside him asked. 'Want to find another girl? Aren't I good enough?' she said, sliding her hand up the inside of his trouser leg. 'Good enough for the likes of you, I reckon!'

The punch sent her reeling backwards into one of the stone pillars. With blood oozing between her fingers, she pressed on the tooth that was sticking through her bottom lip.

'Bastard!' she cried as he walked away.

Amos Dodd ignored her. He had other things on his mind.

9

The Rises

The sound of rushing water woke her. She could feel the barge rocking slightly and wondered if they'd turned around and gone to the coast. But the sea was a long way off, and how could the barge have turned? Didn't Helen say the canal was barely broad enough for two barges to pass and that there was nowhere up ahead wide enough to turn a short-boat which measured sixty-five feet in length?

After rubbing the sleep from her eyes, Amy looked out of the tiny window. It was dull outside, like daylight veiled by an afternoon storm. Little more than an arm's length away from the barge, she was confronted by a brick wall glistening with blackened slime and it was slowly sinking beneath the boat. Dragging her skirt up over her petticoat, she fastened the buttons of her stained blouse and opened the cabin door. *Milkwort* was rising slowly in the lock. Ahead were the gates which held back the waters of the canal. Above, the sky was dappled blue and grey.

The boatwoman with the gold earrings was standing at the stern, her hand on the tiller.

'Stay by the cabin!' Ben shouted when he saw her. 'Don't go near the edge.' Amy glanced down to the water pouring into the lock and bubbling around the bow.

Joel's muffled call could be heard from the main cabin at the other end of the barge. 'Keep clear of the gates!'

Helen didn't answer. She knew the danger of being inside a barge while it was in the lock. Knew that if the rudder caught on the sill, the boat could tip and be inundated by the rising water. It didn't happen often, but she'd seen it once on the cut. A barge had flipped in a chamber, causing chaos on the canal. It had taken several days for the boat to be righted and the forty tons of limestone bucketed by hand from the bottom of the lock. She'd also seen boats flooded due to carelessness, and she'd heard of a few experienced boat folk who'd died in the locks.

She glanced along the length of the boat at the distance between the walls and the side of the barge. There was a gap of less than a hand's span, but there was a yard from the gate to the bow.

'Can I do anything?' Amy shouted.

'Just stay still. I don't want you slipping over. You'd drown for sure if you fell. That's if you didn't get crushed first.'

Leaning against the cabin door, Amy watched the froth churning, as water poured in from the pound above. Ben observed from the gate.

'Keep clear of the sill!' Joel shouted from the cabin, his frustration at being unable to control his own boat obvious.

'I'm not daft,' Helen mumbled as she monitored the gap between the rudder and the gates. The chamber filled slowly.

Once the level in the lock was the same as the canal ahead, Ben opened the gate and pulled the short-boat out on to the canal. It drifted for a while. A stump made a good bollard to bring it to a stop.

'Give Amy a hand off,' Helen said. 'She can help with the gates.'

From his expression, it was obvious Ben didn't need any help. Nevertheless, he stuck out his hand.

Taking one beam each, the pair pushed the huge gates together until the breast posts met and sealed out the water as tight as a drum.

'Don't forget the paddles!' Joel shouted.

Ben shook his head and handed the cotton rope to Amy. 'Go down the path and start pulling when I tell you to.'

Amy looked stunned at his request.

'It's not hard once she starts to move,' he

said, smiling. 'You're in luck — we're not carrying slate or stone!'

Amy walked almost fifty yards along the path, dragging the rope through the water, while Ben ran back, quickly closed the paddles, then returned to the barge. With his foot, he pushed *Milkwort*'s bow from the bank. 'Pull now!' he shouted.

'Pull!' echoed Helen from the stern, her hand guiding the large rudder.

Shaking the stone dust from the wet rope, Amy placed it over her shoulder and pulled. As she glanced back, the rope snaked up from the canal and splashed back on the surface like a skipping rope spanking puddles. As she stumbled on, the rope stretched, then tightened, and the barge slowly started to move. From the deck, Helen steered a course down the centre of the channel. A few minutes later, Ben joined Amy on the rope, laid it on his shoulder and leaned on to it. 'Once she's moving, it's easy,' he said. With the pair of them pulling, *Milkwort* slid along at a steady walking pace.

Amy had expected them to stop once they were well clear of the locks, but Helen said nothing and Ben kept walking, with *Milkwort* drifting silently behind. Though Ben said it was easy, Amy could feel the sweat running down her legs.

'Is it far to the next lock?'

'Over three miles to Hirst Lock. That's just past the mill in Saltaire so we won't be locking through it. Nice clean pound between here and the mill,' he said. 'Not like the Basin in Leeds where all the rubbish gets thrown in. Do you live in the city?'

'I did.'

'Going back there?'

Amy shook her head though the boy on the rope in front couldn't see her.

'Do you have to haul the barge by hand very often?' Then she remembered the dead horse and wished she hadn't asked. 'You must be strong,' she said.

'That's what folk think, but it's not hard on the cut. Pa says a carthorse can pull two tons on land. A boat-horse can pull thirty to fifty tons on water.'

'Was she a good horse, the one that died?'

'Aye,' Ben said.

As the River Aire snaked lazily towards Shipley, the canal nudged up alongside it and the Midland Railway shared the course with them. Unlike the city where the narrow strip of land between the two channels bore barely a blade of grass, here the vegetation was overgrown. Masses of white elderflowers attracted bees, and pink mallow bloomed prolifically from old bushes. The sycamores on the bank provided a canopy of shade while willows teased the water with graceful sweeps of their slender branches. Birds flitted through the hedgerows, dragonflies hovered, and the air hummed with the sound of busy insects.

In tiny coves where the canal's bank had collapsed, moorhens and ducks waddled ashore. A pair of haughty swans circled slowly, ignoring the passing boat, but a heron flew off as soon as the short-boat approached.

When another barge passed, Helen spoke to the man on the tiller, but Amy didn't hear what was said. As it chugged by, the smoke puffing steadily from its chimney hung like a cloud over the damp marsh.

'Will you have one of those one day?' Amy asked, as they watched it pass.

'No. Not me or Pa,' he said. 'We like things the way they are.'

With Ben hauling, Amy walked beside him listening to him talk about the cut, the canal folk who worked it, and the places they'd visited to pick up or deliver cargo. She'd never heard of most of the towns and wondered where they all were.

Suddenly the *clickety-clack* of a passing train interrupted her thoughts. She turned her head from the sound, aware of the faces framed in the compartment windows gazing in her direction. What if her father was on the train? What if he was waiting for her at the next town? She hadn't thought about him since she'd woken that morning but now the fear of him finding her returned.

★ ★ ★

With little over half a mile to the point where the Bradford Canal joined the Leeds and Liverpool, Ben slowed to let three coal barges pass. Though they were all steam powered, they moved little faster than the barge they were hauling by hand.

'I want to stop at the Red Terret,' Joel shouted. 'We'll moor there for the night. Too late to get into Saltaire today.'

As they got close to the inn's wharf, Ben slowed the boat and Helen steered it gently up against the bank.

'Go steady,' Joel shouted, from below.

Helen raised her eyebrows. 'We're already alongside,' she answered, before turning to Amy. 'Poor Joel. He hates being stuck inside.' She pushed her hair under her pleated bonnet before throwing the aft mooring line to her son. 'Normally he'd never say a word when we moor or lock. He knows darn well me and Ben can work the boat with our eyes closed, and that goes for the staircases too. But it's eating him up, having to stay below. Still, it'll be better when we're at Jentz's Yard. At least, in a way, we'll be off the cut.'

There were several barges moored on that stretch of canal — the three which had passed them earlier, two Hargreaves' boats from Blackburn and three others. Amy remembered what Joel had said about company boats and noted how dull they were in comparison to *Milkwort*. Apart from the names and numbers and a little scrollwork decorating the panels on either side of the stem post, they displayed little or no fancywork, and the mooring ropes and fenders were engrained with coal dust. So different from the white rope fenders Joel had woven, which Helen scrubbed daily.

The Red Terret Inn was located not more than twenty yards from the towing path. Joel knew the boatmen would be at the inn and he wanted to talk with them. He needed to make enquiries about a boat-horse, find out if there were any for sale.

'You can come up with me if you like,' Helen said, but Amy declined. She'd had her share of inns and the types of men who frequented them. Thanking her, she said she preferred to stay on the barge. Ben was happy to go with his mother.

While they were gone, Joel explained, 'It's not like a city inn, lass. There's stables at the back for the horses. We used to stop here and put old Bessie in at times. You can't walk a horse all the time, you know.'

It wasn't long before Helen returned, carrying a tray with three jugs of ale. Ben followed behind, hands in pockets, talking confidently to two of the boatmen. Amy considered, by the likeness of their gait and faces, they were father and son. The colour of their clothes and the black dust engrained in the creases of their skin confirmed what cargo they were carrying.

While it was customary for the men to sit out on the bank to talk, because of Joel's incapacity, they were invited into the cabin. Ben and Amy sat on the bales of fibre and listened to the conversation. It was obvious from his voice how pleased Joel was to have some company, and even though the bargees weren't Number Ones, like himself, he respected their knowledge of the canal. They'd been on this navigation longer than him and they knew every inch of it and everything that happened on it.

Over the next hour, they enjoyed their ale, telling jokes and laughing and exchanging yarns. The company men told of a narrow-boat that had sunk in the Trent.

'That's a dangerous stretch of water,' one said.

And there was a barge had burnt out at Crown Point.

'Nearly set fire to Timber Island,' the older man said.

'Company boat?'

'Aye.'

Joel asked if they'd heard of any good horses that were for sale.

'There was one,' the father said, 'but I think it's been sold. Belonged to Faraway Farley, the old boatman who never spoke to anyone. His horse was found on the path in Skipton, fifteen miles from where *Faraway* was moored. Must have followed the path on its own. When it was walked back, they found him stone dead in his cabin. Must have been there a week. They said the cabin stunk to high heaven.'

'And that horse of yours — you could smell that too. It were still on the bank when we came through yesterday.'

'The knacker was supposed to take it nearly a week ago,' Joel said angrily.

'He'll not take it now. It'll end up in the River Aire.'

'Aye, and it'll not be alone. When I were a lad, they were pulling fifty animals a day out of that stretch in Leeds. Filthy river, it were.'

130

The other man laughed. 'No much better now.'

'Hard to believe it were once a salmon stream.'

'Anyone been asking questions about a lass on the cut?' Joel asked.

The younger man drained his pot. 'Aye,' he said. 'At Victoria Wharf, there was a fellow said he was looking for his daughter. Said she'd got herself in trouble and run away. Said he was worried to death about her.'

'I didn't think he looked worried,' the other man said, turning to Joel. 'That's what one of the boys told him — made a bit of a joke of it. But this fella didn't take kindly to the jest and pulled out a knife. Then everyone clamped up.'

From her seat on the top of the tarpaulin, Amy listened.

Later that evening, when the men had returned to their boats, Amy spoke to Helen. 'I should go away,' she said. 'I don't want you or Joel to get into strife because of me.'

'What are you afraid of?'

'The man they were talking about with the knife was my father. And from what Ben has told me, a man on foot can easily beat a barge in a day's travel, especially if there are locks along the canal. What if word gets back from the bargees that they've seen me? What if my father catches up to us? What if he knows the name of the boat I'm on?'

'Trust me,' said Helen. 'The boatmen out there won't whisper a word that they've seen you and that's the truth. What goes on on the cut stays on the cut.'

'You'll be safe with us,' Joel added. 'See those brasses hanging on the wall over there? Supposed to be magic charms, to keep us safe. The idea were passed to the boatmen from the gypsies.'

Helen smiled.

'As for the name of *Milkwort*, I'll tell Ben to take care of that. When we get into Jentz's dock tomorrow, his first job'll be to scrape the old paint off. Any boatman can recognize a barge without its name, but anyone who's not off the cut will never identify it.'

'Why would you do that for me?'

'Well,' he said, looking across at his wife. 'It ain't just out of the goodness of my heart. We've got a cargo to unload tomorrow and a boat to scrub down after it's gone. We could use another pair of hands to help us out, at least for a couple of days.'

★ ★ ★

'Where is she?' Dodd demanded, pushing open the front door and forcing Mrs Medley

132

back against the wall.

'Watch what you're doing, you stupid oaf!'

'Where is she?'

'Amy's not here. I told you that the last time you called. And I doubt she'll come back while you're around!'

Amos Dodd sneered at her as he shoved her aside and stepped into the cluttered kitchen. For a moment the two children on the mat froze, then the youngest dropped the tin soldier from his hand and ran to his mother, grabbing her tightly around the leg.

'It's all right, kids,' Mrs Medley said quietly. 'Now, you get out of my house, mister, before I call for a constable!' she yelled.

'I bet you know where she's hiding.'

'Ain't got a clue and if I did I wouldn't be telling you. Last time I saw young Amy was at Lisbeth's funeral. Strange,' she murmured sarcastically, 'I didn't see you there.'

Dodd didn't answer as he bounded up the stairs.

'Get down here, you! That's private up there!' The sound of his mother's anger set the boy at her leg crying. His brother crawled over to join him just as Dodd's boots thudded down the stairs. He'd found no sign of his daughter.

'Just as well my hubby ain't here!'

Dodd laughed. 'What would he do? He don't scare me for all his size. Lump of whale blubber, that's all he is.'

'Ten times the man you are, Amos Dodd,' she said, slamming the door hard behind him.

On the street, two women pegging washing looked over to see what the shouting was about. A boy playing with a bottle in the gutter stood up and sidled away.

Fire rose in Dodd's cheeks. With every passing day, the urgency to find his daughter grew, but it was no longer a case of wanting her to bring him money. He'd almost forgotten that. No. Now he wanted to pay her back for tricking him. How dare she run away? Make a fool of him? Now the neighbourhood knew all about him: who he was, what he'd done, where he'd spent the last fifteen years. They laughed behind his back. Not that that worried him — he'd not think twice about slicing the throat of any man who insulted him to his face. But he wasn't going back inside Armley Jail! He'd promised himself that.

When he'd looked up at the turreted towers, when he'd been searching the streets of Armley, he swore they'd never haul him in there again. But that didn't mean he wasn't going to find his daughter and when he did, he'd give her what she deserved. But while he was looking, he'd make sure he kept his nose clean.

He didn't see how high the bottle lifted when he kicked it, but he heard the crash as it broke, showering slivers of glass across the pavement at the other side of the street.

'I'll find you,' he yelled, 'if it's the last thing I do!'

10

Saltaire

The company boats all left the mooring before sunrise and by the time Amy got up the waterway was empty. Helen prepared a good breakfast for everyone. She said they would have a long, hard day ahead.

As she helped haul the short-boat through Shipley, Amy thought about Leeds. Though the small town was surrounded by fields and hills, its mills and wharfs and warehouses encroached on the canal. They were little different to Fanshaw's or the other factories which backed on to the water in the city.

Once they were through the town, the countryside opened up again. The hills were wooded and the distant moors tinged with heather.

At about nine o'clock that morning, *Milkwort* was in sight of the tallest of the chimneys of the Saltaire Mill. As they got closer, the two main buildings came into view, the canal cutting a path between them.

'Over there!' Helen pointed. 'That's Jentz's Yard.'

Amy looked. On the right, a short stub ran off the canal for a distance of no more than fifty yards. Halfway along was a pair of lock gates rising little higher from the water than a farm fence. They were old and black with grass and weeds sprouting from the joints in their damp timbers. Beyond the gates the channel extended for a further boat's length, but it appeared dry.

'The dock is empty!' Helen called, as she quickly ducked her head into the cabin to tell her husband.

'Good. The sooner we get this load off at the mill, the sooner we get her in.'

As the barge slid past the disused dock, Amy gazed at the buildings ahead. She'd seen lots of mills — Leeds was filled with them, dismal soot-blackened, ugly structures, crowded together, surrounded by dirty streets and the stench of the refuse and hardship. But the mill ahead was different. In the sunlight the yellow stone glowed. And the same colour reflected in every building stretching up the hill from it. The main chimney was taller than most and decorated in a manner never before seen in Yorkshire.

'It looks new,' Amy said.

'Fifty years old,' Joel said. 'Built by a remarkable man. You'll see when you look around the town, he didn't just build a mill, he built schools, hospitals and churches for his four thousand workers and modern houses for them to live in with privvies and yards and gardens. He wanted them to be healthy and happy. And because he was a sober man, there's not an inn or pawn shop in Saltaire. Would you believe in his lifetime he gave half a million pounds to charity?'

Amy gazed in awe at the impressive buildings towering on either side of the canal. On the left, the huge main building, rose six storeys straight from the canal's bank, while on the right, the towing path ran in front of the slightly smaller New Mill. Halfway along the track broadened out into a long loading dock.

Although there was no wharf or horse path on the opposite bank, a loaded barge was moored at the foot of the main building. Beyond the two mills a stone bridge arched over the canal. It led up the hill into the town.

With Helen on the helm, and Ben on the rope, they floated the short-boat up against the loading wharf. Warehouse men spilled from the stores like hungry ants and waited until the boy had moored the barge securely, before scrambling aboard to unfasten the tarpaulins which covered the cargo. Being South American in origin, each bale weighed a thousand pounds and a crane was needed to unload them. Once they were swung off, they quickly disappeared into the mill's underground wool-store.

Chains rattled and clanged and the short-boat rocked as every bale was lifted from it. While Ben sat on the roof of the cabin, watching the cargo disappearing from *Milkwort's* hold, Helen joined Joel in the cabin to discuss their plans for the work to be done over the next few weeks. Wanting to keep well clear of the men and machinery, Amy wandered along the path to the end of the wharf, took off her boots and dangled her feet in the water.

It was early afternoon by the time the last bale of fibre was lifted from the barge. *Milkwort* looked odd with an empty belly. It smelled of damp hair and rats, though only a few mice and a large hairy spider had made their homes amongst the bales. Once the cargo was off and the quantities checked, Helen and Ben visited the office to collect the balance of payment they were due.

While waiting for them, Amy watched a new loom being hoisted into the building opposite from the barge which was moored to the other bank. A pulley operating from a landing on the fourth floor was lifting it slowly. The job looked difficult and the men were having problems securing chains around the machine to ensure it would lift without tipping. It was a slow, laborious procedure and as the cable was lowered there was a lot of shouting. Some men were giving orders, others advice. There was concern it was not fastened adequately and that the cable wouldn't support it. If it crashed down on to the barge, it would sink the boat and crush the men who were on it. The men operating the pulley looked down from the fourth floor. Their faces were grave but they waited patiently and said nothing.

As she watched, Amy thought about Fanshaw's and its old looms and combs which had been in the mill since it was built. She thought about Mr Lister and the loom he was designing and amidst the noise of the voices, she imagined she heard him call her name. Then she realized it was Ben who was shouting.

'Amy! Get on board. We're getting hauled up to Hirst Lock; there's a winding hole up there where we can turn the boat around.'

Amy looked along the canal, expecting to see a steam barge ready to tow them, but there was none. Then she smiled as she saw a young man parading himself along the wharf like the strongman at the circus. He wore a singlet and trousers and a broad leather belt tight around his waist, which accentuated the dimensions of his chest. With the jeers and whistles from the men on the loading wharf, Jem Carruthers obliged his workmates with a pose. He was a popular man, soft as butter inside and always happy to lend a hand.

When word had reached him that the bargee was crippled, Carruthers had asked permission to help haul the boat to the old boatyard. It wasn't just out of the kindness of his heart, but as a local heavyweight boxing champion, he enjoyed a little free advertising.

Hirst Wood Lock was no more than half a mile up ahead. Digging his toes into the towing path and with the rope over his shoulder, Jem floated *Milkwort* gently from the wharfside, creating barely a ripple. Once he had the empty barge moving, leading it looked no more arduous, for the athlete, than walking a dog. With an audience of onlookers, the boxer relished the occasion and lengthened his stride. Tiny waves began to curl from *Milkwort*'s bow and a line of rippled wake fanned out on the canal behind. Helen was concerned that the line was too short and he would pull the boat into the bank. On the tiller, Ben was afraid he was going too fast and wouldn't slow before they reached the lock. Amy stayed in the cabin out of the way.

'We don't have any brakes!' Ben shouted.

Being some distance from the mill and hidden from the view of his fellow workers, Carruthers slowed and followed Ben's instructions.

After stopping and manoeuvring the boat around in the winding hole, the pugilist returned to the path to pull the short-boat back to Jentz's Yard. As soon as he felt it moving he leaned forward and lengthened his stride. The boat responded, slipping smoothly across the still surface. Once he'd passed under the bridge and had the New Mill in sight, he increased his pace yet again and by the time he reached the start of the loading wharf he was almost running. Helen and Ben were alarmed. *Milkwort* was approaching the barge which was unloading the loom and the canal was little wider than the width of two short-boats.

Jem Carruthers, buoyed by his own bravado, was oblivious to any danger. Cheered on by the workers, he raised one arm, flexed his muscles and kept going. But he was going too fast.

Gripping the tiller with both hands, Helen shouted for Amy to hold tight in case they hit the other craft. Ben watched anxiously, but his mother guided it through the channel. There was less than a foot to spare on either side. The wake *Milkwort* created, however, was another problem. It set the other barge tossing dangerously and brought a barrage of curses from the men on board. Fortunately, the loom was suspended well clear of the boat, and the barge, being light without its load, rolled but came to no harm.

'What's happening?' Joel yelled from the cabin, but no one answered.

★ ★ ★

For Carruthers the self-indulgent event had been a thrill. It was brought to a sudden end by the urgent cries from Ben and Helen.

Releasing the rope, Jem let the boat swim by. He watched as it drifted almost to a stop, mid-channel, only fifty yards from the entrance to the dry dock.

'How was I?' Jem asked, flashing a gold tooth as he grinned broadly.

'Grand,' said Helen sarcastically, while Ben murmured something less complimentary.

'You could have pulled it with one hand,' Ben said, as Amy emerged from the cabin. 'Light as a leaf with no cargo. Like a stone skimming on a lake.'

Jem Carruthers chose to be oblivious to the comments, his broad smile not faltering as he followed Helen's directions and hauled the boat's bow around ninety degrees into the overgrown channel. Being unused, reeds had grown up along its length and the bottom had filled with layers of silt washed in by the passing boat traffic. The channel was not only shallow but narrow — wide enough for only one barge.

As Carruthers hauled, his biceps bulged and the reeds bent beneath the bow, brushing the barge's bottom, hindering its forward movement. As he dragged the boat the short distance to the pair of lock gates, the perspiration glistened on his face. He glanced back to the mill but fortunately his audience had lost interest.

'I doubt this will be here in ten years,' Helen said, looking over the lock gates at the derelict dock. 'If the canal don't fill it in itself then the company will.'

'Don't they need a dry dock here?'

'Did once. This one was built long before they ever built a mill at Saltaire. There were lots of boatyards up and down this navigation then. There's new yards in Shipley nowadays, but they do more repairs than boat building. Not so much demand for new boats these days. I shudder to think what'll happen to the canals in twenty years' time.'

Ben jumped on to the bank. It was damp and clods of earth crumbled into the dock.

'Careful when you jump off,' he called.

Beyond the lock gates was the dry dock,

though it contained a small lake, fed from the water which constantly seeped through the seams in the old gates. The base of the dock was on a slight incline so that the furthest point was much shallower. It ended at a timber wall with a sluice gate in the bottom corner.

'Make sure the sluice gate's closed before you open the lock gates,' Joel shouted. 'Don't want to empty the cut into the River Aire.'

Ben checked, then cranked the rusty paddles on the lock gate, allowing the water to flow in from the canal and flood the chamber. Once the level of water in the boat dock was level with the canal, all that remained was to open the old gates and slide the boat in.

That task was not easy with the amount of silt and weed lodged around the gates. It took the four of them, including Carruthers, all their strength to push the gates open. Thankfully, once the boat was through, it was easier to close them behind it.

The job of manoeuvring the broad timber supports into position under the sides of the boat was even more difficult. Without Jem's help Ben and the women couldn't have managed it.

The gap between the boat's side and the dock's bank was very narrow and the timbers to be set beneath the hull very heavy. They all knew that they had to be positioned correctly otherwise the barge wouldn't sit squarely on them once the water had been sluiced out. With Helen's advice, Jem set the stocks beneath the hull. There were six on each side.

As Ben opened the sluice and the water gushed out, forming a fast-flowing stream which headed straight down to the River Aire, Helen held her breath. If the supports were not properly set, the barge could slip over — and Joel would be tipped from his bed in the cabin.

The short-boat creaked as it shifted slightly once the water was no longer supporting it. Finally, it settled on its stumps with only a slight lean to one side.

'We're high and dry,' Helen announced, jumping back on deck and popping her head around the cabin door. 'Thanks to the help of Jem here. We couldn't have managed without him.' She beckoned the young man. 'Come aboard and meet my man.'

Jem's smile was less confident as he bent his back and poked his head into the cabin. 'Jem's the name, boxing's me game,' he announced, stretching out his grubby hand to Joel.

'I'll pay you for your trouble,' Joel said gruffly.

'Don't worry about it. I like to exercise the muscles when I can. Perhaps you'll come and see me fight one day.'

'I'll do that, and I'll buy you a beer when me leg's fixed.'

'And I'll be pleased to drink it. You'll be around for a while, will you?'

'A few weeks at least,' Joel said. 'But if anyone's enquiring for us, say you ain't seen us.'

'Don't you worry, mister, I can keep my mouth shut.'

Jumping ashore, Jem turned to the two ladies, and bowed as only a showman could. 'If you need me, you know where to find me,' he said.

Amy smiled.

'Thanks,' Helen shouted after him.

* * *

With no money to pay for his lodgings, Amos Dodd laboured for three days at Kilbey's Forge. It was heavy work but Dodd was strong as an ox even though he did little exercise. The job might have lasted a few days longer had he not argued with the overseer and threatened to maim him. Though he was turned off, he collected his pay. There was enough to pay his dues to his Mill Street landlady and to drink a gallon of ale in the Hungry Crow.

'Did you find her, then?' the man said, wiping the beer from his whiskers.

'None of your business.'

'Might have seen her the day of the ruckus at the mill.'

'Might you now?'

'Might be worth the cost of a jug of ale?'

Before the man had chance to put his glass on the table, Dodd knocked it out of his hands and grabbed him by the throat. The blade he suddenly produced drew blood on the man's temple. 'You tell me what you saw or you'll see nowt else, ever again!'

'I'll tell! I'll tell!' the man squawked. 'Let go of me.'

Somewhat reluctantly, Dodd released him.

Rubbing his throat, the man coughed.

'I saw her on Wellington Bridge. She were about to take off on the canal path.'

'Go on.'

'When she saw me, she ducked back and hid. Didn't want me to see which way she were heading.'

'And which way was that?'

'She were heading towards Kirkstall.'

'What then?'

'I didn't see her after that, honest, I didn't, but I reckon that's where she'd gone.

Kirkstall or maybe Rodley, or Horsforth. Plenty of mills along there where a lass can get a job.'

'She might be in Liverpool by now,' a voice shouted.

The men laughed and Dodd spun around but no one volunteered another word.

'What about me beer, then?' the hairy man asked.

Dodd cuffed him with the back of his hand and walked out. He was aware that lots of barges carted coal to Kirkstall Forge. She was probably hiding out on one of those, he thought.

11

Jentz's Yard

'I should go, shouldn't I?' Amy said.

'And where are you going to?' Joel asked. 'And what will you do? You can't keep running all your life.' He shook his head. 'These stories you've told us about your father makes it hard to believe you're the same flesh and blood.'

'I wish to God we weren't,' she sighed. 'But we are and I can't let him find me! He'd kill me.'

'Not while you're on my boat, he won't!' It was the first time Amy had heard venom in the boatman's voice.

'Listen, Amy,' Helen said quietly. 'Me and Joel were talking last night. And there is something we want to put to you. Now it's not permanent, mind — just for the few weeks till Joel's back on his feet and *Milkwort* is back on the cut.'

'We're asking you to stay here with us,' Joel said. 'There's a lot of work to be done and I'm in no fit state to help. That means Helen and Ben will have to do everything

— painting, scraping, varnishing. Not to mention getting underneath the hull and caulking the bottom, if she needs it. Then, of course, Helen's got all her ordinary chores which she's left this past week while I've been stuck down here. What we'd like is for you to stay with us, lend a hand with the jobs and when you find some spare time, you can give our Ben some lessons.'

'Lessons!' said Amy. 'I'm not a teacher.'

'Ben says you know how to read.'

'That's right, I do, but my father took me out of school and sent me to work in the mill.'

'Aye, but you did go to school, and that's more than me and Joel did, and Ben's never stepped inside a school. That's the way it is.'

Through the small leaded window, Amy could see the boy sitting cross-legged on the grass, splicing an eye into the end of a rope. Watching him over the past few days, she had seen how he worked the boat and operated the locks like a man. She'd heard he could handle a boat-horse as well as his father. He knew the names of all the weeds and flowers that grew along the bank and he appeared to know every town in Yorkshire. Amy had learned some geography at school but she'd never heard of half the places he spoke about. It was hard to believe he'd had no schooling.

151

'There's no time for the kids to go to school when you're working the canal,' said Helen. 'It's something you keep putting off — then all of a sudden it's too late and they've grown up and they're off to get a boat of their own.'

'One thing's for sure,' Joel said, 'if a boatman can hold a pen and not just a tiller, he's better off for it. He'll not get conned with contracts he can't read, or miss what's happening around the country. Not that there's much out there I'm interested in.

'Things are changing on the canal,' he said with a sigh. 'Good boat-horses are being replaced by steam engines, and barges are being replaced by railway wagons. Before long they won't need boatmen any more. It's too late for me and Helen to change — but it's not too late for the lad.'

'But shouldn't he go to a proper school? Surely this town has got one.'

'Saltaire's got everything. A school and a college to my knowledge. But it's summer now and school's closed. And when they start up again, we'll be off and that'd mean leaving Ben here on his own. He'd have to find lodgings, and that's not easy. Everyone here works for the mill. And besides,' he said, smiling at his wife, 'how can you part with a boy when he's your only one? We're not short

152

of a bob or two, but we can't afford one of them live-in private schools that fancy folk send their youngsters to. Besides, Ben wouldn't fit in. Not a lad straight off the cut.'

'Trouble is,' said Helen, 'we don't stay in one spot long enough for him to go to day school. It's the same for all boat folk. Always on the move. Got to go where the jobs are and that can be anywhere on the cut. We never know where we'll end up next — Goole, Rotherham, Nottingham.'

'As for worrying about your father,' said Joel, 'you take my word. You'll be safe here for a while. Forget about him and stop worrying about what might happen till you get there. If you're like me, you'll never look further than the next set of locks.' He smiled wearily at Helen, sitting on the edge of the bed, her hand resting on the wooden casing around his leg. 'You give my missus a hand, and give the lad a bit of learning, and you can stay here as long as you like.'

* * *

Harold Lister's apartment was adequately furnished and comfortable. It consisted of two spacious rooms on the second floor of one of the larger houses in Saltaire. Albert

Road housed most of the company executives, school teachers, and the church minister. That row of houses was the best in town.

Harold had used those rooms since his first year at the Science and Art School, and they'd been held for him when he was away at university in Edinburgh. He never had to concern himself about rent payments. Expenses, such as that, came out of the trust fund and the bank took care of all his financial matters.

As he always ate out, he had no need for staff, though a woman serviced his rooms every day. She also took care of his laundry and kept the apartment warmed in winter and aired in summer if he was working away. For Harold, the rooms on Albert Road were his home. It was the only one he had known in over ten years.

Slipping a bookmark between the pages, he closed his book, stretched and walked over to the window. With the mill and town to the rear of the building, his outlook was to the west and the hills and moors of the West Riding. In the distance were the dense groves of Hirst Wood and through the treetops he could see the roof of Hirst Mill. He'd heard there'd been a corn mill on that site for 150 years. Immediately ahead was a green meadow divided by the railway cutting across it. From the window the tracks weren't visible, but the signal poking up from the bottom of the embankment indicated there was a train due shortly.

Not far from the line, the canal and river ran parallel and beyond the River Aire the land rose sharply through Trench Wood and Shipley Glen to the open tops of Baildon Moor. Harold considered those places some of his favourite walking tracks.

As he gazed at the scene, a short-boat disappeared behind the gates of Hirst Lock and he thought back to the barge he had seen at the Saltaire wharf that morning. It was a handsome boat and it had attracted his attention. Even from the fourth floor he had admired its faded decorations. Though weathered and worn they reminded him of the designs on some of the gypsy caravans which rumbled along the country lanes.

He remembered the girl he'd met at the mill in Leeds and smiled as he considered that she alone had caused the greatest commotion Fanshaw's had ever seen. The last time he'd seen her, she was sprawled out on the dirt of the mill yard and yet here she was in Saltaire, dipping her feet in the canal. His expression changed as he thought of her hands, scored by the gravel, and the anxious look on her face. What was she doing with the barge? Didn't she live in the streets near the mill? Then he remembered he'd heard rumours her father was searching for her. Heard she'd run away. He couldn't imagine why that would be; nonetheless, he felt relieved to see her safe. And she appeared content in her new environment.

The working class are hard on their womenfolk, he mused, as he dusted a cobweb from the corner of the window pane. Casting his mind back to his own childhood, he thought about his father, a man he hardly knew. Robert Lister was an amiable man, he was told. Generous in proportions, intelligent, but shrewd and uncompromising when it came to business. Harold hoped that his father had been a good husband and that when he had become successful he had been kind and generous to his mother. But that was something he would never know.

The last he'd seen of the girl from the mill was when Carruthers pulled the empty barge away from the wharf heading towards Hirst Lock. He presumed by now it would be near Skipton if not heading over the Pennines. In a way he regretted being unable to go down to the wharf to speak to her. He'd remembered her name and though she'd turned her face and appeared to look up at him when he'd called, he knew, because of all the noise, that she'd neither seen nor heard him. Hoisting the new machine up from the barge and into the mill without causing damage, or losing the loom in the canal, or injuring any of the men, had been his major concerns.

A train whistle distracted him. He watched as a trail of smoke crawled towards the town like a large grey caterpillar. Somewhere beneath the billowing cloud was a railway engine.

In the distance the lock gates slowly closed. The coal barge moved off, disappearing behind the pocket of trees as it continued its journey to Liverpool.

'Good luck, Amy Dodd,' he whispered, as he turned from the window and returned to the chair and his book.

★ ★ ★

The first morning in the dry dock, Helen rifled the many storage compartments on the boat to see what equipment they had and what was required for the jobs Joel wanted done. As Joel decided what should be bought, Amy listed them on a piece of paper. A little later Helen and Ben went shopping. They brought back brushes and soda and scrapers. The red-lead, oil-based paints and varnish,

157

linseed and tar were delivered by cart in the afternoon and the following day an unwritten work schedule developed.

If the morning was fine, work started early. Ben did the heavy work, hauling buckets of water from the main canal and carrying them back to the boat. The water that had seeped into the bottom of the dry dock was unsuitable. It was rotten with detritus: dead leaves, branches, rotted timber and small, noisy frogs. It smelt rotten too.

For a week Amy and Ben scraped, scrubbed and caulked the carvel-planked hull. The following week the pair daubed tar on the bottom with a long-handled brush. It was exhausting work. Up top, Helen scraped and sanded but she cooked too, and made preserves. Spent a day at the wash tub boiling Joel's shirts and the yards of lace-work which decorated the inside of the boat. Inside the main cabin, Joel worked on anything portable — scraping, sanding or painting, using his leg's wooden casing as a table to rest things on. It took him almost a week to remove all the layers of old paint and varnish from the tiller, before sanding it satin smooth. Then he set to with a camel brush, adding the traditional designs in bright blues, yellows, greens and reds. When the painting was completed, it sat in the cabin for a week before the two coats of varnish were added. He was pleased with his efforts.

In the evenings, while Helen cooked the meal, Ben had his lesson on the small deck at the bow. Joel supplied them with pencil and paper — sheets torn from the notebook in which he recorded his figures. Though Joel couldn't read, he did arithmetic quicker than anyone else Amy had ever seen before.

For reading practice, the only book on the boat belonged to Helen. It had been given to her years ago but it still smelt as if it were new and Amy could see its pages had never been turned. Helen held it in high regard because it was written by a woman. She had always wanted to be able to read it and now she hoped her son would be able to read it to her one day. Amy was grateful to her for the loan of the book and promised to mind it carefully.

Once Amy discovered that Ben could already recognize some letters of the alphabet, she embarked on her task of teaching him how to write.

The month spent in dry dock was one of continual work. The days began early and finished late. But at least it was summer and the weather was mainly fine.

On days when it rained and showed no signs of clearing, they worked inside. The jobs were the same — scrubbing, scraping, painting, varnishing. Though Helen was skilled in the traditional crafts and Ben was learning quickly, it was Joel who was most skilled with the brush. He added scrolls, swirls, patterns and sprays of roses to any item which could be carried into the cabin. Happy to be useful again, he painted everything Helen handed to him: the scoop, the water jug, even the new chamber pot. Anything plain was transformed into a work of art, and for two or three weeks the cabin reeked with the smell of fresh paint and varnish.

Once the painting was done, Ben and Joel sat together for hours, twisting and turning old rope into traditional buttons and fenders for use on the barge. There was plenty available as they had to replace the tow-rope every few weeks, as it was dangerous for the horse once the rope had lost its elasticity.

'We can sell these,' Ben announced proudly. 'And pa lets me keep half of whatever we get.'

Amy listened while they worked, as Joel told stories about life in the south. About the canals he had worked and the previous narrowboat he had owned. About the canal at Devizes with its sixteen straight rises. About the navigation at Bristol and the tall sailing ships he'd seen. And of the demise of the canals, and the reason they had left the Kennet and Avon.

Helen always had a smile on her face, but said very little. She was content to listen to her husband and son. Amy admired her courage. She was strong in limb and had a heart as big as a ton of wool. Like most wives on the barges, she'd been born on the cut and lived her whole life in the confines of a boat. She'd never slept in a bed which had legs or looked out of a window that was much bigger than a bundle of washing. She'd never cooked in a real oven yet the food she prepared was as delicious as any from a bake-house kitchen. She never asked for anything. *Milkwort* was her home and she wished for none other.

Though she'd travelled the length and breadth of England, she'd no thoughts about fashion. The most she ever needed were her old-fashioned boat clothes and bonnet, plus a bobbin of cotton thread to make lace. The large earrings she wore made her look like a gypsy but Amy doubted she ever considered her appearance. The canal was her life, her bath and her mirror. The reflection it gave satisfied her needs.

In the evenings, when tea had been cleared away from the main cabin, Amy would open the book and read from its pages. Helen listened to every word Amy uttered, watching her lips as closely as the women working on the looms.

As the novel's story unfolded, Amy knew her friend would never exchange her home on the water for one on land. As she read them the passages of *Mary Barton*, she too wondered about a new life in Lancashire. Somehow the idea seemed less appealing than she had previously thought.

Though Joel often appeared to be sleeping, he was listening intently. Ben's eyes were wide as he followed Amy's finger as it ran along each line of print.

The evenings were a time they all enjoyed.

Working hard and long made the weeks pass quickly. Amy's fears that her father would find her were slowly subsiding; nevertheless, she never strayed far from the dock. It was doubtful, she thought, that he'd got a regular job, but he'd have to do something if he wanted to stay out of jail.

Their only visitors while they were in the dock were a few passing boatmen and Jem Carruthers. The first time he called he arrived carrying two buckets of milk.

'You look like a milkmaid,' Ben dared to

call. In a whisper, the pugilist told him he really didn't like ale, but because of his image he was expected to swallow his share. He sparred with the lad and ruffled his hair and said he would give him a boxing lesson every time they came to Saltaire. Jem returned three times after that, each time with at least a gallon of milk.

Though he couldn't quite walk, Joel threw the long splints from his leg and accepted shorter ones which Helen insisted on. He fashioned a crutch from a tree branch — and painted it with patterns, of course. Though he wasn't tall, hopping about in the cabin wasn't easy, but being able to sit at the table gave him pleasure.

When other boatmen visited *Milkwort* after unloading their cargoes, he'd sit out on deck and listen to the gossip. Learn what was happening along the cut. He was told of the horse which had drowned after a tow-rope snagged on a tree and of the two boat-horses which had disappeared from the canal — replaced by boilers and steam. Of a pair of young boatmen he knew who were leaving for jobs on the land. Of a fire on a coal barge at Kirkstall Forge. And of news that the state of the Kennet and Avon was not good. Trade on the Leeds and Liverpool canal, however, could not have been better.

'It's about time we got a new horse,' Joel said to his wife. 'And time *Milkwort* got its name back.'

12

Shipley Glen

A spot of paint splashed from Ben's brush on to Amy's cheek. She wiped it with the rag and watched as the name, *Milkwort*, appeared in bold letters on the side of the bow. A curling line beneath it added the finishing touch.

'Come up for a cuppa,' Helen shouted.

Amy didn't wait for a second call. After standing for some time in the mud at the bottom of the dock, she was pleased to climb out. Ben followed her.

'Where are all the people going?' she asked, as she dipped her feet into a bucket of water to wash the dirt off. 'It's too late for church. Is there a rally in town?'

Helen glanced at the stream of folk heading along the path towards Saltaire; couples arm in arm, ladies with parasols, families with baby carts, boys with dogs. 'They're off to the Glen,' she said.

'What's that?'

'Shipley Glen. You must have heard about it.'

Amy shook her head.

'I thought everyone in Yorkshire knew about it. It's got rides that swing through the air and a switchback railway and all sorts of unimaginable things. Folk come from miles about to visit the Glen. I've heard tell that Bradford's near empty on a Sunday.'

'Hyde Park of the north, it's been called,' Joel added, from inside the cabin. 'Ain't you never been?'

'No,' she replied, as she jumped on board. Amy's concern was there would be people from Leeds who might recognize her.

'Is it far from here?' she asked as she ducked her head and joined the pair sitting at the table.

'On the other side of the river,' said Joel. 'Do you want to go?'

Amy shrugged. 'I don't think so.'

'I bet our Ben wouldn't say no to a ride on the tram,' Helen said.

'Yes, please!' The voice, loud and clear, came from the far end of the barge.

'What about us finishing the painting?'

'You've been scraping and painting these past four weeks and you've not even taken a stroll into town. It's about time you took a trip out. Besides, it's Sunday and ma says you shouldn't be working.' Joel reached for his leather pouch on the shelf beside his bed. The coins rattled. 'Here, take this.'

166

Amy shook her head.

'Take it, before I put it away again. Thruppence'll take the pair of you both ways on the tram. A penny up and halfpenny down, if I remember rightly.'

Helen nodded and smiled her approval. 'You best tidy yourself first,' she said. 'Take a look at yourself.'

Even in the reflection of one of the polished brasses, Amy could see her face was streaked with paint. She laughed, then suddenly her smile disappeared. 'What if someone sees me? What if my father's there?'

'Don't be daft!' Joel said. 'There'll be hundreds of people on the Glen, and all out to enjoy themselves. They'll not be interested in you, miss.'

Helen pulled her bonnet from the cupboard. 'Here,' she said. 'No one will see your face under this.'

Amy took it and thanked her.

'Pa,' Ben said rather timidly, 'can I buy a toffee apple?'

'Away with you, boy!'

'But they only cost a penny.'

'You work that out with Amy. If you buy yourself a treat, then you'll have to walk back. It's a fair way, remember?'

'I'll get him an apple,' Amy said. 'We'll walk back. The exercise'll do us both good.'

As they climbed up from the cabin, Ben smiled as Amy sat the voluminous bonnet on her head. The row of tucks at the front radiated from her face like a patterned halo, while at the back the broad frill, from the gathered crown, covered her shoulders and fell almost to her waist.

★ ★ ★

Half an hour later, the pair were on the towing path heading past the New Mill. Amy looked like a boatwoman with the blue pleated skirt Helen insisted she wear, and the ample hat which hid most of her head.

As they reached the canal bridge, they joined the crowds of people who were pouring from a train which had just arrived. Everyone was heading for the bridge across the River Aire. At first Amy felt anxious. It was a long time since she had been among so many people, but she quickly relaxed and followed Ben, who was always half a stride ahead of her.

From the bridge they headed to the wooded hill, which rose steeply from the river flats. On the way, Amy stopped and gazed at the men dressed in white playing cricket in the park. It was a sight she had never seen before. Halfway across they joined a long queue, which snaked out to meet them. It seemed odd to stand in line at the bottom of a hill. 'What are they waiting for?' she called.

'For the tram!'

After waiting for twenty minutes, the pair reached the tramway's pay booth.

'Two, please,' Amy said, placing her threepenny bit on the counter.

'Single or return?'

'Single.' 'Does it go far?' Amy asked.

'No. Just to the top of the hill.'

As the man handed her the tickets and her penny change, Amy heard the noise of the cable turning its pulley wheel. Coming down the track on the right-hand side was the tram. It had two cars, each seating twelve people. The seats were leather padded and the wooden backs could swing to face which ever direction the tram was travelling. The lower end of each car was raised so that the floor appeared flat as it went up the incline. As soon as the tram stopped, the folk waiting on the small wooden platforms took their seats ready for it to convey them up the hill. There was an air of excitement among the trippers. Amy shared it.

No sooner had she and Ben squeezed on to the front seat than a bell clanged and the small carriage juddered and started its

169

quarter-mile journey pulled by a thick hemp cable. As they neared the halfway point, where the track curved slowly around the hillside, Amy saw the other tram approaching on the other track. There were only a handful of passengers on it but they waved as they passed. Overhead, the old trees of Walker Wood touched to form a canopy of shade.

It was a short walk from the ticket office to the green at the top of the Glen. The pathway was crowded with families who had followed the footpath instead of taking the tram. As on any other fine Saturday or Sunday afternoon, Shipley Glen was teeming with visitors. Amy was astounded. It was like May Day but so much better. Ben took her hand and pulled her across the oval. He wanted to show her the Switchback Railway and the gondola on the Aerial Flight which swung high above the edge of the valley. The structure of the building which housed the ride was amazing. For the less adventurous, a convoy of horse-drawn trams offered rides around the green. Both adults and children vied for the open-air seats on the top deck, which provided wonderful views across the surrounding countryside. And for the elderly and more refined, there was tea in the British Temperance Tea and Coffee House or a glass of home-made lemonade from a vendor on the green.

Those families who didn't take rides enjoyed the atmosphere with their own games and a picnic. There were donkey rides, a juggler, Morris dancers, and a Punch and Judy show. Apart from the shrieks of the children's voices, there were cries from the vendor selling postcards, and from the man with the tray selling toffee apples.

'Go buy one,' said Amy, handing Ben the penny.

After offering Amy a bite, they wandered through the crowds. Ben compared it with the fairs and shows he'd seen on his travels. He talked of towns and described many different events he'd seen and Amy realized how much she had missed while she had worked in the mill. She remembered an old neighbour in the street, who boasted that she'd never strayed further than two miles of where she was born. Amy was thankful she would never have to say that.

Looking round at the crowd, she examined the faces, wondered where they all came from, and what they did. Some were rich. Some were poor. But they all looked happy — as if they didn't have a care in the world. So different from the chalky-cheeked faces she'd seen heading to the mill on a winter's morning.

But the man's eyes she alighted on were not those of a stranger. A surge of fear ran through her.

'Ben!' she yelled, alarming him as she grabbed him by the hand and tried to pull him in the opposite direction.

'What's wrong?'

'This way, Ben!' But her efforts were useless. The boy was confused and too big for Amy to drag through the slow-moving crowd.

She felt a hand grasp her arm.

'Amy!' the voice said.

'Let go of me!'

'Amy Dodd!'

'Please let go!'

People looked and a man called to her. 'You all right, miss?'

She stopped, turned and caught her breath.

'What's the matter?' Ben asked, but Amy didn't reply.

She was looking at the man who had startled her. 'Mr Lister, I'm sorry I ran. I was scared.'

'Why would you be afraid of me?'

'I didn't want to see anyone from Fanshaw's Mill and seeing you was a shock.'

'Well, I must admit you are the last person I would have expected to see here, though, if

I'm not mistaken, the last time we spoke you were running — as though all the hounds in hell were after you. But I can understand your desire not to be recognized. You are quite a celebrity around Fanshaw's Mill.'

Amy looked at him quizzically. 'A celebrity? You mean I made a nuisance of myself when I left,' she said, allowing a grin to warm her face.

'Too right! And your father caused a worse one when he found out that you had duped him.'

'You know about him?'

Harold Lister nodded. 'He was searching for you for almost a week. Up and down every street he went, morning and night, shouting your name. Drove folks crazy, I heard. Then the children took up the chant and made up a rhyme of their own. Everyone was singing it. I even heard it sung in the mill. You're quite infamous, I'm afraid.'

Amy flushed. 'Tell me, what did it say?'

He paused for a moment, trying hard not to smile.

'Go on,' she said. 'I should know.'

Harold shuffled uncomfortably, smiled and then repeated the ditty:

Amy Dodd slung her hook,
Set a fire, run amok,

173

Took off like a butcher's dog,
You'll ne'er catch our Amy Dodd.

'But I never set a fire!' Amy said indignantly, her face fixed in a frown.

'I know that, but it did take some time to search all the floors to make sure that there wasn't one smouldering somewhere. You must have heard how many woollen mills have burnt down in the last ten years. And it happens so quickly too. Then there was the fire brigade. They were none too happy about the false alarm, and a constable came because there was talk something may have been stolen and the fire been used as an excuse to cover the theft.'

'But I never stole anything,' Amy argued. 'Was anything else said?'

'I heard tell you'd run off to meet a young man, but after hearing about your father, I didn't think that was true.'

'Goodness gracious,' Amy said, 'I'll never dare set my foot in the neighbourhood again.'

'Well, apart from Mr Fanshaw, I'd say most folk wouldn't hold it against you. It was the most exciting thing that had happened at the mill in years. Gave the girls something to talk about for a couple of weeks at least. I think everyone was singing your song.'

Amy pondered her question. 'Did you hear

174

anything more of my father — about him looking for me?'

'No, but I heard rumours about him — that he was not a pleasant man.'

'They're not rumours, Mr Lister. It's the truth, and I hate him.'

His eyes met hers and for a moment they said nothing. Remembering Ben was with her, she felt embarrassed. 'This is Mr Lister, Ben. He's an engineer. He works at one of the mills in Leeds.'

Ben nodded and shook hands in a gentlemanly fashion. 'Can I go watch the Punch and Judy show?'

Amy agreed. On the other side of the oval, the gaily striped tent had attracted a large crowd. As they wandered across the green, Amy smiled at the smartly dressed gentleman accompanying her. She felt pleased. Sitting on the soft grass, facing the miniature stage, were more than forty infants. Behind them, standing in a large semi-circle, were the older children and parents. From the stage, the puppets' antics raised jeers and excited cries from the crowd. Amy found herself laughing with them.

'Actually,' Lister said, as Ben found a place to sit, 'I work at Salt's Mill.'

'Here in Saltaire?'

He nodded. 'This is where I have lived

since I was a boy, and I work here most of the time.' He paused till the sound of cheering died down. 'I knew you were in this area.'

Amy looked puzzled.

'I saw you a few weeks ago,' he said. 'You were with a barge at the time which was unloading cargo. I saw you sitting on the edge of the canal near the loading wharf with your feet in the water. I was on the fourth floor supervising the pulley which was hoisting the new loom. I called out but you didn't hear me.' He breathed heavily. 'That was quite a job. By the time we got it on to the floor and bolted into position, the barge you were with had gone. I thought that you would have been in Liverpool by now and never expected to see you here at Shipley Glen. Are you still travelling the canal?'

'Not at the moment. The boat's in an old yard not far from the New Mill. Jentz's Yard. You won't tell anyone where I am, will you?'

'Of course not,' he said as he turned towards her. 'Would you walk with me across the Glen? I find my leg aches if I stand for any length of time.'

She'd forgotten his limp.

'That'd be nice,' Amy said. 'I'd like that.' She tried to attract Ben's attention, but the boy was engrossin the puppet show. All the audience were laughing at the cruel, repetitive beatings Mr Punch was administering to his wife and baby. What was it about the performance that made everyone laugh?

'Mr Lister, can I ask why you were at Fanshaw's and when you came back here?'

'Please call me Harold or Harry, not Mr Lister,' he said. 'I get called on by Fanshaw's and other Leeds mills for special jobs, but I must admit I prefer Salt's Mill. It's more modern than the others, and the work is less taxing, even enjoyable.'

Amy screwed up her nose but Harold didn't notice.

'As to when I arrived, I caught the train from Leeds, the day after' — he coughed — 'the supposed fire! But I've been back to Leeds a couple of times since then.'

'Are you staying in Saltaire now or going away again?'

'I was going to ask you the same question,' he said. 'I have a little more work to take care of here, then I must return to Fanshaw's to finish my business with Mr Fanshaw. But I'll only be in Leeds for a few days.'

'And after that?'

'Back to Saltaire. But what of you? Where will you be going? Will you be staying with the folk on the barge?'

A lost expression settled on Amy's face, though the shadow of the bonnet shielded it from Harold. 'I don't know,' she said slowly. 'I'd planned to go to Lancashire. Maybe get a job there in a cotton mill.'

Harold tutted.

'Ben's family are kindly folk but I can't expect them to keep me for ever. And I can't go back to Leeds because of my father. I'm afraid he will follow me, afraid of what he might do.'

'Shall we sit for a moment?' Harold said, indicating a large flat boulder worn smooth over the years, now covered in a fine cushion of green moss. It was perched at the edge of the oval and at the head of the track which zigzagged down to the bottom of the valley. Though the pathway was steep, it attracted a lot of walkers who trudged down to the beck at the bottom. No one, however, was climbing back up the slope. Instead they all chose the easier but much longer walk back to the town.

'Saltaire is a remarkable place, don't you think?' Harold said, not waiting for an answer. 'Imagine the brain of a man designing a town which would be more fitting in the suburbs of Florence than in the centre of the woollen district of Yorkshire.'

'I've never heard of Florence,' said Amy, wondering why this well educated young man was taking time to talk to a girl like her. 'This is the first time I've been out of Leeds,' she admitted. 'And coming here, I saw nothing more than the horse path while we were on the cut.'

'The cut?'

'That's what the boatmen call the canal.'

'And you were running from your father? You are truly afraid of him, aren't you?'

There was a softness in his voice, the sort of gentleness Amy had only ever heard in her mother's tones. She stood up, resisting the temptation to allow tears to form in her eyes, and gazed blankly at the happy throng milling around the green. 'I caught a glimpse of the church with the fancy tower when we walked here today.'

'Have you stepped inside it?'

She shook her head.

'Then you must allow me to show you both the church and the town while you are here. Perhaps I could join you and your friends for service next Sunday?'

'You'll not get Joel to step into the churchyard,' Amy said with a laugh, 'let alone in the church itself, but I'm sure Helen will be pleased to have your company.'

'And perhaps afterwards you would like to ride the tramway again. I'm sure Ben would enjoy that. I'd like to tell you more about it and about the man who built it.'

'Sir Titus Salt?'

'No, not Sir Titus. Sam Wilson built this railway only three years ago. And he built all the other rides and entertainments you see around here. He too is a remarkable man.' He turned to Amy, his eyes filled with admiration. 'I was here when the tracks were dug and timber rails were laid. I even lent a hand when they installed the cable and I've worked with Wilson on the problem which they have had with the supply of gas.'

'That is what the bad smell is?'

'I'm afraid so, but Wilson is looking into it and you would not believe the projects he has in mind. He intends to construct a huge toboggan slide completely out of wood. And alongside it he'll build a track for cable cars so that after sliding down the slope, the riders can return to the top of the hill in a tram. He says it will be the longest, wildest and steepest ride ever erected anywhere in the world. The man is a genius,' he said. 'Today there are hundreds of people at the Glen, but before long there'll be thousands flocking to Saltaire from all over West Riding. The wonders of engineering are unbelievable. There is something new every day.'

Amy was surprised at Harold's enthusiasm. It reminded her of Ben's when he talked of the fairs he had seen or the lad's excitement

180

when he discovered a shilling on the canal path. But never before had she seen such fervour in a grown man. It excited her, listening to him talk.

'If only you could see the lifts which operate in Scarborough. They have huge carriages which travel almost vertically up the side of the cliff.' He paused. 'My dearest wish is to visit San Francisco and see the cable cars in that city.'

'Then I'm sure you will go there one day. But I heard a rumour at the mill that you were going to build bridges.'

Harold looked into Amy's eyes. 'I didn't think you would know that.'

She smiled.

'It's true. But I would like to build a funicular railway also.'

Amy waited for him to continue, but the thoughts of trains and trams and railways were crowding his thinking.

'I think we should find Ben before he gets into any mischief.' Lifting her skirt, Amy allowed Harold to hold her hand as he led her between the boulders.

'May I accompany you and the lad down on the tram?'

'We've only got single tickets,' she said. 'The extra penny paid for the toffee apple.'

'Then allow me to pay.'

'Thanks,' Amy said. 'Me and Ben are off down to the bottom of the Glen. I know it's a fair walk but we don't get much exercise on the barge.'

'How long will the boat be in the yard?'

'Joel says for as long as the yard's free and there are no other boats waiting to go in. He's been laid up with a bad leg but he hopes to be up and around in another two weeks.'

'And then they'll be heading on to Liverpool?'

'No. They're off back to Leeds or to the coast to pick up another load of wool for this mill. It's special wool that comes from South America,' she said knowingly.

'South America. That is a place I would also like to go to.' He thought for a moment. 'Will you go with them?'

'To Leeds? I don't think so.' Amy leaned down and touched Ben on the shoulder, distracting him from the show he was watching. 'Come along, lad, we'd best get off.'

'Then I'll wish you good afternoon, and hopefully see you next Sunday morning.'

'Aye, maybe,' Amy said, as she nodded and smiled, then watched the young gentleman with the limping gait stroll towards the ticket office at the top of the tramway.

After glancing at the children seated in

front of the puppets' tent, she and Ben headed to the path which led down to the bottom of the valley. In response to the actions on the miniature stage, a chorus of high-pitched voices were screaming a warning to Mrs Punch: 'Watch out! He's behind you!' And every time Mr Punch appeared from behind the wings, the same cry went up again, and every time it was louder.

Amy walked carefully down the inclining path into the verdant gloom but Ben ran on ahead, slipping and sliding down the slope and leaving her far behind.

'Don't fall! Wait for me!' she called. But the boy didn't hear her. The only voices she heard were those of the children screaming in chorus.

'Watch out! He's behind you!' they cried.

13

Harold Lister

'Hello.'

Amy recognized the voice instantly. It was Tuesday and she hadn't expected to see Mr Lister till the weekend. She felt embarrassed and looked around to see if anyone else was on the canal bank, but it was empty. It would be a while before Helen and Ben were back from shopping.

'What are you doing here?' she asked.

'I had some time on my hands, so I thought I'd take a walk. Seemed a shame to be indoors on such a fine day.'

Before Amy could respond, a voice bellowed from the cabin. 'Who's that, lass? We don't want no hawkers round here!'

Amy popped her head into the cabin. 'It's the young gent from the mill I told you about.'

'Huh!' said Joel. 'Suppose you'd better bring him in and let me get a look at him.'

It wasn't quite the way she'd have expected Harold to be greeted but she knew what Joel was like. She was also glad to see that her visitor was carrying his coat over his arm and had his sleeves rolled up above the elbows, making him look less like a gentleman.

'This is Harold Lister,' Amy said.

'Huh! Can't get up. Broke me bloody leg.'

'I'm sorry to hear that,' Harold said, sniffing at the smell of paint and glancing at the ornaments and the garlands of roses decorating the cabin. Stretching out his hand he said, 'I'm pleased to meet you, sir.'

'Come in. Sit your body down,' Joel said, pointing to a three-legged stool. 'You'll not stand for long with your back bent over like that.'

Harold thanked him and did as he was bid.

'Do you know anything about boat-horses, lad?'

Taken aback, the engineer replied, 'Afraid not, sir, though I know a little about carriage horses. My father ran a string of coaches on the Leeds to Peterborough run, three times twice a week, regular as clockwork for nearly twenty years. Did Middlesbrough too and some local routes. I'm told his was the best service of its time. He died ten years ago.'

'So that's where your brass came from?'

'You guessed right, Mr . . . ?'

'Call me Joel or Milkwort — that's the handle I'm known by on the cut.'

Harold relaxed. 'My father didn't want me

185

to follow him into the business. He knew the days of coach travel were numbered. He wanted me to do something worthwhile. 'Build bridges, travel the world, lad,' is what he used to say. I'll always remember that. He even suggested I should build more canals.'

'Maybe he was right when you were a lad, but things have changed. Now there's steam barges and soon there'll be no need for a towing path and boats like mine. Before long everything'll be carried by rail and they'll not need these navigations any more.'

'You could be right, Joel.'

'I know I'm damn right. But that's not the point. If you know coach horses, you know drays and shires.'

'I did in my younger days.'

'Never mind your younger days, I'm not interested in them. What I'm interested in is right now. What I need is another boat-horse. Listen to me. There's a field at the back of the Gate and Gander Inn in Skipton. The innkeeper runs the overnight stables for the passing barge horses. We've used it many times,' he said. 'I've heard word that he's got three horses grazing at the back. Good horses, I'm told. Ones that know the path, coast to coast. I gather they're not young. All three been passed in by bargemen who've moved over to steam.' He sucked in a deep breath. 'It's one of those nags I want. Trouble is, I can't get out there to look at 'em. My lad can pick a good animal and he'd got a way with 'em. Some people seem to be born with it, and I guess your father would have been or he'd never have made his living with coaches.'

Harold nodded.

'But I don't want the lad to go alone, not that I don't trust him. What I'm asking you, young man, will you go with Ben and pick me a horse?'

Harold shuffled a little nervously. 'I'd be pleased to do that for you. Would Saturday suit?'

'Fine. Now how about you get out of me cabin and off me boat, and have a talk to the lass outside. I guess that's what you came calling for.'

Harold couldn't stop himself from grinning broadly, though Joel's fixed expression never wavered.

★   ★   ★

The following Saturday, as arranged, Harold Lister and Ben left early but at the engineer's suggestion, and expense, they caught the train to Skipton rather than walk along the canal bank and back.

Once they had looked at the animals it

didn't take long for them to agree on a horse. She was a mare Ben recognized as soon as they walked into the field. A handsome part-shire, which he had spoken to many times when they had passed on the towpath. He even remembered her name: Mallow.

After looking over the two other horses on offer, Harold settled on the mare, and once the price was agreed on with the landlord, arrangements were made for it to remain stabled there until Joel was on his feet again. Ben wanted to walk Mallow back to Saltaire that afternoon, but Joel had been specific in his instructions and Harold followed the boatman's instructions to the letter.

When the pair got back to the boat, Joel was pleased with the details of the purchase and the price that had been paid. His only aggravation was that he couldn't collect her right away.

'Mallow,' he said. 'I know her well. She'd be eight or nine years old, at least, and she's got a good temperament. Belonged to old Featherspoon. Fool he was going over to steam. He won't admit it but I know he hates it. Still, that's his loss and our gain. Mallow,' he pondered. 'She'll serve us proud for a good number of years, you wait and see.'

* * *

The following morning Harold arrived early to take the ladies and Ben to church. Amy wondered what the congregation would think of the pair of them in boat clothes but Helen wasn't the slightest bit concerned and Harold didn't seem to notice either. Ben would have preferred to stay with his father but his mother insisted he came along.

'You can try reading the hymns,' she said. 'You know all the words. I heard you singing them.'

After the service, Harold accompanied them back to the barge and was invited on board to share Sunday dinner. When the meal was over, Harold thanked them then turned to Joel. 'Would it be all right if I took Amy for a walk up into the town? She's not seen much of it, I gather.'

'Don't ask me,' Joel said. 'Ask the lass. She can make her own choices.'

Harold looked across to Amy, who was squeezed between Helen and Ben on the short bench in the cabin.

'That'd be nice,' she said as she eased her way out, not wanting to appear too enthusiastic. Stepping from the cabin, she noticed Joel wink. It was directed at Harold.

'You bring her back safe, young fella. She's a dab hand at polishing brasses.'

Harold took Amy's hand to help her along the gangplank but released it when she had both feet on the firm ground. They chatted as they walked on the path in front of the New Mill. He talked about pulleys and cranes and she talked about caulking and tarring the barge's bottom. Crossing the bridge, they turned towards the town. They stopped at the entrance gates to the congregational which they had attended and looked down its pathway to the elegant fretted tower with cupola and the Corinthian columns supporting the portico.

'A wonderful example of Italian architecture,' Harold said.

They passed the works dining room on the right and the huge six-storey main mill building on the left.

From the top of the railway bridge, they could see the well-tended allotment gardens and on the opposite side the three-storey buildings which Harold explained were the boarding houses. Victoria Road was the main shopping street, with shops on one side: grocer's, butcher's, stationer's, and a post office.

Heading up the main street, a pair of reclining lions guarded the grand Institute building and at the other side of the road the school, with its curved pagoda-like masonry, resembled an oriental temple. The garden in front was planted with roses, sweet briar and honeysuckle.

'It's so beautiful,' said Amy. 'Nothing like the dark mills where I come from.' She laughed. 'And fancy a pair of lions sitting on the side of a mill street. It's not surprising no one ever leaves here.'

She could also understand why Harold respected the man who had designed the town and why he aspired to be like him.

'It'll still be here in hundreds of years' time.'

'Really?' said Amy.

'The Romans built roads and bridges here in England nearly two thousand years ago that are still standing. Did you know that?'

Amy shook her head. He knew so much and she knew so little. She wondered why he had time for her.

'Here we are,' he said, as he stopped outside a corner shop. The sign above the shop read Salt and Pepper Tea Shop. 'Shall we go in?' he said.

Amy was nervous. Not only had she never walked out with a gentleman before, but she'd never stepped inside a tea shop either.

Sensing her apprehension, he took her by

the hand and led her to the round table next to the window. It was set with a lace cloth and in the centre was a small pot containing a bunch of violets. 'Don't be nervous,' he said. Two elderly ladies sitting in the corner exchanged pleasantries. Amy smiled nervously.

'Isn't it pretty?' she whispered, running her hand across the cloth and picking up the flowers to smell them.

'Shall I order?' he said.

'Yes, please.'

The lady who waited on them was rather plump, as if she had eaten a few too many of the shop's delicacies. Her smooth skin belied her age though the flounce of snow-white curls which framed her rather ruddy face could not deny her sixty-odd years. A pair of dark, beady eyes peered at Amy from over the metal-rimmed spectacles, which rested on the end of her rather sharp nose.

'Just visiting Saltaire?'

'The young lady is,' said Harold.

'Two teas, is it?'

'Yes, and perhaps a piece of cake,' he said, looking at Amy.

She nodded and smiled. 'Yes, please.'

'Now,' said Harold, as the woman disappeared into the back room, 'I want you to tell me a little about yourself.'

'Me?' said Amy. 'There's not much to tell. I've worked at Fanshaw's for the last three years and I've lived in the shadow of its chimneys since the day I was born. I went to the local school, and I liked that, but that stopped when my father came out of' — she hesitated and lowered her voice — 'jail.'

Harold touched her hand. 'It's all right, I heard. I think everyone at Fanshaw's knows about Amos Dodd. Just like they now know about Amy Dodd.'

They stopped talking as the woman approached. After sweeping the cloth with a bone-handled brush, she placed a plate of cakes in the centre of the table.

Harold thanked her.

'Why did you stop to talk to me?' Amy said.

'Where?'

'At the Glen, when you saw me. You could have ignored me, but you didn't.'

'I told you, I was surprised when I saw you with the barge. Then when I thought about you afterwards, I was a little concerned. If you remember, the previous time I'd seen you was in the mill's yard. And with all the talk about your father and him spending time in jail and the rhymes they were repeating about you, I was worried.' He paused. 'You are such a nice girl, Amy, and if you'll excuse me for saying so, I find it hard to believe you are related to such a terrible man as Amos Dodd.'

The two china cups and saucers, the sugar basin and milk jug crashed on to the floor beside Amy. The metal tray landed on top of them. Amy jumped up immediately to assist the woman, who was also in danger of falling to the floor. The ladies seated at the other table looked worried.

Taking the woman's arm, Harold helped her into a chair. 'Is there someone I can call? You look ill, madam.'

'I'm sorry,' she said. 'I'll be all right. My niece is out back, but I don't want her to see this mess. This is her place, you see. I'll be all right, if you just give me a minute. I'm terrible sorry, sir, I think I scared the young lady.'

'Don't worry about me,' Amy said. 'Did you trip or are you sick?'

The woman scooped in a chestful of air. Her cheeks were no longer red. 'No, miss, it were the shock of hearing the name the young gentleman mentioned.' She shuddered. 'Amos Dodd! I knew a man of that name once and, I have to say, I hoped I'd never ever hear that name again.'

'That's my father's name,' Amy said.

The woman put her hand to her heart and

sighed. 'Then it can't be the same man. A rogue and a murderer, this fella was, and if you'll excuse me for blaspheming, I hope he's roasting in hell!'

Harold's eyebrows lifted.

'I'm sorry,' said Amy, 'but I think that is my father. He spent fifteen years in Armley Jail, but he's out now.'

At the other table, the two women whispered behind their handkerchiefs.

The woman shook her head. 'God save us all,' she said. 'I've feared this day all my life. If I've ever wished a man harm it were him.'

'But why?'

'I can't talk about it, love. It would bring too many memories flooding back.'

'But I need to know. There are things I want to find out. How did you know him?'

The woman took a cloth from her apron pocket and dabbed her cheeks. 'You say he's your father? Then I'm sorry for what I said to your face, lass.' Straightening herself in the chair, she continued. 'Years ago, I worked at a place for a reverend and his wife. That's where I first came across Amos Dodd. He worked there too. Did the garden and odd jobs about the place.'

'My mother worked for Reverend Upton. She said that was where she met my father.'

'Then your mum was Lisbeth Eccles?'

'That's right.'

'And your aunt was her sister Rose?'

As Amy nodded, she watched the woman's eyes glaze before a stream of tears flowed over her dumpling cheeks. There was nothing Amy or Harold could say to console her.

A sudden shriek announced the owner's entrance as she burst through from the back of the shop. Harold stepped back as she rushed over, her cries even attracting the attention of passers-by on the street. 'Goodness gracious, Auntie, what have they done to you?'

Despite Harold's pleas to be allowed to explain, and Amy's obvious concern for the elderly waitress, the shopkeeper continued her abuse. As the woman was visibly distressed and inconsolable, Harold took Amy's arm and pulled her away.

'If we stay we'll only make matters worse. If you must speak with her, I suggest we return another day when she's less upset. Now is not the right time.'

Though she didn't want to leave, Amy knew Harold was right and allowed him to take her arm as they left the shop.

As they walked down the hill, they spoke very little. Amy's head was spinning. She wanted to know the truth. What was it the woman was concealing? Was it the same thing her mother had promised to tell her before she died? She wanted to know about Rose and what had really happened to her and felt sure this woman could answer some of those questions. Taking Harold's advice, however, she decided to wait a few days and then visit the teashop again. Hopefully next time the lady would be more willing to talk and would answer her questions.

When they arrived back at the boat, Helen was surprised to see them both in a quiet mood.

'He didn't upset you, did he?' she asked later.

'No, it wasn't Harry, it was some talk I heard about my father.'

'Not him again! Word certainly travels. Trouble is, it's always the bad news which travels the furthest. Don't worry, love, you'll be safe in here. Joel won't let anything happen to you.'

Amy was warmed by Helen's hug. They were kind folk, and no doubt Joel, when he was fit, was a strong man. But from her own experiences and from what the woman in the teashop confirmed, Amos Dodd had an ugly reputation and it would take more than a good man to defend her against him.

★　★　★

For the next three days Amy hardly stuck her head out of the boat. She was glad of the rain. There was less work to do and she found more time to spend with Ben on his writing and reading.

She always felt safe inside the main cabin and though it was crowded with the four of them around the small stove, she never felt that she wanted to get out. At night, the cabin in the bow seemed a long way from Helen and Joel. And though she shared it with Ben, she often felt anxious and confused. She feared her father and hated him and wanted nothing more to do with him. Yet she wanted to know the truth about him and her mother. The things her mother had never told her.

Pacing the bank beside the dry dock, Amy thought about the woman in the tea shop. She knew she must go back and speak with her. She decided to go alone and arrive just before the shop shut for the day.

*   *   *

Stamping the rain from her boots before entering, Amy glanced through the window. Three ladies were occupying one of the tables. The rest of the shop was empty. A bell tinkled as she walked in. The patrons looked around and smiled. Amy waited by the door.

Within a minute, the woman who owned the establishment appeared but her cordial expression changed as soon as she recognized Amy.

Speaking in a loud whisper, she attracted the attention of the other customers. 'I didn't think you'd dare come back here again. You can't imagine the state you left my auntie in. It took all afternoon for her to get over it, and even then I think she was just putting on a brave face.'

'I'm sorry,' said Amy. 'I didn't mean to upset her.'

'I don't know what you said to her but she's not set foot in the shop since then.'

'I didn't say anything to her. It was what she was telling me that distressed her.'

'Well, I don't care who was saying what to who, all I know is she's not been back to work since, and I can't manage without her.'

'Perhaps if I talked to her, it'll make her feel better. I need to ask her some questions. She knew my father, you see.'

'I don't care if she knew Prince Albert, God rest his soul. You leave my auntie alone. You've done enough damage already.'

Amy sighed and turned back to the door. The other customers, looking uncomfortable, reached for their empty teacups.

'I didn't mean no harm,' Amy said. 'If she changes her mind, would you tell her she can find me at Jentz's boatyard. It's on the canal, about half a mile past the New Mill. The boat's name is *Milkwort*.'

*   *   *

About a week later, there was a cry from the bank.

'Hey! I'm looking for Miss Milkywort.' The voice was that of a young lad, no more than seven or eight. His cap was several sizes too big for him.

Helen stepped out on to the small deck. 'What you want?'

'I've got to take the lass to see my great aunt. I've to say she met her at the Salt and Pepper Tea Shop.'

Amy dropped her sewing and grabbed her coat. She was anxious to meet the old woman and find out what she could tell her about the past. In her eagerness to go, she forgot to take Helen's bonnet.

'Will you be all right on your own? Ben can go with you.'

'I'm sure I'll be fine.'

'Take care,' Helen said.

*   *   *

Amy followed the boy along the canal path, finding it hard at times to keep up with him. Though his legs were short, his gait was somewhere between a skip and a trot. They passed the New Mill building and Amy recognized one of the barges she had seen before. It was unloading bales of cargo similar to the ones Joel had carried. Looking up to the pulley wheel protruding from the fourth floor, she wondered if Harold was up there but there was no sign of him.

Following the boy, she retraced the route she had taken to the tea shop. But when the boy trotted past the doorway and crossed to the other side of the road, Amy felt a tinge of concern. Had he been sent by the woman who worked there or was it a trick her father was playing? Surely he couldn't know about the incident in the shop.

When the boy crossed over from the last of Saltaire's streets to a narrow track which led up the hill, she stopped.

'Where are you taking me?'

'Up there,' he said, pointing to a small farm cottage. It was more than a hundred years older than the model village built by Sir Titus Salt.

As they approached, Amy recognized the woman who was waiting on the doorstep.

'Thank you, Sam,' the woman said, as she

met them at the door and handed an apple to the boy. 'Come inside, love.'

The cottage was cosy. It smelled of jam on the boil. The ceiling beams were so low, Amy's unruly hair brushed across them. Ducking her head, she was led into a small living room. Despite the compact size of the window, the room was bright. There was not a speck of dust anywhere and everything was spick and span. Even the lace mats on the chair arms and back looked freshly ironed. They were bleached as clean as fresh snow.

Amy didn't dare disturb anything.

'This is my niece's place,' the woman said. 'Her that owns the tea shop. She lets me have it rent free. In return I do the baking, and help out in the shop. I'm a lucky woman, aren't I?'

'It's very nice,' Amy said shyly.

'Don't worry, I won't bite your head off,' she said, 'or bawl like a baby. Quite a performance I put on in the shop. That's something I've never done in all my life, and I'm sure I won't do it again. It were just the shock of hearing that name again after all them years. Aye, and the surprise at seeing you. Fancy you being Lisbeth Eccles' child. Here, sit down here, love. The kettle's boiling. I've been waiting for you.'

Amy smiled and thanked her and while the

woman busied herself in the kitchen she tried to think. She'd followed the boy without much thought, and now she was here she didn't know what questions she wanted to ask.

As if recognizing the puzzled expression on Amy's face, the woman poured the tea and said, 'My name is Maisy Jones. I've been in service all me life as a cook, and Cook's the name I answer to. So you can take your choice. You can call me Maisy or Miss Jones, or Cook. I'm not fussy.'

'I'll call you Miss Jones, if you don't mind.' As the woman looked old enough to be her grandmother, the title seemed more respectful. 'As you know, my name is Dodd, Amy Dodd.'

For a moment neither spoke. Both sipped their tea.

'You want to know about your father, I suppose. What he was like. What he did for a living, that sort of thing.'

'I suppose so,' said Amy cautiously. 'But I also want to know about my Aunt Rose, and what happened to her, and to my mother when my father went to jail. I don't know how she managed on her own when I was born. There were things she never got around to telling me. She died not long ago.'

'I'm sorry. I liked your mother. She was a nice girl.'

'But she took her secrets with her when she died and now I've met you, I think you might know the answer to some of my questions.'

'Some things are best left unsaid.'

'I've thought about that too, but I want to know the truth and I won't be satisfied until I do.'

Miss Jones nodded. 'I thought that might be the case.' She paused. 'Well, I'll tell you what I know, but it's quite a story. It's twenty years since I was at the Manse — them last few days were the worst days of my life and I can remember them like they happened yesterday.'

Amy interrupted. 'Can you start at the beginning and tell me what happened?'

14

Cook's Story

Miss Jones kicked off her slippers and stretched her legs out in front of her. 'I knew your mother as Lisbeth Eccles. We worked together at a big house called the Manse for the Reverend Upton and his young wife. An odd couple they were, each in their own way, but I blame him for the way she went. 'Suffer little children . . . ' he'd preach on Sundays, especially if there was a christening, but for all that, he didn't want none of his own. Mrs Upton told me that one day, but I'd guessed as much, as they always slept in separate rooms.'

'I don't understand. What has that to do with my mother?'

'You must let me explain. I think it was her hankering for children that made Mrs Upton fuss over her young maids. Treated them almost like they were her own. It was weird in a way. But she got rid of them in quick sticks if she caught them talking with any of the local lads.

'Like I said, I remember when your mother

first started at the Manse. Only fifteen, she was. Fresh faced and healthy. Or as healthy as any child can be growing up in a city like Leeds. For a time after Lisbeth started, Mrs Upton stopped talking about having a child. Then after a spell it started again. She used to natter the reverend, even while he was at the table. 'Wouldn't it be nice to hear the patter of little feet in the house?' she'd say, or, 'Imagine how nice it would be to christen your own child.' That sort of thing. But she didn't know when to stop and went on and on, morning, noon and evening. Eventually, he had no choice and had to bend to her whim. I think the fact the whispers had spread around his congregation might also have had a bearing.'

Miss Jones continued, gazing straight ahead. 'But it was right odd. It wasn't like he made her that way, if you know what I mean. No, he agreed for her to have a child — but not his. Said she could mind an infant for a spell to see if she could handle it. Then he said, if all went well, she could keep it.

'Lisbeth and I decided he must have done that because she couldn't have children of her own. Anyway, one Monday — I remember it was Monday because I was outside hanging the washing — this man arrived at the gate and presented me his card and asked to see 'the reverend and his good lady'. He was a nice chatty gent, but I didn't know his business. What I do know is he spent almost three hours in the house talking. When he left, Mrs Upton couldn't contain herself. She announced to Lisbeth and me that she was getting a baby at last.'

Amy smiled sympathetically.

'Well, that put the house in a right stir,' Miss Jones said. 'We had to whitewash the walls and make up baby linens from old sheets. We were sewing from morning till night. Never worked so hard in that house as we did that week.'

'And did the man bring a baby?'

'Three weeks later, he was back with an infant in his arms. He was a pretty little lad, finest of fine fair hair you ever did see, and a right bonny little face.'

'And the child thrived?'

'No, it didn't. It got sick after a matter of only a couple of weeks. Colic, I think, from over-feeding. Every time it cried she fed it. Then, when it was in pain, it wouldn't stop crying. Mrs Upton was beside herself — couldn't stand the sound of its screaming. She used to go out for walks to get away from the noise, and leave it for me and your mother to try settle.' She looked across at Amy. 'Poor little mite, I felt that sorry for it. I must say your mother was much better than me. I've never had children. But Lisbeth, well, she'd just about brought up her little sister, Rose, so she was pretty good with the young one.'

'So what happened to the child? Did it get better?'

'I don't know.'

Amy looked puzzled.

'It was sent back.'

'Sent back?'

'That's right. Mrs Upton went berserk one day. We all heard her screaming at the child. I was in the kitchen and the reverend was in his study. I don't know where Lisbeth was, but we all rushed upstairs at the same time, and when we got to the nursery she was shaking the poor mite like it were a piece of carpet. It took the strength of all three of us to get her to stop.

'The very next morning, Lisbeth was given her fares and sent off with a letter for the man who'd delivered the baby to them. It was a terrible business.'

'Did he take the child back?'

'Aye, he came the next day. Polite and businesslike he was. Never a cross word. Never asked what had happened. And Mrs Upton didn't say anything, but I think that was because the doctor had given her some potion to settle her down. Anyway, the man left with the little lad in his arms. Carried it just the way he had when he'd arrived. Cuddling it, he was, like it was his own. I could hear Lisbeth crying as he walked down the street. I don't know how she'd managed to choke the tears till then.'

'Was my father working at the Manse at that time?'

'No,' said Miss Jones, as she filled Amy's cup. 'He didn't arrive until about a year later.'

'And was the reverend's wife all right by then?'

'To outsiders, she seemed fine, but your mum and me, we knew different. She did odd things, like carrying a rag doll around with her. And she'd talk to it and dress it like it was a real baby. She even got me to fill the tub to bath it in. I didn't like to argue with her, the state she was in. At times she appeared all right for a week or two. And then there were the letters.'

'The letters?'

'Aye, she'd sit down and write long letters and put 'em in envelopes and give them to your mother and tell her to deliver them to the gentleman who'd brought the child.

'Lisbeth and me, we never knew what she wrote in them, but we guessed she were asking for another chance. She wanted another infant to look after.'

Amy shook her head.

'Of course, your mother didn't mind delivering them messages even though it was quite a way off. The address was over in Roundhay, at the other side of Leeds. A nice house, from what your mother said, but it took the best part of a day for her to get there and back, and she was often right weary when she arrived home. But Lisbeth was always happy to go. It was a treat for her to have a day out. Imagine a young lass having her fares paid to take a trip. It gave her plenty of time to stop and look in Leeds markets when she was passing through the city.'

'And after all her letters, did the reverend's wife get another baby?'

'No, she never did. And she never got pregnant either, poor soul, so that was the end of that.'

Miss Jones closed her eyes, and for a moment Amy thought she was falling asleep. 'Tell me about my father, Amos Dodd. When did he start working at the Manse?'

Leaning forward in the chair, Miss Jones continued. 'He came to the Manse about a year after this terrible baby business. It was early summer and the rhododendrons were in flower. Beautiful, they were. But if it weren't for them damn blooms, he'd have never got a job at the house.' She paused and drained her cup. 'Fred the old gardener was sick. Well, he was ninety, if he was a day. Too old to work, really, but the reverend insisted on keeping him on. Anyway, Fred didn't come in to work that week, and Mrs Upton got a bee in her bonnet about the rhododendrons. The bushes had grown out over the path and you could hardly see where to walk, so she decided to cut them down — there and then. That was exactly the time Dodd turned up on the doorstep. His timing couldn't have been better. He was a strong man, said he wanted a job and said he was prepared to do anything.

'It took him over a week, but he cleared every last rhododendron bush in the garden. And it was a big garden too. Such a shame. Beautiful blooms they were, and had been since spring. Hacked them down to ground level and burnt the lot. Talk about smoke! Anyway, that same week, old Fred sent word he wasn't coming back to the Manse, so Dodd was offered the gardener's job. Walked straight into it. Not only that, he was allowed to have the garden shed to live in, on condition that he tidied it up a bit.

'Mrs Upton seemed quite taken by the new man. It seemed odd to us. She was a well bred woman, educated and talked proper, whereas he was as common as muck.' She paused for a moment as she realized she was talking about Amy's father. 'I'm sorry, love,' she said.

'Don't worry,' Amy said. 'He's not changed.'

Miss Jones continued. 'Lisbeth and I couldn't figure out what the attraction was with the new gardener, till he told us. Boasting, he was. 'I keep telling her,' he said, 'if she wants a baby, I'll fix 'er up.' Then he'd laugh. 'Stupid woman, dumb as a dead dog she is, believes I'll fetch her one.' She shuddered. 'Then he'd laugh again. Evil it was. I hated that laugh of his. Even now when I think about it, it sends shivers down my spine.'

'Did anything happen between my father and Mrs Upton?'

'No, I don't think so. He just played with her. Teased her. Lisbeth and I used to watch him, joshing with her in the garden, and her eyes would sparkle — sadly, it was the only time they ever did. I reckon it was cruel the way he made a fool of her.

'But he had a glib tongue, that man, and before long he had young Lisbeth's eyes lit up too. He used to invite her to his shed — big one, it was — and he furnished it out like a real room; table, chairs and a bed. Don't know where he got them from! Well, I don't have to tell you what happened. One afternoon, when the Uptons had gone away, he got your mother drunk. She came to me afterwards in a terrible state and I had to sober her up. That were the beginning of the end.'

'So that was how Mum got pregnant. So her and my father weren't married?'

'No, not then. Lisbeth was ashamed of herself when she found she was pregnant but she daren't tell anyone except me. And she made me swear I wouldn't tell because she knew she'd lose her job if the missus found out.'

'So how long was it before she left?'

'She managed to hide her belly till she were about five months gone, but then it got to a stage her dresses wouldn't fasten in the middle. When Mrs Upton found out about her condition, she sent her packing that same day.'

'And my father, did he lose his job too?'

'No,' said the cook. 'That was all a bit odd. Mrs Upton insisted that Dodd stay on in the garden even though it was February and there was nothing to do. Surprisingly, the reverend agreed to it. The only condition Reverend Upton made was that Lisbeth and Dodd get married and make it official. Your mother accepted that because of the baby.'

213

Amy nodded.

'The other thing Mrs Upton insisted was that Lisbeth sent her sister, Rose, along to the Manse to work in her place.'

'So Rose went to work at the Manse where my father was working?'

'That's right. But it put your mother in a right bind. She didn't know whether to send her sister to Mrs Upton, partly because the girl was not much more than a child herself, also because she knew how odd and highly strung Mrs Upton was at times. And then, of course, there was Amos. On the other hand, it was a job for the little lass, and a good one at that. I think Lisbeth hoped and prayed that when she and Amos married, he'd mend his ways and wouldn't start his games with young Rose. Only thirteen she was — the sweet child.' Miss Jones sighed and shook her head. 'Some men never change, do they?'

'Some men never do.' Amy took a deep breath. 'Tell me what happened at the Manse after my mother left.'

The woman leaned back. 'I guess you can imagine. Everything was fine at first. Mrs Upton was in her element with a young girl fussing around her. And she fussed around the lass like a mother hen. Because of the cold, the pair of them were indoors most of the time. As for the reverend, providing he

214

was left alone, he was happy. As for me, well, I'd got my kitchen and that's where I stayed. And Dodd wasn't allowed in there, I'm pleased to say.'

'But what happened between him and Rose?'

'There was nothing to see for quite a while, then it developed slowly, like mould on a piece of cheese. You tend to ignore it at first, then suddenly it's green all over. He was polite at first. But it was put on. Then he started fussing over her. Talking to her every chance he got. Silly talk. Always trying to impress her. But I think your mother had warned her what he was like, because she used to spend all her time indoors. Of course he wasn't allowed in the house and young Rose managed to keep her distance from him for over three months.

'But Dodd was cunning,' she said. 'He never missed a trick. He'd be out there if Rose had errands to run or washing to peg out. He'd lurk about in the garden and stalk her every time she went anywhere. But she was a smart lass and wilful, and she wouldn't give in to him. She told me he'd tried to grab her twice and drag her into his shed, but said she'd managed to get away, but that made him downright angry. I told her she should tell the reverend, but she was afraid she might lose her job. As for Dodd, you could see him simmering, ready to boil over. It was obvious what he wanted and he couldn't get it. I tell you, it was a terrible atmosphere to live and work in.'

'How did Rose die, Miss Jones?'

The elderly woman took several deep breaths. 'There was a fire. The garden shed burnt down.' She pulled a handkerchief from her sleeve and screwed it around in her hands. 'Unrecognizable she was when they brought her out. She was burnt to a crisp. Dodd pretended he was upset. Said she must have been looking for something in his shed and knocked the lamp over. I didn't believe a word of it.'

'What happened to him?'

'Nothing happened right away. The reverend and I were concerned about Mrs Upton and the effect it had on her. She started behaving stranger than ever before. Seeing things and hearing things, she was. It was scary. As for Amos Dodd, no one saw him for two weeks. Then the reverend got word that the police had caught up with him in Wakefield. They brought him back to Leeds and charged him with Rose's murder. Of course he denied it, but at the inquest the doctor, who'd examined her remains, said her wrists had rope fibres burnt into the skin. He also said that she'd burned up more than the rest of the shed. It was like someone had deliberately set her on fire. He'd tied her up and doused her with paraffin!'

'God help us!'

'I warned you, lass.' After taking a few moments to calm herself, Miss Jones continued. 'That was the end of the cook's job for me. That was when I came to stay with my niece here in Saltaire. They closed up the Manse when they carted Mrs Upton off to the asylum at Menston. She spent five years there. If I hadn't recognized her dress, I wouldn't have known her when she came out. White like a ghost, she was — face and hair — and she walked like one of them undead.' She shuddered again. 'She's in a nursing home not far from here. I go and visit her occasionally. Very sad.'

Amy nodded slowly. 'What happened to Reverend Upton?'

'I never saw him after he asked me to pack his bags and books. After the trial, he went off to Colchester or Winchester or some such place to take up a post at the university. He was teaching theology, of all things! I reckon I could teach him a thing or two about godliness!'

'And did you ever see my mother again after that?'

'Aye, just once, at Rose's funeral. There were a lot of people there, but she wasn't interested in well-wishers. I felt so sorry for her. Almost full-term, she was, and her clothes hardly fitted. She looked terrible. I spoke to her when the service was over and offered to help if I could. But she was in such a state, what with losing her little sister, Rose, and with the baby due at any moment, there was nothing I could say or do that would help. She told me then that she hated Amos and the last thing she wanted was to have his baby. She told me what she was going to do, but made me promise I'd pass it on to nobody. In all these years, I never broke my promise, but as your mother's dead and gone, I suppose I can tell you now.'

'Please,' Amy said.

'She told me she was going to see the man who had delivered that little blond-haired infant to Mrs Upton.'

Amy looked puzzled. 'Do you think she was going to ask him to take her baby?'

'I don't know what she had in mind. And I didn't ask her.'

'Do you know where I can find this man?'

'I don't. All I know was that he lived in Roundhay. Somewhere near the park, Lisbeth said. She was the one who visited his house to deliver those letters.'

'I don't suppose you know his name.'

'Oh, yes,' she said. 'I remember that. It was written on the card he handed me the first time he called.

'His name was Ogilvy. Mr Charles Ogilvy.'

15

Charles Ogilvy

For two days, Amy considered the cook's words, and though she knew Helen sensed something was troubling her, she never mentioned the conversation. Nor did she mention it to Harold when he called that day after work.

Though she still wanted to get away from her father, unravelling the mystery lurking in her past now seemed more pressing. It was a chance to find out what secrets her mother had taken with her to that plot of unconsecrated ground.

Maybe Mr Ogilvy could fill in the missing jigsaw pieces — no matter how black they were. Nothing, she thought, could be worse than the conversation she had had with Miss Jones, but she was prepared for anything.

During the previous weeks, while she'd been busy working on the barge, thoughts of her father had slowly been pushed to the back of her mind and her feeling of fear had ebbed. She'd heard no word of him in almost a month and thought it unlikely she would bump into him in Leeds but that was a chance she must take. There was no choice. She had to go back. It was the only way to discover the truth.

'Are you sure about this, lass?' Joel asked, after Amy finished telling him and Helen the cook's story. 'Seems daft going back into the lion's den when you're safe and sound with us here. Why not wait and speak to Harold. He'll be here in the morning to go get the horse with Ben. Talk with him. He'll know what's best. And if it means going back to the city then maybe he'll go with you.'

'I can't wait,' said Amy anxiously. 'I've been thinking about it since I talked to Miss Jones and I know I have to go even though I don't know what I'll discover.'

Joel shook his head. 'Well, it's your life, Amy lass, but I think you're foolish. And I reckon Harold would agree with me on this one.'

'How do you plan to get to Leeds?' Helen said.

'I'll walk there — along the towing path.'

'Now that's the daftest thing I've heard yet. You're planning to walk the way you came, when round every corner, under every bridge and behind every bush you'll be thinking your father's waiting to grab you. You'll scare yourself silly!'

Amy looked at Helen for support. 'I have to go.'

'Don't try to stop her, Joel,' Helen said. 'It's best she finds out what she needs to know. Only then can she put it to rest. Tell me, love, when you've seen this man, Mr Ogilvy, where will you stay in Leeds? You'll not get your business over and done with in time to get back to Saltaire the same day.'

'I'll stay with the Medleys. They were neighbours on the street near Fanshaw's Mill. Mrs Medley will let me stay with them for a night or two.'

'When you go you'll wear my bonnet and skirt so you look like a boatwoman and not a mill lass. And you'll take money for your fare,' she said, handing Joel his purse. 'You've earned a few shillings with the work you've done on the boat.'

'When are you taking this trip?' Joel asked glumly.

'Tomorrow morning. I'll catch the early train.'

'And when will we expect you back?'

'I'll be back on Monday, I promise.'

★　★　★

The journey to Leeds didn't take long. Gazing at the canal from the train window,

Amy thought back to her trek to Saltaire and the state she was in when she met *Milkwort*. How lucky she had been.

From Leeds the journey to Roundhay, though much shorter, took longer than she had anticipated. Having reached the area, she then had to find where her mother's old landlord lived. She was fairly confident that with a tongue in her head, the local shopkeepers or the postmaster would be able to direct her to his house. Unfortunately, not being familiar with that part of Leeds, Amy hadn't taken into account the types of residences in the area. Many of the houses in Roundhay were big and fancy. Many stood in their own grounds surrounded by well-kept gardens and stone walls. Iron gates, reminiscent of those at Fanshaw's Mill, blocked some entrances. The streets of slightly less opulent houses seemed to stretch for miles, and shops were few and far between. On finding a grocer's shop, she enquired if the shop-keeper knew where Mr Ogilvy lived. The man seemed suspicious of the strangely dressed girl asking after the premises of a gentleman and said he didn't know. She got the same response from the next two shops she tried.

It was the coalman, just finishing his rounds, who stopped his cart and gave Amy directions. He remembered Mr Ogilvy well. He was the gentleman who gave him a couple of shillings each Christmas.

★ ★ ★

A small kindly lady answered the door at the Roundhay residence. She smiled sympathetically when she saw Amy. 'You'd be looking for Mr Ogilvy, I presume?'

'Yes.'

'Does he know you are coming?'

'No, I don't expect so.'

'Then just wait in the porch while I go tell him you're here. What's your name, love?'

'Amy Dodd.'

'I'll be back in two shakes.'

It was quite hot in the porchway. It was more of a conservatory than a porch with two cane chairs and a table. In the centre of the table was a large, round glass bowl with two orange fish swimming in circles. Amy was used to seeing fish at the markets hung up by the gills, and dead ones floating on the surface of the canal, but she'd never seen live ones sitting on a table. She wondered why they were there. They were too small to eat.

'Amy, please come through into my study,' Charles Ogilvy said.

The housekeeper stood back, and smiled

again, as Amy followed the elderly man down the hall.

'Two teas, Mrs Smith, please.'

The room, which was at the back of the house, was light but bare and colourless. The curtains were chocolate velvet and the armchairs a dark walnut shade of leather. Scores of books vied for places on the two tall bookcases and more were half hidden behind the swirling glass in the door of the chiffonier. Apart from the portait of a young woman above the fireplace, there were no ornaments to colour the room, no sprays of roses painted on the walls, not even a pattern on the wallpaper. Though it was summer and the sun-porch had been very warm, the air in the study was cold.

Mr Ogilvy's manner, however, compensated for that. 'Please sit down,' he said, showing Amy to a chair. 'You look well, Amy. But tell me, what brings you here?'

'Are you my father, Mr Ogilvy?'

The man looked shocked. He smiled. 'Goodness! No, girl. Whatever gave you that idea?'

Amy suddenly felt deflated; foolish and embarrassed. Since she had spoken with the old cook, the silly notion had been festering in her head. A notion that something had transpired between her mother and the man she had delivered Mrs Upton's letters to. For Amy the idea seemed quite feasible. He had provided a home for her mother and her for almost eighteen years. And the thought that Amos Dodd was not her father appealed to her. And it wasn't just the conversations or wishful thinking that had led her to consider the idea. After all, she looked nothing like her father in build, or face, or eyes, or the colour of her hair.

'I'm sorry,' she said, wiping the tears on the cuff of her blouse. 'I've been told some terrible truths recently about my father and the horrible way Rose, my mother's sister, died. I was told that before I was born my mother had nowhere to go and you were the only person she was asking to see. I thought perhaps you were my father and not Amos Dodd. I wished you were, because I hate my real father.'

Mr Ogilvy handed Amy a handkerchief and waited until her sobbing stopped.

'I'm sorry that you feel like that. Are you living with your father?'

'Not for more than a month. He made me work and took all my money so I ran away from him. I think you know what sort of man he is.'

Mr Ogilvy nodded. 'Where are you staying now, Amy?'

226

'In Saltaire. On a barge on the canal with a family of canal folk.'

'Then I am pleased you are free of him.'

'I don't know if I am free. I heard he was searching for me, trying to find me.'

'Then why have you come back to Leeds?'

Amy looked into his eyes. 'I came to see you. I spoke to a lady who told me you helped my mother. I know that was the case after I was born, because you gave her the cellar to live in. But I want to know what happened when she came to you after Rose was buried and father was put into Armley Jail. She had no one to turn to, but she asked for you. Did she want you to take her baby? Did she have me in the workhouse?'

'Who suggested you speak to me? Surely it wasn't Mrs Upton? I gather she is not a well woman?'

'No, it was their cook. She was at the Manse when . . . '

'When those tragic events happened.'

Amy nodded as the housekeeper interrupted them with a tray of tea and sandwiches. Amy didn't realize how hungry she was until she saw them on the plate.

'Cold pork,' the housekeeper announced.

'Please help yourself, Amy. Mrs Smith knows I don't eat a great deal, yet she is forever bringing me extra morsels.' He stood up and faced the window, his fingers intwined behind his back. Outside a passing breeze fluttered the leaves on the beech tree but the branches remained motionless. There was no sound save the ticking of the clock in the hall.

'Did my mother come to see you after my father went to jail?'

'She did.'

'Did she want you to take her baby and find it another home?'

'She did.'

Amy caught her breath. 'She didn't want me, then?'

'Amy,' he said, drawing up a straight chair and facing her. 'It is not as simple as that, believe me. I have seen instances like that dozens of times. Your mother was distraught. Her sister had suffered a horrible death. Her husband had been convicted of the heinous crime of murder and sent to jail for life. Her past employer had been certified insane. She was only seventeen years of age with no family or obvious means of support. On top of that she was due to have a child within days. When Lisbeth Dodd came to me she was at her wits' end. She didn't know what she wanted but I could see she needed help. Taking a child from her as soon as it was born would only have added to her despair.'

'But you were able to help her, though?'

'In a small way,' he said, as he leaned back. 'I arranged for her to see a midwife and directed her to a place where she would have the baby.'

'Was it the workhouse?'

'No, it was a home for unmarried mothers.'

'Are you a doctor or something?'

Charles Ogilvy smiled sadly. 'Unfortunately, no. My roles over the years have been several, but have included a seat on the Board of Governors of various charitable organizations, one being a home for unmarried mothers — for girls who, for one reason or another, had become pregnant. It was from this very establishment that a child was procured for the Reverend and Mrs Upton at the Manse which you mentioned. Unfortunately, that arrangement did not work out well.'

'So, you arranged for a midwife for my mother, and for her to have the cellar room to live in when I was born.'

Mr Ogilvy pondered over his answer. 'Yes.'

'And that is all that there is to know?'

'Did you expect something different?'

Amy sighed. 'I wanted it to be different. I wanted you to be my father. I want anyone to be my father other than Amos Dodd.'

Though she could feel his warm eyes on

her and feel his sympathy, she was lost and disillusioned and could not respond.

After a moment, Mr Ogilvy excused himself, walked over to the desk and took out a sheet of paper. After writing something on it, he placed it in Amy's hand.

'The home for unmarried mothers, which I mentioned, was closed several years ago due to lack of financial support. I believe the building still stands, but it has fallen into disrepair. Shameful,' he said, shaking his head. 'What I have written here is the address of the midwife who attended your mother. Her name is Mrs Sneddon. If you decide to visit her, I do not know what condition you will find her in. Let me warn you, she is now an old woman. She is also a drunkard. If you choose to speak to her, I suggest you call around noon. And if she asks you for money, you would do her a favour by not giving her any. She will only waste it on drink. A gift of food would be better.'

Amy looked puzzled. 'But what can she tell me that you haven't said already?'

'I cannot say. My advice is, speak to her. She was there when you were born. There may be things about your birth which you should know.'

'What things? You must tell me! Did my mother have twins? Do I have a brother or a sister somewhere? Tell me! I must know!'

'All I will say is Lisbeth Dodd was a good woman, and a good mother, and for all the years I knew her, I know she loved you dearly.'

'And I loved her more than words can tell. She was the only family I had.'

'Then always remember her in that way.'

'What are you saying?'

He hesitated. 'I believe Amos Dodd was not your father.'

Amy was lost for words. It was the best news she had ever heard. She didn't care who her father was. He could be anybody. But he wasn't Amos Dodd.

'But,' he added, before she had chance to respond, 'there is more.' He paused. 'I also believe Lisbeth Dodd was not your mother.'

Amy swayed on the chair as a swirl of light-headedness smothered her thinking. She could feel her cheeks tighten. For a moment she couldn't comprehend what she was hearing. Then a torrent of thoughts started tumbling into her head: memories, conversations, bathtimes, hugs, Christmases, songs her mother sang to her, arguments they had had over silly things.

'What are you saying?' she cried. 'I came here longing to hear the news that Dodd was not my father, but this . . . I didn't come to hear this!'

'I'm sorry, Amy, it is something which, if you hadn't come here, I would've never revealed.' He spoke gently. 'I believe Lisbeth Dodd is not your mother but, let me add, I am not sure. The only person who knows the truth is Mrs Sneddon. She was with your mother when she gave birth — the day you were born.'

16

No One's Child

If Amos Dodd was not her father and Lisbeth Eccles not her mother, then she belonged to no one.

What had happened the day she was born? Where did her mother go to have her? If she wasn't her mother's child, then whose child was she? Did Mr Ogilvy really know the truth and was he purposely withholding it? Had he something to hide? Had money changed hands?

Questions bombarded her brain as she left Charles Ogilvy's house. She had no recollections of saying goodbye, of fainting in the sunporch due to the heat, or of the hug Mrs Smith gave her as she helped her with her coat.

She didn't remember how she found her way into Roundhay Park or notice the time she spent gazing into the lake. But she was conscious of the still water, black and inviting, just like the canal. Like a dark winter blanket she could slide under; hide from her past and block out the facts she didn't want to hear.

Sitting alone on the grass, she knew what her mother had always wanted to tell her, but never did. Why did she wait so long? Amy thought. Was she afraid I would have loved her any less? Surely not. Lisbeth Eccles was everything to her. Then she thought about Amos Dodd. Was she afraid I would tell him that he was not my father?

So whose child was her mother carrying? Was it his? Or was she pregnant to another man? She hardly dared imagine what would have happened if that had been the case.

A family of ducks swam towards her, fanning the dark surface with tiny waves. The adults quacked as if demanding attention. When they received nothing they swam further along the bank, the cluster of ducklings paddling frantically in an effort to keep up.

Had Charles Ogilvy told her the truth when he said he wasn't her father? And if he wasn't, why had he allowed her mother to live rent free for almost eighteen years? Would a man do that if he was not in some way responsible? Surely no man was so charitable to forgo access to that income for so many years? Yet from the little she had seen of him, Mr Ogilvy was just that — kindhearted and charitable, a man of principle. Though he lived in a large house he did not live to excess and the trappings in his room were not those of a spendthrift. More questions kept coming. Was Charles Ogilvy hiding something? Did he really know the full story? Was his honest appearance merely a deceitful ploy? She had heard he'd arrived at the Manse alone with an infant. Strange for a man to be bringing a child, she thought. Stranger that he called back and took it away. Strange there was no nurse or nanny to accompany him. Were his dealings with infants legal? Was he in the business of buying and selling babies?

A thousand and one thoughts whirled through Amy's head, but one cold fact always emerged — Amos Dodd was not her father. And if he was not her father, then he had no right to hold her, chastise her or make her work for him. If she could prove that fact then she would be free of him. But proving it would not be easy. Speaking with the midwife was the first step and from what Mr Ogilvy said, Mrs Sneddon may hold the key to the truth.

★ ★ ★

The sound of the tram's wheels screeching along metal lines and the *ding-ding* of a bell brought Amy to her senses. Looking up, the dome of the Corn Exchange building was in front of her. As she gazed up, a mob of pigeons flew from the roof and fluttered down to the pavement, settling around the feet of a shabbily dressed woman broadcasting crumbs. A group of men talked outside the entrance of a private club, thick cigar smoke swirling round their top hats like smoke from a stack of chimney pots. They ignored the young lad who extended his cap, begging for a few coins. On the corner, the lady selling posies smiled as she stood in her usual position, patiently waiting for trade to come to her. Most folk were in high spirits. They were looking forward to the evening.

Instinct had brought Amy safely back to the city. But where to from here? she asked herself. Though her plan was to stay the night with the Medleys, for a while she considered trying to find Mrs Sneddon. But Mr Ogilvy had said it would be futile to visit the old midwife in the evening. Accepting his advice, she decided to wait till the following day and go at noon.

Walking back near the mill brought mixed memories. The iron gates of Fanshaw's were still open though work had finished early that afternoon. Amy shook her head. It was Saturday — the day that the cost of a week's labour was exchanged for a jug of misery and heartache. It was a ritual in most alehouses in the West Riding and the Hungry Crow was no exception. With the smell of the public bar already in her nostrils, she pulled Helen's bonnet forwards over her eyes and kept her head bowed. She had to pass the front door of the Crow on the way to the Medleys.

A cat miaowed, from a window-sill, but Amy never looked up. A small girl on a doorstep smiled shyly. A couple walked by, talking quietly.

How nice it will be to see the Medleys, she thought, visualizing the compact kitchen, crowded with children, and the smell of fresh tarts straight from the oven, oozing with lemon curd. She would ask Mrs Medley if she could stay for two nights and on Monday morning she'd catch the early train back to Saltaire. If she didn't arrive as promised, she knew Helen would worry.

'Well, look what we have here! If it isn't Amy Dodd!' The voice, like a breath from the grave, sent a chill through Amy's spine. He was on the pavement not more than five yards ahead — legs apart, hands on hips — waiting. A half-smile twisted on his lips as he spoke. 'Decided to come back to your father, did you?'

'You are not my father!' she yelled. 'And you can't make me work for you.'

'Huh!'

'Do you understand? I'm not your daughter and I'll be able to prove it!' She wanted to sound pleased as she announced the news, but her voice was flat and emotionless. 'Did you hear what I said?'

Amos Dodd's answer was to latch his hand around her wrist and almost pull her off her feet. 'You dare cross me, you little bitch!' he said, swinging his other hand across her face. 'I'll teach you to run off from me.'

Amy grabbed her bonnet. 'You can't make me work for you,' she said. 'You're not my father!'

'What do I care whose brat you are?' he said, dragging her along the pavement.

'Let her alone!' the woman shouted from a doorway.

'You mind your own bloody business, else you'll get a dose of what she's going to get. Try to run off from her pa. Ungrateful little hussy.'

'He's not my father!'

The sting of his hand across her cheek sent her reeling, but he pulled her back to her feet and tugged her behind him. Across the street, a couple walking arm in arm stopped and looked. The woman whispered to her husband, then they hurried on, not wanting to get involved.

It was pointless to shout on a Saturday

night. House doors remained shut to a woman's wails. If a man chose to chastise his own daughter then it was likely she'd been misbehaving — in which case she deserved it. Most folk stayed indoors and minded their own business.

Amy knew he was taking her back to the room they had shared after her mother died. If only Mr Ogilvy had let her stay in the cellar and her father had been forced to go elsewhere. If only her mother had not died. If only Amos Dodd — had died in jail. Or even better — if only he'd been hung for his crime.

The cat squealed as he kicked it from the doorway. Three boys playing in the street stopped and watched.

'Out of the way!' he yelled to the landlady.

'In a bit of a hurry, are you? Not even so much as a beg your pardon or by-your-leave.'

'Bugger off, you old bat. Keep out of my way. I've paid for my lodgings.'

Amy's feet hardly touched the steps as he dragged her along behind him up the three flights to the attic. As the door banged behind them, he turned her around.

She never felt the punch which knocked her out.

The rag was tied tightly across her mouth. Her dry tongue felt swollen and the smell of blood filtered through her nose. Her wrists were tied to the bed's head posts. There was no sign of Amos Dodd. She couldn't check but Amy was sure the money Joel had given her would be gone from her pockets. She wondered if the return train ticket was still in there.

★ ★ ★

Sharp at eight o'clock on Saturday morning, Harold strolled along the canal path towards Jentz's old dock. It was a lovely morning and the good weather promised to attract hundreds of visitors to the Glen that afternoon.

Harold was looking forward to the day's outing even though he knew it would take most of the day. It was several miles to Skipton, but he intended to walk the distance there and back, and a jaunt along the river flats would make a change from his usual hikes which took him over Baildon Moor.

Striding out, he considered the letter in his pocket and was pleased at the thought he had some good news to share with Amy. Hopefully, when he returned, there would be time to take her for a ride on the tram. He was sure she wouldn't say no.

He was also looking forward to taking young Ben along and collecting Mallow. Walking the horse along the towing path would be a new experience for him, and it would provide an opportunity for Ben to acquaint himself with his new animal before harnessing it to the barge. From his childhood, Harold had always loved working with horses. What a treat, he thought, walking back on the bank, beside the boy and the boat-horse.

The still water of the canal glinted in the sun, reflecting the buildings like images on a photograph. Bees buzzed busily on the wild flowers colouring the bank. On the waterway a pair of richly coloured mallards swam apart while an empty barge chugged slowly by, leaving a stream of smoke to dissolve into the otherwise clear sky.

Harold was looking forward to seeing Amy and had planned to ask her to accompany them on the outing. He hoped she would agree.

'Good morning,' he called, when he caught sight of Ben sitting on the deck. But when he waved, the boy got up and disappeared into the cabin. A moment later, Helen appeared.

'What's wrong?' Harold asked.

'Amy's gone to Leeds.'

'What?'

'She left this morning — only an hour ago.'

'What on earth for?'

'She was talking to the lady from the tea

shop during the week. It seems there's more to Amos Dodd than meets the eye. And there's a man in Leeds who knows more about him. He also knew Amy's mother. She's gone to find him.'

'And you let her go alone?'

Helen looked guilty. 'She promised she'd be back on Monday.'

Joel appeared from the cabin, dragging his foot along the deck. He straightened as he slipped the crutch under his arm and leaned up against the cabin roof. 'She's got a mind of her own, that girl, and so she should have. There's a dark side to that man Dodd, and Amy wants to know the truth, and if there's a chance he's not her father, she wants to know that too. If she can get him out of her life, she'll rest easier in bed at night. But it don't make it no less of a worry, her going off on her own.' He rubbed his leg. 'I couldn't go with her and besides I think she wanted to go alone.'

'Did she have money with her — for fares, I mean?'

'Aye, she did,' said Helen. 'I made sure of that. And she'll be safe. She's going to stay with a family by the name of Medley. They were neighbours in the street near the mill.'

'That's good,' said Harold. 'I know Moses Medley. He's a gentle-giant of a fellow.

Good-hearted bloke — works in the ware-house at Fanshaw's. I'm glad Amy is going to stay with them.'

After a cup of strong tea and piece of warm teacake running with honey, Harold and Ben set off for the Gate and Gander Inn at Skipton. Since hearing about Amy, Harold's enthusiasm for the trip had waned. Now he wished he had not committed himself to collecting the horse — but he knew Joel didn't want Ben to go on his own. He had offered his services and he wouldn't go back on his word. But now Harold wanted to get back from Skipton as quickly as possible so that he could travel to Leeds that afternoon. They would still have to walk the horse back along the canal, but by catching the train to the market town, they would save at least three hours.

Having started the day feeling elated, Harold now felt angry. If only Amy had told him and waited. He was planning on going to Leeds on Monday. They could have travelled together and he could have made sure she arrived safely and was all right.

★　★　★

The big shire was as meek as a kitten and didn't object to being bridled and blinkered.

In fact, Mallow appreciated the attention. The enforced rest had improved her condition and her black coat shone in the sun.

'Wait till we get her home,' Ben said. 'I'll plait up her mane and comb her feathers. And when I dress her in her collar and brasses, and add the swingers and terrets, she'll look a real picture.'

Harold could understand how pleased Ben was.

On the way back, they stopped briefly at the Five Rise in Bingley and Harold chatted to a boatman locking through the gates while Ben gave the lock keeper a hand. The man obviously knew the boy well.

As they strode at a steady pace, Ben talked about locks, their names and numbers, the ones that leaked or jammed and the mishaps that had occurred on the cut. His knowledge of the navigations from one coast to the other amazed Harold. But Ben had been born on a narrowboat, he'd ridden a boat-horse before he could walk, and walked on the towing path since the time he could toddle. The canal and its bank were his home.

He told Harold how Amy was teaching him to read. That he planned to read to his mother one day.

In turn, Harold told him about the letter he had written applying for a job with the

Chilean government.

'What sort of job?' Ben asked.

'Building tramways.'

'Like the one at Shipley Glen?'

'Something much grander than that,' he said.

'Is that place far from here?'

'Chile,' Harold said. 'It's at the other side of the globe almost.'

'Is it like Yorkshire with canals and coal mines and factories and farms?'

'Quite different, I think. It's got mines, though, but they dig for emeralds and gold, and it's got rivers which flow fast from great snow-capped mountains. But it's got good land too on the hillsides for farms. A wonderful place to grow grapes, I would say.'

'How will you get to Chile?' Ben asked.

'On a sailing ship. Or maybe a steamer,' Harold replied. 'It's like the canals. Things are changing so fast these days. Soon there'll be no sailing ships crossing the ocean.'

'I saw some big ships down at Grimsby — we took the barge right down there once but the waves came in and rolled over the deck and I was afraid they might sink us, but pa got us through. I bet the waves in the ocean are big,' he said.

'I imagine they are,' said Harold.

On the opposite bank, a tree had fallen. As

its massive root system had upended, it had taken with it a large bite of the canal's bank. Where the tree had stood, a small nub had formed. Over time it had lined with silt and mud and the reeds had grown up, forming a tiny beach. A swan, who had adopted it as her home, was busily tending five fluffy grey cygnets. Ben rested the horse for a while before continuing on their way, but no sooner had they set off again than the swan's squawking made them turn. With wings flapping and head outstretched, the swan was heading over the field after a fox which had one of her young in its jaw.

'Cunning,' Harold said. 'He'd been waiting until we passed before pouncing.' Cunning, he thought. But how cunning was Amos Dodd? Dangerous too. That man had a black streak running right through his heart.

17

Amy's Back

In the attic, Amy struggled to loosen the ropes binding her hands to the bed but they cut deeper into her wrists. Her fingers felt hard and swollen. As she tried to turn, her stomach hurt from the punches he'd thrown at her. As she leaned back against the bed head, exhausted, the image of the man she hated flashed through her brain — his twisted smile, his pale eyes and the tarry black wart stuck on the top of his bald head. She thought about her mother, Lisbeth Dodd, the only mother she had known, and was thankful, at least, that she was not the child of that horrible man.

How alone it made her feel. She had despised him when she thought he was her father. Now she hated him even more. But she also feared him. Having learned the extent of his evil, she could only imagine what lengths he would go to to get rid of her.

She didn't know what time of day it was, or how long she had been there. The day was still bright outside so perhaps only an hour, she thought. She wanted a drink and something to eat. Surely he didn't intend to leave her there and not come back? Or did he?

The scarf across her mouth prevented her from screaming. Her jaw ached from the pressure on it. Her mouth was dry. Tears no longer flowed. She dreaded what would happen when he returned.

As she began rocking, the iron frame bounced rhythmically against the wall. If she made sufficient noise, she thought someone might hear. Swaying backwards and forwards as far as her bindings would allow, Amy continued relentlessly. *Bang. Bang. Bang.* But no one came. Could no one in the building hear her? Her head hit the bed head every time she threw it back, and though the exercise was tiring her, she kept going.

'What the hell is going on up here!' It was a woman's voice. 'Can't you give it a rest for a spell?' Her feet pounded up the stairs. A key clicked in the lock. The hinges rasped as the door slid open.

'What the . . . ' The words trailed away when she saw Amy tied to the bed. 'The lout!' she said. 'All the same, they are. Bastards every one of them.'

Amy recognized the woman but doubted she'd remembered her face or the rations she'd sold her for sixpence over a month ago. Likely a lot of lasses passed through her premises hiring rooms by the hour both by night and by day.

'How long's he had you trussed up like this?' she said, as she slowly unfastened the scarf. 'I'll need a knife to cut these off.'

Even with the gag from her mouth, Amy couldn't speak. Her jaw was stiff. Her throat raw. She needed a drink. 'Hurry,' she tried to call, as the woman trundled down the stairs, but her cry was no more than a whisper. Fearing Amos could return any time, she continued desperately pulling at the ropes. The bed head continued banging.

'Hold your horses — I'm coming as quick as I can!' the landlady mumbled, puffing on the stairs. Wielding a large pair of scissors that seemed hardly sharp enough to cut the rind off a slice of bacon, she worried the blade into the knots and cut through the twisted hessian. Amy's arms and shoulders hurt when she tried to fold them across her chest. Her hands were swollen and red and when she stood, her legs were weak. The water on the dresser was tempting but the moths' wings put her off. She cupped her hands and swilled it across her face then sucked a mouthful into the back of her throat, gargled it and spat it out on to the floor.

'Hey, watch what you're doing!' the woman yelled.

Amy didn't reply as she grabbed Helen's bonnet and rushed through the door.

'There's gratitude for you!' the voice called from the attic. Amy hobbled down the stairs as fast as she could. There was no time to stop and say thank you.

* * *

The late afternoon train leaving Saltaire was full. Even all the first class seats were taken. Most passengers were weary but happy after spending a day at the Glen. Only the small children were silent. They slept on their mothers' laps or on the floor of the compartment.

Harold Lister was pleased to have a seat, but his mood was sombre. The more he thought about Amy, the angrier he felt. He was angry with Joel for letting her go to Leeds alone, though he knew the boatman would have had little chance of stopping her. He was angry with himself also, for not offering her more help. Why hadn't she spoken to him first? he wondered. Why didn't she wait just one more day? They could have travelled together. He could have arranged for her to have a room in the small hotel where he lodged. She'd have been safe there and it was a pleasant place where only respectable people stayed. She'd have had time to do all the things she wanted, and he wouldn't have bothered her. He'd have been busy at Fanshaw's, but at least he'd have been close by in case she needed his help.

The most he could do now was find her and make sure she was settled at the Medleys and in no immediate danger.

'Amy Dodd, slung her hook,
Set a fire, run amuck,
Took off like a butcher's dog,
You'll ne'er catch our Amy Dodd!'

Mrs Medley jumped up from her knees and raised her fist to the three boys in the street. 'Didn't I tell you lads to stop singing that song? Amy Dodd's not here any more, and you'll not be calling people behind their backs, especially when it ain't true.'

'Aye, missus,' the biggest boy said boldly, 'but she *is* back. We saw her not far from here early this afternoon.'

'What did you say?' Mrs Medley asked, the

251

holystone she'd been rubbing the step with clasped in her hand.

The three lads stood their ground as she hurried across the cobbles towards them. Their expressions looked somewhat sheepish. 'We weren't giving you no cheek, missus. Honest!'

'And I'm not accusing you of it, lad. I want to know exactly where you saw Amy. Are you sure it were her?'

''Course we're sure! She lived on this street, didn't she?'

'Anyway,' the little one added, 'them words ain't right. Says they'll never catch her.'

Mrs Medley looked at him quizzically. 'What do you mean?'

'Well, they did. We saw t'man that caught her and dragged her off.'

'What man, for God's sake?'

The boy shrugged his shoulders and looked at his companions for help.

'Dunno,' one of them replied. 'Didn't take much notice of him. Must have been someone from t'mill, cos it weren't a bobby.'

Mrs Medley spun her head around. Her son was standing in the doorway. 'Jimmy! Go get your da. Tell him it's urgent. Tell him it's about young Amy. And you three,' she said, turning back to the boys, 'don't you dare move. Stay right where you are and when Mr Medley comes out, you take him to where you saw this fella with Amy. Do you hear me?'

Seeing the stone gripped tightly in her fist, the boys stood rooted to the spot. They hardly even blinked.

★　★　★

A few minutes later, the three boys were trooping along the street with Mr Medley following close on their heels. Soon after they passed the Hungry Crow the boys stopped.

'That's the house with the cat on the doorstep!'

'You sure, lad?'

'Certain. The fella kicked it out of the road when he dragged Amy inside.'

Mr Medley reached into his coat pocket. 'Here, lads,' he said, pulling three sweets from the inside pocket, 'take this for your trouble. Now, get on your way and say nowt to no one.' With that, he glanced at the building, turned and hurried back towards home. He had to get help.

★　★　★

As he walked towards the mill from the station, Harold consciously tried to improve his mood. He wanted to see Amy and, though he was concerned, he didn't want to show his frustrations.

On the streets, the children peered at the smartly dressed stranger, wondering why he was visiting that area. Well-dressed men were often bailiffs or lawyers or rent men and best avoided. Few of them ever brought good news to that neighbourhood.

It was not hard to discover which house the Medleys lived at. Everyone around Fanshaw's knew them. Mrs Medley was very cautious when Harold knocked on the door and introduced himself.

'I'm a friend of Amy Dodd's,' he said. 'And I've come to pay a visit. Wanted to make sure she was all right.'

'Then I hope you haven't come too late. Come in,' she said, peering down the street before ushering him into the living room. 'Outside, you kids,' she shouted.

'Where's Amy?' Harold asked.

'Well, she's not here, as you can see.'

'But she's supposed to be staying with you. She came down on the train from Saltaire this morning and left word she'd beg you for a bed for two nights. She's due back in Saltaire on Monday.'

'Is that where you've come from?'

'Yes, Amy and I are friends. Has something happened to her?'

'I'm not sure. We'd not seen hide nor hair of her this past month. Then about an hour ago I heard the kids singing their silly rhymes and discovered they'd seen Amy being dragged off by some fella. Moses, my husband, reckons it was Amos Dodd and that he's got her locked up in a boarding house near t'mill.'

'Where?' Harold shouted, as he jumped up. 'Tell me where!'

'It's on the same street as the Hungry Crow. My Moses should be there right now. He went to get a crowbar and a couple of strong lads to help him. They'll find her and get her out, trust me, even if they have to break the door down.' Mrs Medley shook her head. 'It worries me, though. My husband is a big fellow but he wouldn't harm a flea. Amos Dodd ain't big but he's a strong bugger and nasty too. I'd not like to see him when he's angry.'

Harold thanked Mrs Medley but didn't wait for any more instructions. He knew where the public house was. If Dodd had dragged Amy away, what did he intend to do with her? He couldn't send her back to Fanshaw's to work for him. She'd never get a job there. His main concern was the way

Dodd had treated Amy and he wouldn't put anything past him. The man had not spent fifteen years behind bars for nothing.

★ ★ ★

The three men talking in the street touched their caps to Harold when he ran up. They'd spent all their working lives in the yard at Fanshaw's and knew the engineer by sight, though they'd never had occasion to speak to him before. After a brief introduction, Moses Medley thanked his mates and they turned and walked off up the street.

'Where's Amy?' Harold asked.

'She's not here. But she was earlier. That father of hers had her trussed up in the attic like a prize turkey, I'm told. God only knows how long for. But she got away from him, thank goodness, and the woman who runs the place said she's been gone about an hour. Said her father went berserk when he found she'd got away. I reckon he's on the prowl again to get her back.'

Harold couldn't hide his desperation. Amos Dodd could have killed her up in that room or done things to her too terrible to consider. Dodd was an evil man who respected no one, not even himself.

But where was Amy now? He'd just come

from the Medleys' house, and she wasn't there. Last time she'd run away she'd gone to the canal, even slept under one of the bridges. She may do that again, he thought. She may have begged a lift on a barge or set off walking on the towing path. Then he remembered that she had some money and considered that she may have caught a train back to Saltaire. There were crowds of people at the station earlier and he'd never thought of looking for her. Now he was annoyed with himself for not being more observant.

'I was surprised to see you, Mr Lister,' Medley said, as they walked back to his house. 'Did the mill send you to look for the girl?'

'No,' he said. 'Amy and I became friends in Saltaire. Good friends. But I'll tell you about that later.'

After a drink and a bite to eat with the Medleys, they resumed their search for Amy. Moses volunteered to scour the local streets. He said he'd search the mill yard if the gates were open. He'd check the schoolyard too and go as far as the main road. Mrs Medley said she'd search near the mill, and the children would help by keeping their eyes and ears open.

Heading down the hill to the canal. Harold looked in all the ginnels and alleys, searched every doorway, feared the worst. He thought of shouting Amy's name, but was worried she may think it was her father calling. Besides, he didn't want Dodd to know someone else was looking for her.

★   ★   ★

The canal bank was empty, the water black and still. Only a narrow strip of inhospitable land separated it from the River Aire which slithered towards Leeds like a great black slug. Gazing at the water, Harold suddenly imagined Amy's body floating to the surface.

Please don't let me find her here, he prayed, and as he wandered on, trying hard to stop his imagination playing cruel tricks.

It was dusk already and in an hour it would be pitch black. After walking to the city and back, he felt satisfied she wasn't hiding there. He'd checked under all the bridges and seen few signs of life; only a handful of drunks curled up in the darkness under the bridges.

As he wandered wearily back to the Medleys', he hoped there would be better news awaiting him, but he doubted it. He would go back to his room in the hotel, sleep if he could, and resume his search in the morning. If he didn't find her soon, he feared he may never find her.

18

Mrs Sneddon

When Amy ran down the steps and out into the street, she had no idea where she was heading. All she knew was that she was free again. She had no idea of the time, save for the fact it was daylight and there was a smell of cooking in the air.

As she hesitated for a moment to get her bearings, a voice called out: 'I'm looking for a bit of fun. What d'you say, love?'

Ignoring the man, Amy picked up her skirt and looked both ways. Her neighbour's house offered a safe haven and it was only a short distance away, but to get there she must pass in front of the open doors of the Hungry Crow. The fact that her pocket was empty indicated that her father was probably drinking there at that very moment. Amy turned in the opposite direction. She would wind her way through the streets and go down to the canal. She'd been safe there once before and since she'd lived on the barge, the area didn't scare her any more. Besides that, in her present confused state, it was the only place she could think of.

Conscious of her boots clacking on the paving, Amy ran. She was conscious too of kitchen doors wide open to the light and warmth of a summer's long afternoon. Conscious of faces peering out. Of men sitting out on the doorsteps reading or smoking a pipe. As she ran by they looked up and watched her pass.

'You'll cop it when you get home!' one shouted.

The words hit hard. She had no home. No family. Nowhere to go. And now it seemed nowhere to hide. She knew he'd look for her at the Medleys', and if he asked for her along the street, a dozen eyes couldn't deny they'd seen her rush by.

The bridges were the only safe places she knew. The only places she felt certain he wouldn't look.

Pushing her hand into her pocket, she fingered the lining. She already knew the money was gone but she'd forgotten about the ticket. That was missing too. She felt in the other pocket. Thankfully the piece of folded paper Mr Ogilvy had given her was still there. She wondered if her father had read the address which was written on it. Would he go there and get to Mrs Sneddon before she did? But he wouldn't know of the woman for Lisbeth had only visited her after he had gone to jail. She remembered her mother had said he couldn't read and she'd always believed her. Now she wasn't sure. Maybe in fifteen years he'd learned something.

She thought back to the conversation she had had with Mr Ogilvy. He had told her to see Mrs Sneddon about noon. That meant walking the streets in broad daylight. Anyone would be able to see her. And now he knew what she was wearing, he could easily recognize her. Perhaps she could go this evening. The night would hide her. But she had no knowledge of the streets or suburb where the woman lived and the only places she could go to get help would be the inns and brothels. Without instructions, she'd find herself walking around in circles. The streets were no place for a lass at night. And besides, come evening, Mrs Sneddon would be in no fit state for talking. The bridge was her only choice.

Climbing down the metal steps, she stumbled in the shadows. At her feet a huddled figure moaned and rolled over, cuddling an empty spirit bottle like some cold, dead infant. Amy squeezed her fingers across her nose. The woman's rancid smell turned her stomach. 'You won't mind if I share your accommodation for the night,' Amy said, not expecting an answer. If Mrs Sneddon was in a similar condition then she had made the right decision not to visit her that night.

Beside the woman was a pile of posters, old but clean. They'd obviously been pushed or dropped from the bridge but the wind hadn't had time to lift them into the river. Selecting the largest ones, Amy climbed up to the darkest part of the bridge, right beneath the arch. The headroom was little more than two feet. After moving the stones from the ground, she spread some of the posters on the lifeless dirt and crawled on to them. Then she pulled the other ones over her. Being completely hidden from view, she was sure no one would find her.

★　★　★

The sun had come up very early — too early for Amy's liking. She had no choice but to stay where she was until later. Sleep had been intermittent, but she felt rested. Now ravenously hungry, she concentrated her thoughts on positive things. She thought about Harold and the tramway and the day they had met at the Glen. About foreign places and the building of bridges and canals

262

and funicular railways. How clever he was, she thought enviously. How nicely he spoke and dressed. She questioned his reasons for liking her but she was convinced he did.

She thought about Helen and Joel also, and young Ben. And the Medleys. How good they had been to her. And she thought of her mother — Lisbeth Dodd. He had killed her too — she was sure of that. Life had been fine for them while he'd been in Armley Jail. It'd been hard at times but they'd enjoyed it together. That all changed on the wet Saturday when he walked through the door.

'She used to smile then,' she said to the river.

Feeling the piece of paper in her pocket, she thought of the midwife. Finding Mrs Sneddon was not something she was looking forward to. She was afraid of what she might learn. Yet she was determined to find out — and felt entitled to know. After all, hadn't her mother said she would tell her everything one day?

In her heart she knew Lisbeth wanted her to know the truth. She'd just been afraid to tell her.

'I'll always love you, Mum,' she said sadly.

*   *   *

It was mid-morning when Amy climbed from under the bridge. The drunk had moved to a different spot but was still asleep or dead. She couldn't tell. She'd decided not to climb back on to the bridge but to follow the canal into the city, go under the Dark Arches, and find her way into Hunslet from there.

The woman lived in an area unfamiliar to Amy though she'd heard it was a dingy part of town. A shopkeeper gave her directions to the street as she looked longingly at the fresh bread and ham which she couldn't afford.

Thirty-seven Holroyd Close appeared vacant. Pieces of wood nailed across empty window frames swung gently in the light breeze. Those upstairs which had retained their glass wore layers of dirt and grease, turning them dusty brown. Four steps led up to the front door with a spiked railing on either side. Amy knocked and waited. There was no response. She turned the knob. The door was locked. From the pavement, another set of stone steps led to a cellar, not unlike the one she had grown up in. She climbed down. The door wasn't closed. She knocked. It squeaked as she pushed it open. Inside, all was dark. There was no sound. After waiting a moment she called out and ventured inside.

Apart from a table and a wooden box beside it which served as a chair, there was no other furniture. There was a gaping hole in the wall where a fireplace had once stood.

Now it contained only dislodged bricks covered in a fall of soot. It was a long time since a fire had graced that hearth. There was no fender, and no rug, and where the drifting soot had blown across the room, black footprints had trampled it hard into the remaining weft of threads which had once been a piece of carpet. The hum of a fly trying to escape from a bottle broke the silence, while other flies sat silently waiting their turn around the rim of a bucket behind the door.

The only window to the room had been boarded up. The only light came from the chute where the coal was once deposited. Fifty years ago the building would have been a fine home.

Amy wasn't sure if Mrs Sneddon was alive or dead. She was curled up on the floor, like the woman under the bridge. Her odour was revolting and Amy wondered how she must smell after spending the night on the canal's bank.

Touching the woman's arm, she remembered how stiff her mother's arm had felt when she found her on the bed.

Mrs Sneddon was still alive. She grunted. 'What's up?' she mumbled. 'What do you want?'

'I want to talk to you.'

'Bugger off. I don't want to talk to no one,'

she said, rolling herself over to face the wall.

'I'll make you some tea?' said Amy, before realizing there were no pans or kettle, no tap and nowhere to heat the water. 'Mrs Sneddon,' she said loudly, 'I've been talking with Mr Ogilvy.'

Like a puppet on a string, the woman sat upright, swayed a little, then focused her eyes on Amy. 'What did you say?'

'Mr Ogilvy sent me to see you.'

'You going to have a baby?'

'No, I'm not. He said you can tell me about my mother.'

As if the string holding her up had been released, the woman collapsed backwards, her head banging on the stone floor.

'Mrs Sneddon, wake up. I must talk to you.'

'Go away. Leave me alone. I got nothing to say.'

'If you tell me some things, I'll give you some money.'

The woman hauled herself up again. 'How much money you got? Let's see it.'

Amy had nothing. Her father had taken it all. 'I'll get you the money when you tell me what I want to hear.'

'Huh! Expect me to believe that.'

'I will, or I'll bring you some food. I promise. You have to help me. Mr Ogilvy said you would.'

'Now there's a gentleman if ever there was one. Salt of the earth,' she drawled. 'Do anything for anyone that man would.'

'Mr Ogilvy sent my mother to see you when she was pregnant. You helped her deliver the baby.'

'I bet you don't know how many babies I helped into this world.' She pondered on her own question. 'Lots,' she said, slurring her words. 'Seen 'em born and seen 'em die, I have. Aye, there's lots of 'em die. They don't all find nice homes to be raised in, though Mr Ogilvy tried hard to place 'em all. God bless his soul,' she said. 'He were the only one of all them governors who ever visited the place. A real gentleman he was.' She paused. 'You're wanting a child, are you?'

'No. I want to know what happened to my mother when she came to you.'

'How should I know? They stayed a while till they'd had their kid, then once it were fed for a day or two, it were put to the bottle and were taken off 'em and given to someone who wanted one. The girls who came in went back to their fancy homes as though nothing had happened. Or back to the street, or back to wherever they came from. Didn't even give their real names, most of them. Too ashamed, they were.'

'My mother's name was Lisbeth.'

'Beth, Lisbeth, Elizabeth — what's the difference? Known hundreds of girls by that name.'

'She was married to a man called Amos Dodd. He murdered her sister.'

A smile cracked across the woman's lips as a drifting memory broke through her addled brain.

'Now I remember,' she said. 'Splashed all over the paper it were and Mr Ogilvy told me I shouldn't mention it to anyone. Aye, and I remember Mr Ogilvy came to visit her, after it were born. Aye,' she said, 'and there was a bit of a to-do.' She scratched at her hair and frowned.

'What do you mean?'

'Don't rush me. G'me a minute.'

Afraid to interrupt the woman's trickle of thoughts, Amy sat silently, hardly daring to move.

'It were dead.'

'What!'

'The baby — a boy, if I remember rightly. Red hair. Born dead. It had the cord around its neck, tight like a noose it were. I remember the poor lass. That confused and upset, she were. She wanted it but she didn't want it, if you know what I mean. She said it died the way her husband should have done — on the gallows — a noose tight round his neck. I remember her saying that.' She shivered. 'I've never heard a woman say that of her infant before.'

'But was that the only child Lisbeth had? Did she give birth to two?'

'Now you're confusing me. Let me think.' She scratched at her parchment breasts under the shawl. 'I remember. That was the time Mr Ogilvy turned a blind eye — only time he ever did. Always so particular about interviews and paperwork and suchlike, he were. It were the only time.'

'What do you remember?'

The woman lifted her wrinkled hands and smoothed her matted hair, as delicately as a girl would if admiring herself in a mirror. 'There were a young lass brought in the same day Lisbeth arrived. More dead than alive she was. Been knocked down in the street and trampled under the horse's hoofs right outside the place. I reckon, when it happened, she was making her way across the road to come here. There was little I could do for the lass, 'cept pull the baby out when it started to come. I remember I was on my own and there was Lisbeth, the wife of a convicted murderer, on the next bed, howling about her dead infant, and this young lass, quiet as the grave, bleeding to death as I watched, and a newborn infant screaming its head off for a feed.

'Then, to make matters worse, another woman started yelling that hers was coming. I tell you, I didn't even have time to clean me hands between them. And the noise were near driving me batty. 'Here,' I said to Lisbeth, 'hold this one. See if it'll take your milk. If you can't feed your own, you might as well quieten this one down.''

'And did she take it?'

'Oh, aye.'

'And was it a baby girl?'

'Boy. Girl. What did it matter? It worked a treat. Too well, in fact. It were later that afternoon, Mr Ogilvy called in to check on Lisbeth. When he saw her, she was sitting up in bed with the infant in her arms, feeding it like it were her own, and the young lass, who it rightfully belonged to, was cold as stone on the next bed. She were covered in a sheet with Lisbeth's dead infant, not even cleaned, lying next to her.

'I could see Mr Ogilvy was pleased she'd survived the birth and he was happy for the child as well. I weren't going to spoil it and say anything about the swap, but I think she must have told him because I saw him lift the sheet on the other lass, and look at the infant beside her. Bright red hair — same as

Lisbeth's. As alike in colour as two fresh carrots. Then he looked at me, and I reckon he knew, but to this day, he never said more about the matter. If he knew about the swap, he turned a blind eye. And if she didn't tell, I think he worked it out himself.'

Amy nodded. 'I understand Lisbeth was not my real mother, but the girl who died — who was she? What was her name? Where did she come from?'

'It were never discovered who she was. She was nicely dressed, though a bit grubby. I think she'd been wearing the same clothes for some time. I remember I got a few shillings for her clothes.' Mrs Sneddon sighed. 'I could do with a bit of that money now.'

'Did she have a purse with her?'

'Not when they brought her in,' she said, rolling her eyes towards the wall. 'Must have lost it when the coach ran her down.'

'Then there was nothing of hers that was kept?'

'No,' she said. Then she remembered. 'Aye, there was one thing.'

'What?' said Amy.

'A handkerchief. She had it gripped in her hand when she died. It took quite an effort to prize it from her fingers, but I managed. I reckoned it was no good to her dead and I could have got a halfpenny for it, but with Lisbeth bawling her head off, I handed it over to her. Aye,' she said, 'I gave the handkerchief to Lisbeth to wipe her tears with.'

19

The Handkerchief

The churchyard was almost empty. Most of the morning congregation had dispersed. Parents with children, teenagers dressed in their best clothes, and the young couples had all hurried home looking forward to their midday meal. Only a few lonely souls remained, loitering by the gate, prolonging the awkward conversations. For them, there was no one at home and therefore no reason to hurry away. They lingered and talked.

As was his habit, whatever town or hamlet he visited, Mr Ogilvy dawdled in the churchyard, not to spend time over idle gossip, but to read the inscriptions on the tombs, chiselled decades ago by long-forgotten stonemasons. Skilled men, he was sure. Like the old men whose names they bore, most gravestones stood upright against the test of time, while others leaned forward, attracting the vestiges of age — the moss and lichen of the passing years.

Pausing at a strip of vacant earth between two monuments, he recognized an unmarked grave. Neglected. How sad, he thought, and wandered on, reading each epitaph carefully.

The ages interested him — young men, old women, wives, sons, daughters. He read the verses, rhymes, religious texts, followed the branches of a family which spread over a century or more. Of a patriarch, his wife and sons, and their sons' sons, and so on. Five lifetimes summed up in a score of words. He shook his head and moved along.

The smaller stones attracted him. The infants' graves. Perhaps they'd hold what he was searching for.

He thought about his wife, so beautiful, so warm, and the two wonderful years they'd shared. But that was more than forty years ago. He remembered how much she'd longed to have their child and how cruel fate had been. So tragic that her wish, once granted, brought about her end. But how were they to know? They were young and very much in love.

He closed his eyes and visualized her face. Her pain. Those images would never ever fade. But death brought peace. Serene, but cold and empty. And once her soul had gone, he laid her in the ground to rest in peace.

As to their unborn child, he never saw its face. Never knew if he was to be blessed with a son or a daughter. Never gave it a name.

Yet he had felt it move within her belly. It had lived a brief life within her womb and made them both feel proud.

But it chose to die, as many did, and it chose to take her with it on its final journey.

He buried her under the shade of a lilac tree and instructed the mason what words to carve upon the stone:

Faith Ogilvy
Born 1835 Died 1857
aged 22 years
SAFE IN GOD'S LOVING CARE

That was all. Nothing more. There was only one name on the tomb. Hers. The child was never mentioned. Only one casket had been lowered into the grave. She had carried the child within her. Never a word was inscribed in its memory.

He asked himself the question he'd raised a thousand times. What words were possible? It had no name. It had no date of birth. And it had no date of death as neither of them had noticed the day on which it had decided to die.

But the words 'IN GOD'S LOVING CARE', had never been enough. And even after forty years, he thought, there should be more. He ambled on. Perhaps one day he'd read the words which told a story similar to his own. A father and husband stripped of all he loved. A grief more profound than any other.

From the trees, a goldfinch flew down and bathed its wings in an ornamental urn. The sun twinkled through the canopy of trees as the breeze rippled a thousand leaves in unison.

Charles Ogilvy moved on to the next inscription. It was a pleasant Sunday and he was in no hurry.

★　★　★

When Mrs Smith opened the front door to the Roundhay house, she almost fell over the girl asleep on the floor.

'Goodness me, girl!' she said. 'How long have you been there?'

Amy didn't know. She couldn't remember anything of the long walk. She did recollect her talk with Mrs Sneddon and of walking across Leeds Bridge. She remembered gazing down at the barges moored along the bank and of longing to be back in Saltaire. She remembered she had no money and no ticket. She knew Mrs Medley would loan her the fare, but she dare not go anywhere near Fanshaw's Mill again for fear of meeting that man — Amos Dodd.

It had taken every ounce of her energy to walk the last mile to Mr Ogilvy's house and when finally she arrived she'd succumbed to her tiredness. Sleep was one of the things she wanted and it came very easily in the warmth of the porch with the afternoon sun streaming through the glass.

'Here, let me help you up.'

Amy gazed up at the woman. She was motherly, middle-aged, with a caring but worried expression etched on her face. She didn't question where Amy had come from or what she'd been doing, or even why she was slumped on the porch floor.

'Mr Ogilvy's not home,' she said. 'He had business to attend to. He left yesterday afternoon not long after you had gone. But he did tell me, if you were to come back, I was to take right good care of you. He's a very good man, you know?'

Amy hardly had the energy to walk inside and allowed herself to be helped into the kitchen. Mrs Smith loosened the laces on her boots.

'First of all, a drink, then a bath for you, young lady, and then something clean to wear.'

'But . . . '

'No buts. I'm used to young ladies turning up at all hours that God sends — used to get the neighbours' chins wagging, but I think they are used to it now. And some would arrive in a far worse state than you. Now tell me, have you eaten today?'

Amy shook her head.

'I thought not. Then it's a bath first — get yourself cleaned up and then you can eat and after that there's a room upstairs you can lay down for half an hour. Till you're feeling a bit better.'

'You're very kind, but I need to talk to Mr Ogilvy.'

'He's not here. He's gone down south on business and won't be back for three or four days.'

'Then I should get going — I promised I'd be back in Saltaire by Monday.'

'Well, as it's only Sunday, there's no rush, is there?'

Lacking the energy to argue, Amy sat at the table, her hands clasped around a large cup of tea laced with honey, watching the woman as she filled various-sized pans with water and brought them to the boil.

'Now upstairs,' she said. 'And get your things off. While I bring up the hot water.'

Following Amy up the carpeted staircase, she directed her into a bedroom. Against the far wall was a four-poster bed with pretty patterned drapes. The bedspread matched, and the pillowslips, though yellowed, were lace-edged. Catching sight of herself in the dressing-table mirror, Amy hesitated. She felt ashamed of her appearance but the woman didn't seem to notice.

'Drop your clothes outside the bathroom and I'll pick them up later.'

Amy had never been in a bathroom before, not one with a real bath and a brass tap which discharged cold water into it. Carting the hot from the kitchen, Mrs Smith emptied the pans in one by one, then added some crystals which melted slowly on the bottom and made the whole room smell sweet.

'There's soap and a scrubbing brush, and I'll fetch you a towel. Now mind you don't fall asleep. And when you are all washed, you sort yourself out some clean clothes. You'll find underwear in the drawers and dresses in the wardrobe.'

'But . . . '

'I said no buts. They're all clean and they've all come from folk who have more money than sense, or poor souls who have no need for them any more. We get more things dropped off than we know what to do with. You have a good look. I'm sure you'll find something that fits.' With that, Mrs Smith closed the bathroom door and left Amy to her toilet.

Amy had never sat in a deep bath before. It was long too. At home, in the tin bath, her knees had touched her chin. In this her legs were stretched almost full length. The water wasn't hot but it was comfortably warm and changed colour quickly as she slid the soap over her skin. How dirty she was.

*   *   *

All three drawers in the dressing-table contained clothes: camisoles, petticoats, stockings, bloomers and nightshirts. Every item was folded neatly and carried a hint of the scent of lavender. Tiny bags of the dried flowers were tucked in the corner of each drawer.

The wardrobe smelled of camphor. It was packed so tight with dresses, blouses, skirts, even coats, it was hard for Amy to prize her hand between them. In the bottom was a box containing belts, scarves and fancy collars, and on top a stack of hat boxes of various sizes. A line of shoes and boots stood in file along one wall. Some looked as though they had hardly ever been worn.

*   *   *

'Now don't you look a picture,' Mrs Smith said as Amy stood in the doorway to the kitchen. Though her hair was still wet, it fell into waves to her shoulders. 'The blue gingham suits your blonde hair,' she said.

'I took a pair of boots,' Amy said guiltily. 'The soles were peeling from mine.'

'Mr Ogilvy will be pleased when I tell him. Now, let's get some food into you.'

As Amy ate, she tried to concentrate on what the housekeeper was saying, but her mind was flitting about as though she were dreaming. When her hand dropped on to the edge of her plate and sent her fork bouncing on to the floor, Amy shook her head with a jerk.

'You're falling asleep. Upstairs right now. Get yourself into bed and rest for a while. I can see you need it.'

★   ★   ★

The sound of knocking was part of her dream, a strange dream. Amy could see herself in a narrow stairwell. It was the one in the boarding house where Amos Dodd had taken her. The door at the top of the stairs was closed. Then suddenly the scene changed. Now the door was on the top floor of Salt's Mill — five floors above ground. How could someone be knocking on that door from the outside, she asked, when there was a sheer drop straight down to the canal below? In her dream, the knocking continued, then the door squeaked open and a woman's voice called her name.

'Amy!' the voice called. 'Amy, there's a man here to see you.'

Mrs Smith's voice was soft as a whisper as she tapped her on the shoulder. 'He says he's been looking for you everywhere.'

'My father!' she cried, sitting upright, her hand cupped across her mouth.

'No, no, dear. It's not your father. It's a very nice young gentleman by the name of Mr Lister. We've been having a bit of a chat. He's been very worried about you and was so relieved to find you were here.'

'Harold?'

'Get yourself dressed and come down and have some breakfast.'

'Breakfast?'

'Well, it's only an hour to noon, but I saved it for you. You slept for more than fifteen hours. I don't think you knew how tired you were.'

★ ★ ★

How pleased she was to see Harold and how relieved he was to see her too. When he held out his arms to her she allowed him to hold her. How good he felt. How long it had been since she'd felt the warmth of someone's arms.

'Oh, Harold,' she said, 'I'm so glad to see you. I've so much to tell you. Things I've found out about my father — no, about Amos Dodd. He's not my father, after all. Can you believe it?'

'Oh, Amy. Dear Amy, I was so worried about you when I heard he'd caught you and locked you away.'

'But I got away,' she said, shaking her head. 'I was so afraid of him, Harold. He's a terrible man. But how did you know?'

'Joel told me you had come to Leeds and that you would be lodging with the Medleys near the mill.'

'That's right.'

'Well, I followed you from Saltaire late on Saturday. Mr Medley told me your father had taken you to that boarding house but when he got there, you'd disappeared and so had Amos Dodd. Mr Medley didn't know where you'd gone and I think he was pleased when I turned up. Oh, Amy,' he said, taking her hand. 'I was afraid something dreadful had happened to you. You should never have come back to Leeds. I don't know why Joel allowed you to leave the barge.'

'I had to come. Joel couldn't have stopped

me. There were things I had to find out.'

'And now you have discovered those things, can I take you back to Saltaire?'

Amy nodded. 'There's just one thing I must get before I leave. There's a small box of my mother's possessions at the Medleys' I wanted to collect it yesterday but I didn't dare go alone in case he caught me again.'

'Then as soon as you are ready, we'll take a cab to the Medleys' house. I'll stay with you while you collect the items you want, then we'll drive to the station and I'll see you safely on the train for Saltaire.'

'But I don't have any money.'

'Here,' Mrs Smith interrupted before Harold could continue. 'Mr Ogilvy left this to give to her if she came back.'

'Five shillings!' Amy said. 'That's more than half a week's pay!'

'Let me take care of her,' Harold said.

'No,' she said. 'Mr Ogilvy would have insisted. He'll be pleased to hear Amy is safe, and in good company, I might add. And if you are able to write, I suggest you send him a letter. That would be thanks enough.'

With Helen's skirt and her dirty under-garments packed in a small leather suitcase, Amy thanked Mrs Smith. Carrying Helen's bonnet in her other hand, Amy boarded a cab with Harold for the journey back to the street in Leeds where she had lived for almost eighteen years.

★ ★ ★

Mrs Medley hugged Amy. She even hugged Mr Lister for bringing her back safely. But she gave the children strict instructions not to go shouting about it on the street.

Of the oddments which Amy had taken to the Medleys' for safe-keeping after her mother had died, only one of them concerned her. It was her mother's shoe box, which had been hidden under the bed for as long as she could remember.

'There's something in here I must show you,' she said, lifting the lid carefully. It wasn't the wooden shoe-last or the bundle of old accounts which interested her — she would look at those later. Nor was it the sketch of two little girls standing hand in hand in a garden. She was interested in the piece of yellowed cloth which was wrapped around a handful of objects.

Scattering the items on the table, her friends gathered around, looking inquisitively at the contents: a military button, the crushed remains of a dried flower, a cheap brooch with most of its coloured glass missing, a pair of brand new leather bootlaces and a crumpled concertina cut-out of a string of paper dolls. There was nothing of value or real interest.

It was the old cotton handkerchief Amy was examining. She opened it and smoothed it gently on the table. It was yellow with age and so thin you could see the weave of threads in the centre. The strip of tatting added to the edge had rotted away in parts but the decorative stitches were still intact. In one corner, the letters AMY stood out in gold. In the other, a horse rearing on its hind legs was cleverly worked in faded blue embroidery silk.

Harold examined it closely. 'A solid-looking steed, indeed.'

'A carousel pony,' Mrs Medley suggested. 'How old were you when you made that, Amy?'

'It isn't mine,' she said, examining it more closely.

Mrs Medley looked puzzled.

'I think it was my mother's.'

'I wonder why Lisbeth put a horse on a hanky.'

'Lisbeth wasn't my mother.'

'What?'

'It's a long story,' said Amy. 'But I think this handkerchief is the only thing which had belonged to my real mother. I believe her name was Amy, and that my mother — Lisbeth Dodd — named me after her.'

Leaning against the door, Harold spoke quietly, as there were other people seated in the compartment. He was apprehensive about letting Amy travel alone, but didn't want to show his concern. While they waited for the clock to tick over, he mentioned the horse on the handkerchief. He talked about Ben and Mallow, and told her about the two dozen horses his father worked when he was a boy. He didn't mention Amos Dodd.

'When will you be returning to Saltaire?' Amy asked.

'In a couple of days, maybe even tomorrow. I don't have much work to attend to here, but if I don't get finished, I'll leave it. I can come back later.' Glancing up the platform, he saw the guard check his watch and return it to his waistcoat pocket. The red flag was poised in his hand, the whistle clenched between his teeth.

'Be careful,' he said, squeezing her hand. 'Stay on the barge and don't venture out on your own.'

'Don't worry about me. I'll be all right.'

'And don't come back to Leeds,' he said teasingly.

Amy smiled. 'I don't have reason to any more.'

The sound of the whistle echoed around the station roof. Steam hissed and the engine's wheels slipped on the rails before making purchase, jolting the train into motion.

'I'll miss you,' Harold shouted. As the train moved slowly along the platform, Amy's hand slipped from his. He stepped back and waved. Amy returned his gesture, then she pulled up the leather strap, lifting the window, and moved back into her seat.

Satisfied at seeing her heading safely back to her friends, Harold's thoughts turned to Fanshaw's Mill and the job he had to finish. The sooner he got back to the mill, the sooner it would be done. Once that was attended to he could return to Saltaire.

In his hurry to get away from the station, he didn't notice the man who strode purposefully across the platform. The peak of his cloth cap was pulled low on his brow, but it failed to hide the evil smirk on his face. Swinging the door of the last carriage open, the man hoisted himself into the moving train and grinned.

20

The Man on the Train

'Good riddance!' Joel cried as he tossed the splints and crutch over the side of the short-boat, and into the pit beneath the boat. The shorter splints, which Helen had bandaged to his upper and lower leg, had allowed him to bend his leg at the knee. Now he could drag himself out of the cabin and on to the barge's small deck. 'I'll have these off in a week,' he said to his wife. 'In a couple of days I'll go down to the mill office and see if they have any loads of cloth for Leeds or the coast. Then we'll be on our way.'

Helen didn't say anything. They'd spoken little that morning. It was Monday and Amy was due back, but Harold's concern on Saturday had worried them both. Though they were glad he had followed her to Leeds, Helen could sense an air of tenseness on the boat. It was a feeling she'd experienced before with Joel, and in the past he'd laughed at her and put it down to the Romany blood in her veins. But it was the first time she'd felt it with her son.

Sitting on the roof of his cabin weaving a piece of rush matting, Ben appeared busy, but watching him she noticed how many times he stopped, stood up and squinted down the canal to the town.

'She'll be coming on the train,' Helen called. 'She's money enough for a ticket. Why don't you go along to the station and enquire what times the trains are due? I'm sure she'll be pleased if you're there to meet her.'

Ben didn't wait for confirmation from his father; he was off like a shot.

'I hope she's all right,' Helen said. 'There's not much of her and from what she says that father of hers is a brute of a man.'

'I was thinking the same,' Joel said. 'I'm glad Ben's gone. I'd not like to see her walking back here on her own.'

★　★　★

When the last afternoon train steamed under the bridge into Saltaire station, Ben was engulfed in a cloud of smoke. When it cleared he leaned over watching each compartment door as it opened, checking every passenger as they stepped down. Unlike the weekend traffic, there were few people on the station at that time of the day on a Monday.

Amy was one of the first off, though

290

initially Ben didn't recognize the blonde-haired girl in the blue gingham dress carrying a shiny leather suitcase. Then he noticed his mother's cotton bonnet held in the other hand. It was grubby but unmistakable.

Though he called and whistled, the sound of the engine muffled his cries and Amy didn't hear him. He watched her as she stopped for a moment, donned her hat, then followed the other passengers up and over the iron footbridge and down the other side to join the queue to hand their tickets to the collector. For a moment he lost sight of her.

On the platform the engine whistled and the train rolled slowly away. As it did, the door of the last compartment opened and a man jumped out. Ben watched as he ran up the steps two at a time. He hesitated for a moment on the bridge then proceeded more slowly down the other side lingering for a moment beside the marble pillar at the entrance to the waiting room. Ben watched as the man reached in his waistcoat pocket, retrieved his ticket and sidled slowly towards the gate.

As Amy climbed the stone steps from the station she was delighted to see Ben waiting for her.

'Come with me, Amy, and don't argue!' he said, taking the suitcase from her and heading up towards the town.

Amy's smile quickly disappeared. 'What's wrong? Why aren't we going to the canal? Where are you taking me?'

'Just walk with me, Amy. I don't know what your father looks like, but a man got off the train and I watched him. I just got a funny feeling and I want to make sure he's not after you.'

Trusting the boy's intuition, Amy quickened her step. She didn't dare look around. She didn't want to see the man she feared. 'He mustn't catch us,' she said.

'Walk, Amy. We'll be all right.'

Hand in hand, the pair hurried up Victoria Road, past the shops and the school and the lions guarding the Institute.

'Is he still following?' Amy asked anxiously.

'Hard to tell,' said Ben, scanning the stream of workers walking home from the mill. 'I think everyone who got off the train is coming this way, and half the town as well.'

Unable to resist the urge, Amy glanced down the street. It was milling with folk all heading in their direction but there was no sign of a man resembling Amos Dodd.

A card in the window of the Salt and Pepper Tea Shop said CLOSED, but inside the owner was still tidying the tables. Banging on the glass, Amy attracted her attention.

Though disgruntled, the shopkeeper agreed — under the circumstances — to let them go through to the back entrance.

'You go,' Ben said. 'I'll stand outside and wait.'

'But what if it *is* him and he comes after you?'

'Why should he? He don't know me, and besides, I can look after myself. I'll hare up the hill and lose him. Don't worry, he'll never catch me.'

With little time to think or thank the woman, Amy hurried through her shop and out to the narrow laneway at the back. Workers wandering home looked at her strangely, wondering what was wrong. Amy didn't care. Running around the back of the school and down George Street brought her to the railway embankment. Along Albert Terrace and over the bridge at the station and the canal was ahead.

By the time she reached the towing path, she was panting. As she ran along the front of the mill, the workers unloading a barge stared at her. It reminded her of the time she ran from Fanshaw's. But Dodd didn't catch her then and he wouldn't now.

From *Milkwort*'s deck, Joel saw her coming. 'Get me the mallet, woman,' he said to his wife. 'I think someone's chasing Amy.'

Helen pulled a heavy wooden hammer from one of the boat's cupboards. 'But where's Ben?' she said.

'Don't worry about the lad,' Joel said. 'He can take care of himself. Just get Amy on board and leave the rest to me.'

When she reached the dry dock, Amy struggled to cross the plank. Her legs were like jelly. Frightened and exhausted, she collapsed into Helen's arms, tears rolling down her cheeks, her words of explanation almost incoherent. The events of the weekend had hit her suddenly like a slap in the face.

'Where is he?' Helen called.

'There's no one on the path,' Joel called. 'Unless he's hiding somewhere.'

'Dodd doesn't hide,' Amy stammered.

'I wish I could get my hands on him!'

'I hope you never get the chance.'

Though she feared for herself, Amy now feared for her friends. If Amos Dodd was on her trail, there was no way they could escape his malicious anger. Joel could barely walk, let alone defend his family. As for getting away, though work on the short-boat was finished, there was no water in the dock. There was no way they could escape. A man on the path could walk faster than the horse could tow the boat. Thinking of the family she had only known for a matter of weeks, Amy asked herself how she could do this to the people she loved.

Joel stood guard on the deck for half an hour, the wooden mallet resting on the roof. But apart from a boy with a dog, no one suspicious ventured along the canal bank. Helen paced anxiously, her eyes set on the path leading from the front of the mill.

Surprising them all, Ben came trotting up the towing path from the other direction. He was swinging Amy's suitcase in his hand.

'I took a detour,' he said. 'Went up to the next set of locks and crossed the canal there. No one followed me,' he announced proudly.

'Where's this man who was on the train?' Joel asked.

'No idea,' said Ben. 'Got lost in the crowd in Saltaire. He never came as far as the tea shop. I guess I was mistaken. He must have lived in the town.'

Amy wasn't convinced. 'Did he have a bald head with a wart on the top?'

'I wouldn't know,' Ben said. 'He was wearing a cap. I'm sorry I scared you. It was just a strange feeling I had.'

Joel looked at his wife.

'I don't like those feelings,' Helen said.

★ ★ ★

None of them slept well that night. Dogs howled. Owls hooted and the frogs who resided on the damp ground beneath the barge croaked throughout the night. Amy was glad it was summer and the hours of darkness were few, but having slept for so long at Mr Ogilvy's, she had trouble sleeping at all. At the other side of the cabin, Ben seemed to be sleeping peacefully, but the bunk creaked noisily every time he rolled over. When finally she dozed, her dreams were troubled.

★ ★ ★

Breakfast, next morning, was a quiet affair.

'When Harold gets back from Leeds, we'll move on,' Joel said. 'There's no money to be made while there's no water under our hull.'

Amy wanted to thank him but didn't know where to start. She told them what she had discovered; about the talk she'd had with Mrs Sneddon, and about the day her mother had given birth. She also showed them the handkerchief with her name embroidered in the corner.

'I loved Lisbeth Dodd dearly,' Amy said, 'and she'll always be my mother. I don't expect I'll ever know who my real father was, but at least I'm not the child of a murderer.' Strong words, she thought, but the truth.

'You've both been kind to me and I don't want to leave you, but I must get away — far away — and make a new start. I know Mr Ogilvy will lend me a few shillings. It's not charity I'm asking, because I'll pay him back one day. But I can't stay in the West Riding. There are too many people here who know my name.'

As the words slipped out, Amy pondered on what she'd said. Amy Dodd was the only name she'd ever known, the name her mother had given her. She thought of her real mother, the girl who had died holding the handkerchief, and wondered if she would ever discover who she was.

★   ★   ★

Though Joel was unable to move far, he was convinced he could stand on the deck and handle the tiller. He was anxious to work again. The following morning, he supervised as Amy, Ben and Helen prepared the barge. They would refloat it the following day. After clearing most items from the bottom of the dock, Ben secured lengths of old tow-rope to the wooden stocks which were supporting the hull.

'When we flood the dock,' Ben said, 'the barge should float off on its own. But if it jams on the baulks of timber, we can drag them out from under the boat.'

'Always a worry,' added Joel. 'There's always a chance the boat might slip, and you wouldn't want to be under it if it does. I'll warn you now. Keep clear of the barge when the water comes in.'

Amy handed a bucket up to Helen. As she glanced towards Salt's Mill, she immediately recognized the gait of the man on the path.

'We've got a visitor,' Helen whispered.

'It's Harold back from Leeds!' Ben shouted.

A broad smile stretched across Amy's face as she collected the remaining cans and brushes from the bottom of the dock. 'There's not much left down here,' she called.

'Come on up,' Helen said, washing her hands.

'You'll stop for a cuppa, won't you?' Helen called to the engineer, before disappearing into the cabin. Harold didn't hear. He and Ben were talking to the horse that was grazing not more than thirty yards from the barge.

'She looks good,' said Harold. 'Has she settled?'

'Sure has,' said the boy. 'She'll be a grand horse, just like old Bessie.'

'Mallow,' said Harold. 'An unusual name.'

The horse pricked its ears and snorted, tossing its mane. As they turned to the dry dock, the shire horse continued to feed contentedly.

Leaning down, Harold held out his hand to Amy and helped her climb up from the dock. She was still smiling as together they dragged the ladder on to the canal bank.

'I'm filthy,' she said, swilling her hands in the bucket.

'It'll not be the first time I've got my hands dirty,' he said. 'But with me it's usually mucky grease, and that doesn't wash off so easily.'

He watched her closely as she dabbed the mud from her skirt and scraped her boots. 'So where's that pretty girl I met in Leeds yesterday?'

Amy blushed and they laughed.

'I'm glad you're all right.' His tone was serious.

'Joel's moving the boat tomorrow. He's decided it's time to go.'

'What will you do? Where will you go?' he asked. 'Had you thought about staying in Saltaire? There are nice boarding houses on William Henry Street, just near the station. I could arrange to rent a room for you there, if you'd allow me.'

'I don't know just yet,' said Amy. 'I'd still rather leave here.'

'Are you leaving tomorrow?' Harold called to Joel.

'We'll float her in the morning, and leave the day after that.'

'I'll watch for you moving from the mill and come down and lend a hand if you'll let me. Do you know which way you will be heading?'

'Depends what we can get. If there's no cargo available we'll slip back into Leeds. Always plenty of work there. But I'd rather cart cloth than a cargo of stone, especially since the boat's been spruced up and is looking so good.'

Amy looked at the barge, which had been transformed over the previous six weeks. The name, *Milkwort*, on the bow stood out in white letters on a blue background edged with gold. A flourish of fancy scrollwork decorated the panels at each end. On the cabin roof the five-gallon water barrel was circled with hoops of green, yellow and red, each broad ring bearing scrolls or geometric patterns of different shapes and sizes. On the barrel ends Joel had painted a house with a garden and trees, and on the horse's proven box a landscape of meadows and rolling hills and sky.

From the red-leaded deck at the stern, the painted bands twisting around the tiller made it look like a maypole ready to twirl and the rudder itself was a patchwork of pictures and patterns. Helen said the designs were the best Joel had ever painted and they made *Milkwort* quite different to the other short-boats on the Leeds and Liverpool canal. As he'd learned his craft on the Kennet and Avon, those were the images he knew and enjoyed recreating. With the new white buttons and fenders Ben had woven, the short-boat was a sight which would make any Number One proud.

'Come with me to the Glen,' Harold said. 'It'll be our last chance. There are things I want to talk to you about. I have so much to say. I don't want you to go and I know I'm going to miss you. I have plans for the future — a long way from here. Amy, please say you will come?'

'When, Harold?' she said.

'Now, if you can. Ben can come too.'

'Take the lass on your own,' Joel said, from the barge. 'I trust you.'

Harold smiled. 'I want to show her the tramway. Explain how it works, show her the mechanism. There'll be no one there right now. But we must go quickly because it'll be closing soon.'

Helen winked at her husband. 'Away with you,' she said. 'Just bring her back safely.'

'I will.'

Harold talked all the way on the towing path about tramways and trains and industrial engines. Only the appearance of Jem Carruthers silenced him for a moment. After brief greetings, Harold and Amy walked on, crossing the river and the field by the park which led up to the Glen. Once they reached the tramway, Harold took delight in showing Amy the cables and surge wheel which tensioned the rope. His enthusiasm was infectious, like a child with a new toy. Amy enjoyed listening though she couldn't understand all he was saying.

'Last tram up!' the man in the pay booth said. 'Penny a piece. Tuppence for two.'

'Two to the top,' Harold said. 'We intend to take the long way back.'

They were the only passengers on the tram. The twin carriages, which passed them on its way down, carried only three.

The green at the top of the Glen was almost empty. A boy ran, chasing a hare, which quickly disappeared into the bushes. A couple with an infant ambled back towards Saltaire with a long-legged hound lolloping behind. Sam Wells' Aerial Flight and his Switchback were strangely silent. The pair crossed the green to the far side.

'It's so peaceful,' said Amy, as they stood together, looking down into the verdant valley. On the slopes, shaded beneath oak and birch, bluebells, goldenrod and honeysuckle grew among the outcrops of rocks, and near the beck weeping willows veiled its course.

'Can you manage the hill?' Harold said. 'It's very steep.'

'Better than you can,' Amy said, challenging him and setting off at a run down the stony slope. Three-quarters of the way to the bottom, the path zigzagged back and forth. When she could hear the sounds of the Loadpit Beck, she stopped. Breathless yet giggling, she turned and looked back up the slope.

But Harold wasn't there! In his place, standing near the top of the path, was the man she hated. His stance was unmistakable. It was Amos Dodd.

21

Amos Dodd

Amy ran helter-skelter to the stream, which gurgled through the valley. Behind her she could hear the sound of his boots slipping on the gravel. Suddenly it stopped. Unable to keep his footing on the incline, Dodd had fallen, tumbling head over heels. Amy watched as he rolled down the steep hillside. Then she lost sight of him.

For a while there was no sound in the Glen, save a single bird's cry and the water trickling over the stones.

Amy dived for the reeds. They were high and rustled loudly. She sank into the silt and waited. Any moment she expected his hand to reach in and grab her. She hardly dared breathe.

Then she heard him again, calling her name: 'Amy Dodd! Amy Dodd!' As she peeped through the reeds she thought back to the bars at the top of the cellar steps, where she had sat for hours looking through them, longing for her father to come home.

'I'm not Amy Dodd,' she murmured.

He was up and running. She could see a cut on his face. It was bleeding. But he was unaware she had stopped. Leaping over the beck, he ran past the clump of reeds and headed up the path leading out of the valley at the other side. Thinking he was following her, he took the longer but easier pathway back to the canal. She was relieved she had waited. He would have easily out-run her before she'd reached Saltaire.

Pulling herself up by the roots of trees, Amy struggled up the steepest part of the glen-side. Her feet and skirt were caked in mud and dripping wet.

'Amy Dodd!' she heard him cry. 'I'll get you this time. And it'll be the last time you cross me!'

Heading in the opposite direction to the voice, she thought about Harold. He'd disappeared and she didn't know where to look for him. Heading across the green, she knew she had to get back to the barge as quickly as possible.

Above the ticket-office window with its painted sign, *Halfpenny Down*, hung a swinging board which read: *Closed for the day*.

A pair of empty carriages was sitting at the platform but the ticket collector had already left. Not knowing where to find the footpath which led to the bottom, Amy chose to run down the hill between the two sets of tramlines.

★ ★ ★

Harold shook his head and stood up unsteadily. He felt dizzy but was aware something hard had hit him on the back of the head and it was still bleeding. Not knowing how long he had been there, he pulled himself on to one of the boulders and looked around. There was no sign of Amy or Amos Dodd at the bottom of the Glen but from his vantage point he could see a head bobbing at the other side of the valley. Dodd was running and obviously taking the long way round to the river and canal. Harold knew must find Amy before Dodd caught her. He was sure she would have headed back to the boat.

Limping and holding his head, Harold made his way across the open ground to the footpath which wound down through Walker Wood, close to the tramway. As he arrived at the clearing near the pay booth, he saw Amy running down between the lines.

'You're all right!' he cried, gathering her into his arms.

'Yes,' she breathed. 'What happened to you?'

'I'm fine,' he said. 'But we must get back to the barge.'

★ ★ ★

Helen heard them call as they neared *Milkwort*. 'Goodness gracious, what happened?'

'I was hit from behind,' Harold said, unaware of the blood colouring his shirt collar. 'When I woke Amy was gone and I saw Dodd running at the other side of the Glen. I imagine he's on his way here right now.'

'Then we'll be ready for him,' said Joel, grabbing the mallet.

They waited.

Half an hour passed. Then an hour. There was no sign of Dodd.

'He doesn't know where I am,' said Amy, trying to smile. 'If he did, he would have been here by now.'

Helen and Joel tried to relax and went into the cabin. Amy and Harold sat on the upturned buckets on the bank. Ben kept watch from the roof.

'It couldn't have taken him so long to get back here,' said Harold. 'He must have gone into Saltaire.'

'He's coming!' Ben yelled.

Jumping up, they all knew who the man on the towing path was and when he saw the large can he was carrying, Harold knew why he had gone into the town.

'It's him, my f — ' Amy murmured, half under her breath.

'On the boat, the lot of you!' Joel cried.

'No!' Harold yelled, looking at the container. He could almost smell the fuel from that distance.

'On the boat!' Joel called.

'You're not going to burn my dad's boat!' Ben shouted as he leapt from the cabin roof and ran headlong at the man, but one swing from Dodd's fist caught the boy's head, sending him reeling along the grass.

Joel slid his hand around the cabin door and reached for the mallet but as Amos saw the movement of the cripple, he opened the can and tossed it into the bottom of the dock. Picking up a boat-hook, he swung it at Joel's head.

Though the bargee's balance was limited, he grabbed the end of the pole and hung on.

'Leave them!' Amy screamed. 'I'll come with you.'

'No you won't!' Harold yelled, as he launched himself towards the man's legs. 'You'll not take her!'

'The paddles, Ben!' Helen shouted, throwing him the handle. 'Open the paddles!'

Ben scrambled to his feet and headed to the lock gates. As he opened the paddles, water started seeping into the dry dock. By the time they were fully open, water from the main canal was thundering in, spilling across the muddy bottom and surging around the struts holding up the barge. As the water flooded the dock, it bubbled back from the gates and swirled to the far end. The empty fuel can turned in the current and the paraffin spilled iridescent colours on the surface.

'Grab the mallet!' Joel yelled to his wife as he grappled the man for control of the pole.

'Get ready to open the gate!' Helen yelled to Ben.

Amy knew what was about to happen and ran to the other gate, ready to lean her weight against the beam.

'I got word there was a fight!' The cocky voice came from Jem Carruthers. No one had noticed him running from the mill. Grabbing Dodd by the shoulder, he turned him and landed a resounding blow on the side of his jaw.

With Harold hanging on to Dodd's legs, the man reeled back, dropping the pole. At the other end, Joel lost his balance and fell heavily to the deck.

Amos Dodd was quickly back on his feet. He kicked out at Harold and turned to face the pugilist. But his jail-yard tactics were not those of a prize ring. His boot came up, hitting Carruthers squarely in the groin.

As Dodd caught his breath, Harold threw himself at him again.

'No, Harry, don't!' Amy cried. 'He'll kill you.'

Just as Dodd opened his mouth to speak, a barrage of punches from the boxer forced him back towards the bank.

'Now!' shouted Joel. 'Open the gates!' He could feel that the barge had floated free from the timbers and knew there was only a matter of inches difference between the level of water in the dock and the canal outside.

With one each side, Amy and Ben both leaned against the lock gates, but the water pressure was still too great. 'Push harder!' Joel yelled.

As the paddles continued feeding water, the level continued to rise and Ben and Amy pushed the beams with all their strength. Then suddenly a torrent spilled between the gates, gushing through like water through a break in a dam.

As *Milkwort* was buffeted by the flow, Dodd's foot caught on the ladder. He stumbled but had nothing to hold on to and his other foot became entangled in the ropes tied to the timber stocks on that side of the dock. Twisting and turning like a barrel of snakes, the ropes slithered into the water, following the baulks of timber to the bottom of the pit.

Turning his head to look behind him, Dodd suddenly realized he was too close to the edge. As he did, the soft bank gave way, sinking beneath his feet. At the same time a wave of water washed the timbers under the boat, carrying them to the head of the dock. Dragged by the ankle, Amos Dodd slid through the gap into the water and was pulled under. *Milkwort* bobbed like a cork, bouncing from one side of the dock to the other. But the canal bank was soft and slimy and the boat suffered no damage. Joel rode his barge clinging to the cabin roof.

Exhausted, Harold hauled himself up on the bank while Amy stood by the open gates, waiting for the water to settle and the man she hated to swim to the surface.

But Amos Dodd didn't come up. The rope wound tightly round his ankle had followed the baulk of timber under the barge. It had settled in the pit and secured him as surely as if he were anchored to the bottom.

Amy waited with Harold until the local constable arrived, but it wasn't until they had sluiced out the muddy water that the body of Amos Dodd was recovered. Once she had identified the body, she was allowed to go back to the boat. Harold walked with her.

By that time, Jem Carruthers had hauled *Milkwort* to the far side of Saltaire's New Mill to a mooring near Hirst Wood Lock. On this occasion, his pace had been slower, knowing Joel was at the tiller watching his every move. Ben had followed on the towing path, leading the horse. The following day he planned to harness her. Till then, she could graze on the strip of meadow between the River Aire and the canal.

★ ★ ★

At midday the following day, Harold returned.

'It's strange,' said Amy, gazing down the canal. 'I hated him and I knew he was evil, but in a way I feel sorry he's dead.'

Harold didn't answer.

'I know he wasn't my father, but he was the only person I thought I was related to. Now I realize I have no one and I feel very much alone.'

'You have me,' Harold said.

'You mean that?'

'Of course,' he said, taking her arm. 'Would you care to walk for a while?'

'I'd like that.'

'There are things I wanted to say earlier, but I never got chance.'

As they crossed the bridge over the River Aire, Amy waited for him to continue. There was an anxious look on his face.

'If you sail away with the barge, I may not see you again.'

'Yes, you will, I'll make sure of it. Besides, I can't stay with the boat for ever. I will have to find my own way soon. Maybe I will go back to Leeds and get a job.'

'Not at Fanshaw's, I don't think,' he laughed.

'Perhaps I could work here in Saltaire. It's a mill after all with the same sorts of looms and combs, and jobs for menders and burlers.' She hesitated. 'You mentioned boarding houses and rooms.'

'I didn't mention engineers doing jobs which they were growing to hate.'

Amy looked at him surprised. 'I thought you enjoyed your job.'

'I do to an extent.'

'But you would rather be building bridges.'

'Come,' he said, taking her hand. 'Can you run?'

'Of course. I've done plenty of running. But what are we running for?'

'Because I just feel like running. And because the tram is coming down the side of the Glen.'

Amy wasn't sure about Shipley Glen, but Amos Dodd was dead and could never bother her again, and Harold had things he wanted to say. Taking his hand, she ran beside him. He hobbled across the grass at a reasonable pace.

★   ★   ★

'One way or return?' the man in the ticket office said.

'One way,' said Harold. 'If that's all right with you, Amy? I thought we might walk down the Glen to the beck and follow the track around the fields back to Hirst Lock.' He released her hand as he reached in his pocket for the pennies to pay the fare, but as they stepped into the open carriage, he took hold of it again and rested it between his.

'I had a letter, Amy,' he said. 'It's about a job.'

'That's nice,' she said, as the bell rang and

314

the cable started pulling the carriage up the hill.

'I sent an enquiry six months ago but only late last week received a reply. I've been offered a position with an engineering company to build a funicular railway.'

'A what?'

'A railway that runs up a hill and works on the same principle as this,' he said. 'See the other carriage coming down. They are balanced together. It's mainly gravity that carries them.'

Amy listened.

'There's a place where they are building elevators which run almost vertically up the side of a cliff. They are far bigger and grander than the Shipley Glen Tramway.'

'Where,' she said.

'A long way from here.'

'Where no one knows the name of Amy Dodd?'

He smiled. The carriage stopped and they alighted. 'This way,' he said.

There was not a soul about at the top of the Glen. Apart from a pair of rabbits, they had the green to themselves. Skirting the open ground, they found the path which zigzagged down to Loadpit Beck at the bottom.

The trees were filled with the sound of

birds though it was impossible to see any of them. Their boots crunched on the loose stones of the path, disturbing a squirrel which skittered away and bounded up a tree, running so high it was lost in the branches. Harold held Amy's hand to prevent her from falling.

In the valley bottom, the beck gurgled over the rocks, spilling out over the soft earth to feed the wild mint and meadowsweet which was growing in abundance. The trickling song of the water was magnified in the silence of the Glen.

The rise up from Shipley Glen on the other side was a gradual one and they helped each other. At the top where they turned, their path was blocked by a swinging gate.

'I've never seen a gate like this before,' Amy said innocently.

After passing through it, Harold stopped at the other side. 'If I told you it was a kissing gate, would you believe me?'

'I suppose.'

'And if I told you you were supposed to kiss the person waiting for you at the other side, would you believe that also?'

Amy laughed. 'So this is why you brought me here?'

'But of course,' he said, swinging the gate wide enough for her to step through. Leading her by the hand, he pulled her gently towards him and slid his arms around her waist. 'May I?'

'Please.'

The thrill of that first kiss ran right through her. He kissed her again. She didn't want him to let her go. 'Oh, Harold,' she said. 'I've never felt like this before.'

'Amy, I want you to come with me. I want to take you away from Leeds and the mills. Away from Yorkshire and England.'

'And where are you going to take me?'

'To Chile.'

'Where?'

'South America.'

'When, Harold?'

'As soon as a passage can be arranged.'

★ ★ ★

Amy had no idea where Chile was but she didn't care. At times she had to pinch herself and ask herself if she was only dreaming. But it was true. Harold explained he had no family. No ties. There was nothing to hold him and he was tired of living his life in rented rooms. How he had longed for a new life and a wife to share it with.

It was hard for the pair to part but Harold had work to finish at Fanshaw's and Joel had heard that there was a cargo waiting in Bradford to go to Leeds.

Amy didn't see Harold when *Milkwort* stopped in Leeds but while the cargo was being unloaded on a wharf near Leeds Bridge, she went shopping and bought bread and preserves and fresh milk and delivered them to the cellar Mrs Sneddon lived in. The place was empty, but Amy left them anyway. It was the least she could do.

* * *

Amy stayed with the barge for a month and by the time they sailed back into Saltaire, Harold had completed his contract with Fanshaw's and was prepared to close up his rooms in Albert Road.

When he offered the premises to Joel, for Ben to live in rent free while attending school, the lad jumped at the idea. Joel wasn't too happy. But when Miss Jones, the old cook, said she'd keep an eye on him, he agreed. Helen was delighted and it was agreed Harold should secure a place for him at the elementary school.

Joel said that once his boy had started they would only take cargoes that kept them near Saltaire, so that at the weekends the lad would be able to visit his mother.

Helen said she was going to miss Amy. And Amy knew that to be true. She was sorry too that Harold and Amy were planning on leaving England and that she would never see them again.

'We'll be back in a few years for a holiday,' Harold said. 'Who knows, I may be building bridges in Yorkshire. The Humber could be a future challenge.'

⋆　⋆　⋆

It was October when Amy and Harold were married.

A dozen barges lined the towpath that afternoon, but *Milkwort* looked the prettiest with garlands of flowers from the river bank adorning the cabin roof. Ben led the horse, its terrets plumed in vermillion and blue and its polished brasses swinging freely, flashing with the gold of the sun.

Joel sat proudly astride the mare, holding Amy in front of him, her legs resting to one side. Helen walked proudly beside her son.

The bride's gown and shoes were gifts from Mr Ogilvy's stores and no one guessed they were not brand new. In one hand Amy held a bunch of pink mallow flowers, in the other the old handkerchief which had belonged to her mother. As the horse clip-clopped up the pathway to the elegant church, Harold waited on the stone steps to lift his bride down.

It was a lovely ceremony and afterwards on the canal bank the passing boatmen joined in the celebration. It was a happy affair, with music from banjos and accordions. Some sang, others danced, while others were content to sit and watch, clapping their hands and tapping their feet to the rhythm. Miss Jones attended and the Medleys came with four of their children.

Jem Carruthers was dressed like a show-man, complete with his championship belt. The lucky young lady who accompanied him hardly left his side.

Mr Ogilvy sat quietly enjoying the scene but excused himself after a couple of hours. 'I would like to take a walk around this wonderful town and take another look in the church and its interesting yard. But first, a present for you both,' he said. 'When your ship sails away you can gaze through this glass and look forward to a new life in a land far away. And when you arrive, you can gaze back towards England and remember those loved ones you have left behind.'

Amy kissed him and thanked him for everything he had done for her and for the woman she would always regard as her mother — Lisbeth Dodd.

That night in the quiet of Harold's rooms, they watched a train from the window. It was heading to Leeds.

'I'll have to learn to talk nicely like you, or everyone'll know I come from the streets.'

'I think you'll find accents don't matter a jot. There are people from all over the world moving to Chile. Besides,' he said, 'I love the way you speak and when we get there we can both learn to speak Spanish and no one will guess where either of us come from.'

'And tell me again what it is you will build.'

'A funicular railway that will slide up the side of a steep cliff.'

'And what else?' she asked, smiling.

'I will build us a house at the top of the cliff which will look out over the blue Pacific.' Harold folded her in his arms.

'I don't think I'll miss this town, or the mills or the memories. Perhaps some memories I'll take with me, but I'll remember my friends.'

'In a few years we will come back for a holiday and we'll search the canal for *Milkwort* and you will wear Helen's hat and be the barge girl that I fell in love with. I promise.'

'Are there canals in Valparaiso?' she said,

gazing into his eyes.

'I don't think so. But there are in America. And maybe one day we will get the opportunity to go there also, and I will build my bridge.'

'I hope so.'

22

AMY

Charles Ogilvy sauntered along the canal bank near Hettersley. It was a fine afternoon for a walk, and after the exhausting journey from Leeds on the previous day, he wanted to relax before embarking on the business which had brought him south. He always enjoyed taking a walk on Sundays, particularly if he was visiting places he'd never been to before. He believed the fresh air was beneficial to his lungs and the exercise good for his stiffening joints. The canal banks were ideal to wander along. The scenery was pleasant, the air was clear and the terrain was flat.

From the hull of a barge in a dry dock, the sound of hammering echoed across the waterway. The smell of tar and paint drifted across the path and he thought of the tales Amy had told him of Joel's boat when it had been at Saltaire. It seemed like more than three years since Amy and Harold had been married. How quickly time had marched along since then.

As a narrowboat steamed by, he raised his

hat to the boatman. The man's head twitched imperceptibly, but Charles knew his greeting had been acknowledged. Nearing the village, he could see a church spire poking up from the woodland surrounding it. On first glance, it appeared slightly crooked. He decided to investigate.

A footpath, between two giant privet hedges, led to a lych gate decked with a climbing rose. He ducked his head as he swung the gate. It opened wearily and led into the graveyard.

The church was built in Norman times, he estimated, but the spire had suffered damage later in its history and had been rebuilt at a later date. The use of a lighter coloured stone was the reason for its twisted appearance. An optical illusion. He smiled and sauntered on.

Many of the old gravestones leaned at precarious angles. Some had fallen. Those which formed part of the pathway had been worn smooth beneath countless Sunday feet scurrying across without even stopping. Such a shame, he thought.

Of the carved inscriptions, many had fallen victim to wind and weather, their eroded words masked with clumps of moss in mottled shades of rose and yellow.

At the far side of the church, shaded by boughs of knurled trees, four raised tombs graced the silence. As he passed, he stopped and read each epitaph. The last monument stood four feet high and eight feet long. A family tomb, he thought. He stood and read:

Andrew Madeley Yellering
Born 1801 Died 17 December 1866

Alice Margaret Yellering
Born 1842 Died 1867

Alphonso Maurice Yellering
Son of Andrew
Born January 1829 Died October 1885
Aged 56 years
Rest in Peace

Sophia Grace
Beloved wife of Andrew Madeley Yellering
Born 1805
Followed him from this life on
16th March 1887
Aged 82 years

Algernon Michael Yellering
Son of Andrew
Born 18th May 1827 Died July 4th 1894
Aged 67 years

The inscription told him little of the lives of

those departed. Only the size of the grave indicated the family had money. Skirting around it, he glanced down at the far end and was immediately attracted to a carving on it. His eyes widened. It was not a religious symbol such as a cross or shield or angel, as was expected. Here was a stallion, rearing boldly on its hind legs, its hoofs pawing the air. How odd, he thought. Looking closer, he read the inscription chiselled beneath it.

AMY
El Caballero
Rest in peace

'Amy!' he said out loud, remembering the handkerchief she'd shown him on her wedding day.

Turning quickly back, he scanned the names appearing on the epitaph. Every member of the Yellering family, except the wife, bore the same familiar initials. He was intrigued and wanted to learn more.

* * *

The village of Hettersley backed on to the canal. It was small but scattered with outlying farmhouses dotted between fields of rye and barley. It was not hard to locate members of the Yellering family; the village consisted mostly of them. After speaking to one of the young Yellering wives who worked in the local shop, Mr Ogilvy was directed to speak to the family's matriarch, who lived close by.

Mrs Phoebe Yellering's house was a substantial two-storey eighteenth century cottage. It stood at the end of a lane lined with lime trees. Vines graced the south-facing slope and the garden was dotted with lemon and orange trees. The glasshouse windows were speckled red and green with ripening tomatoes and on the loamy ground outside, yellow pumpkin flowers bloomed on the same stems as the mature prize sized vegetables. In the orchard, green-leaved almond trees lacked evidence of fruit but the branches of the apples trees were already bent.

Mrs Yellering, a nimble seventy-year-old with faded blonde hair, welcomed the stranger and invited him to sit in the parlour while she prepared some tea.

As he entered the room, Mr Ogilvy gazed around in astonishment. Above the mantel-shelf a pair of glass eyes gazed coldly at his from the head of a huge black bull. Much of the hair had shed from its leathery skin but tufts still sprouted at the base of its curling horns. On the wall a pair of barbed banderillas hung beneath a feathered fan fashioned in ivory and trimmed with black lace. Foreign trinkets decked each piece of furniture — postcards from distant ports, plates and vases decorated with exotic scenes. But the item which interested him most was the statue of a horse carved from a solid piece of cherry wood. Standing almost two feet high, it was perfect in every detail. Rearing up, the stallion's powerful hoofs flailed the air, its thick tail trailed on the ground and its nostrils flared.

'May I?' he said, reaching towards it.

'Of course,' she said. 'His name was Fernando. He was Andrew Yellering's prized Andalusian.'

'A magnificent animal,' he said, placing it carefully back on the table. 'Would you care to tell me a little about it?'

Mrs Yellering poured the tea into fine china cups. 'My husband's father was Andrew Yellering. You may have heard of him in your younger days. He was known as the great El Caballero,' she said. 'He had a troupe of magnificent Andalusian horses, the best outside Spain, it was said. His wife, Sophia, and all the Yellering family were involved in the performance. They toured the length and breadth of England, a little like a circus.' She laughed lightly. 'Most people thought he was a Spaniard, but he was born right here in

Hettersley.' Her old eyes sparkled as she continued. 'The items you see in this room are things he collected on his trips to Spain almost eighty years ago. They were passed to me when his wife died.'

He smiled. 'Andrew Yellering is dead now, I presume?'

'He died in 1866 and sadly the troupe died with him. His eldest son tried to keep the show alive, but he was not nearly the showman El Caballero was. I remember the day the horses were sold. I hate to think what happened to them.'

'And the rest of the family returned to Hettersley?'

'Yes,' she said. 'Sophia Yellering, Andrew's wife, lived another twenty years. This was her house. I cared for her till she died only three years ago. She was eighty-two.' She paused and looked quizzically at her visitor. 'Are you involved with horses, Mr Ogilvy?' she asked. 'Is that why you are interested in my family?'

'No,' he said. 'You must excuse me for not explaining the reason for my visit, but I enjoyed listening to you reminisce.' He looked across at the stallion standing on the table. 'It is the horse engraved on the family's tomb which has brought me here.'

She smiled. 'That symbol was the emblem of the troupe. The family have retained it to this day, though the show's been gone for more than thirty years.'

'It interests me,' he said, 'because I've seen it once before — stitched on a handkerchief.'

'Ah,' she said. 'Then you would have seen one which I made. I've embroidered so many over my lifetime, I've lost count.'

'Do you sell them?'

'Oh no, Mr Ogilvy. I make one for every child born a Yellering — the children, grandchildren and great grandchildren of El Caballero. I have been sewing them since I was a young mother myself and now it is a family tradition which I maintain.'

'Are they always the same?'

'I have no pattern but I know the work by heart, so, yes, they are identical. Let me show you.' Taking a tapestry bag from the dresser, she placed it on her lap. Inside were several white cloths. She took one out and showed it to her visitor. In the corner was the outline of a horse.

'And here,' she said, 'are Andrew's initials — AMY.'

It was the same as the one Amy had shown him on her wedding day.

'Mrs Yellering, I would like to ask you a question which may be painful.'

She touched his arm. 'I've seen much in my life, and like you, sir, I'm growing old. But

I feel I'm strong enough to face most things. Please, ask me your question.'

Charles Ogilvy spoke tenderly. 'Did you have a grown daughter who you lost over twenty years ago?'

The woman caught her breath. 'I did,' she said. 'Her name was Angela.'

'Will you tell me a little about her?'

Mrs Yellering folded the handkerchief and rested it in the palm of her hand. 'She was the second oldest of my seven children. Five of them are still living here in Hettersley with families of their own. My Angela was a quiet girl and because of that I think she got the least attention. By the time she reached twenty-one she had seen two of her sisters marry. Then without us knowing, she took up with a young fellow we didn't know. He wasn't from this village and, as we'd only seen him here at harvest time, my husband thought he was an itinerant. The first I knew of their affection was when she told me she was in trouble.

'Unfortunately, when her father discovered what had happened, he sought out the young fellow and took to him with a horse-whip. It was no wonder he went away. We never saw him again for almost a year. As for Angela, her father hardly spoke to her again. Said he'd not have a loose woman living under his roof.

'Those were the worst days of my life,' she said. 'No matter how much I begged, he'd not listen to me. Stubborn as a mule he was. Said she should leave rather than bring shame on the name of Yellering.

'It broke my heart when she left. I never forgave him and he knew it, but he was too proud to go back on his word. Angela loved her father and, though he wouldn't admit it, I think he loved her more than the others.'

'What happened to your daughter, Mrs Yellering?'

'She went away. She said she loved the man and wanted to have his child. Told me she'd go up north and find where he was working. She said she knew he'd marry her.' The woman heaved a heavy sigh. 'I remember the day she left this house as if it were yesterday. She looked so bonny. She was wearing the green dress I'd trimmed with ribbon, the matching bonnet too. I watched her walking down the road, a suitcase packed with her clothes and special things in one hand, a purse with money in the other. I made sure of that.'

'Did you ever see your daughter again?'

'No. That was the last time.'

'And what of the young man?'

Mrs Yellering sipped her tea. 'He came

back a year later looking for Angela. He was a nice young fellow. He'd been busy working up north and had built himself a small carting business. He was doing well. Wasn't a vagrant after all but even so, I was surprised my husband didn't take to him with the pitchfork. But by that time the fight had gone from him. Seeing the young man again dashed our hopes. We'd prayed she'd gone to live with him, but when he turned up, we knew our worst fears had been realized.'

'You considered something untoward had happened?'

'What other could we think? Deep down, I knew she wasn't coming home.'

'And the young man?'

'He didn't know she'd headed off in search of him. Never even knew she was with child. He looked for her for years, travelling round Yorkshire, hoping he might bump into her somewhere. Eventually he stopped looking, sold his business and bought himself a small house in the next village. Angela never did return and we could only guess what fate had befallen her.'

The old woman looked into Charles Ogilvy's damp eyes. 'Do you bring news of my daughter?'

'I do,' he said. 'Your daughter died twenty-one years ago in Leeds. She was run down by a coach on the road.'

The woman sniffed as her head nodded. 'I always thought it, but I never gave up hope that one day she'd walk through that door. Alphonso, my husband, God rest his soul, went to his grave a few years later. He rued the day he'd sent her off. I'm sure it was a broken heart which took him.'

'Mrs Yellering, I spoke of a handkerchief. Did your daughter have one with her when she left here?'

'She did indeed; in fact, she had two. She carried her own in her pocket. It was something she always had with her, though she never used. That handkerchief was a keepsake she would never part with. It was more than twenty years old by then.'

'And the second one?'

'Brand new. I'd made it especially for her unborn child. I remember giving it to her and watching her fold it neatly. It was the last thing she laid in her case before she closed it.'

'Dear lady, that child was born. It survived the accident,' he said. 'You have a grand-daughter. Her name is Amy and she is living in South America.'

The tears that flowed had been held for over twenty years. Mr Ogilvy sat patiently beside her and held her hand.

'May I ask what happened to the young

man who was the infant's father?'

'His name is David Bliss. He is a gentle, quiet man. He lives in the next village only a few miles from here. Seven years ago he married a local girl and now they have three daughters.

'But please,' she begged, 'tell me about Amy. I want to hear her story.'

23

Valparaiso, Chile, 1901

From the house, perched on the edge of the cliff, Amy stood at the window gazing out across the bay to the vastness of the blue Pacific Ocean. She'd watched the sky change slowly from mauve to rays of burning orange, as the ball of sun slipped into the sea. The Chilean coast certainly boasted the most magnificent sunsets she'd ever seen.

Beside their residence on the cliff top, elegant tall houses vied for the best views over the extensive panorama. Standing like candles decorating a cake, each building was different, reflecting the builders' origins — French, German, English, Swiss. A kaleidoscope of colour, shape and style.

Below, on the narrow strip of coastal land, the busy port of Valparaiso bustled with the trade of foreign ships thankful to make port after battling the Horn. Captains were anxious to make repairs while the seamen were eager to challenge their land legs in the taverns before embarking on the voyage north. New immigrants arrived tired but excited to be stepping foot in their new land. For other ships the storms of the Southern Ocean awaited. But once safely through the Magellan Strait, they would be heading home to Europe and to England.

Glancing left, Amy's eyes were attracted to the graceful movement of the great funicular as it began its descent across the cliff face. She watched it sliding like a sled on snow to the city streets where waving palms and historic Spanish buildings were testament to Chile's Iberian background. The ascensor, Cerro Artillería, was the longest in Valparaiso. Others were steeper.

'I love this view,' she said, as Harold joined her in the sitting room. 'I love to watch the sailing ships drifting over the ocean. They're like balls of fluff rolling across a floor when a draught blows.' She sighed. 'Sadly we are seeing less and less of them. Now it's the trails of smoke drifting from passing steam ships. It reminds me of the soot and ash which poured from the mill chimneys in the West Riding. How things are changing.'

'And if the canal they are planning in Panama is ever cut this port will suffer, but what a feat of engineering it will be. Imagine a canal broad enough to carry the huge steam ships which you mention.'

Amy thought back to the canal at Saltaire.

'Things are changing,' he said. 'But for the better, and these are exciting times we live in.'

'They are indeed,' she said, turning her face from the window. 'Why are you smiling like that, Harry, dear?'

'We have a letter,' he said. 'You will excuse me for opening it but it was addressed to both of us.'

'From England? Is it from Ben?'

'No,' he said, handing the large envelope to her. 'It's from Charles.'

She smiled. 'I think every ship that sails from England must carry at least one letter from Mr Ogilvy. How is he?'

'He is well and his fundraising for the orphanage is keeping him busy. But it is a long letter and you must read it all.'

Amy sat down at the rosewood table, slid the pages from the envelope and began:

My dearest friends

Sincere congratulations on the birth of your second child. I am delighted to hear that young Joel is doing well. It seems like no more than a few months ago that I was with you in Saltaire celebrating your marriage.

How quickly the years fly by!

I read with interest that you are considering travelling to the United States and wish you well. I wonder if we will ever see you back in Leeds again.

When you left England three years ago, Amy said she would miss the friends she had left here, but, as neither of you had family in this country, it was unlikely you would return to these shores.

Before I go on, let me divulge to you a pastime of mine which may sound a little strange. For many years, I have taken an interest, nay, delight, in wandering around graveyards reading the epitaphs on tombstones. It was on one of my recent expeditions that I made a startling discovery.

Last week when I was in Berkshire on business, I happened to visit the tiny village of Hettersley. It was here I discovered a family by the name of Yellering.

Enclosed is a letter from a dear lady I met there . . .

Without finishing the letter, Amy reached for the envelope. It was empty.

'I was saving it,' Harold said, revealing another letter he had concealed behind his back. After handing it to her, he placed his hand gently on her shoulder, leaned forward and kissed her hair.

Amy smiled at her husband and squeezed

the envelope between her fingers. It was soft and fairly thick. Opening it, she took out a sheet of writing paper in which a small package was enclosed. It was wrapped in plain brown paper.

'You must read the letter before you open it,' Harold said.

She looked puzzled and read:

My Dearest Amy

My name is Phoebe Yellering and I am your grandmother.

Let me explain. Over forty years ago, I gave birth to a daughter. Her name was Angela. When she was almost twenty-two, she left home. I have never heard from her again, but now I learn she had a child and that you are her daughter.

To hear this news, after so long, has been the most wonderful gift any woman could receive. I can never thank Charles Ogilvy enough for giving this to me.

He also told me you are married and have two young children — my great-grandchildren. I am enclosing a small traditional gift for each of them which I send with my fondest affection.

Without reading more, Amy laid the letter on the table and reached for the soft package.

Within the wrappings she found two cotton handkerchiefs, each edged with lace and folded neatly. She opened one and laid it on the table.

In gold thread, embroidered in one corner was her name in bold capitals: AMY. On the opposite corner the outline of a stallion was sewn in blue silk.

Harold slid his arm around her as tears glazed her eyes.

'I don't understand,' she said. 'It's the same as my mother's old handkerchief. How is it possible?'

'You will understand when you have finished Charles's letter,' he said. 'But let me read the rest of your grandmothers' message to you.'

She handed it to him and listened.

Amy, dear, you cannot believe how excited the family were to hear of your existence. I wept when I learned of the dreadful times you have been through but am pleased to hear your life has changed now you are married.

Though you are not aware of it, you have aunts and uncles, cousins, and three half sisters all living here in Hettersley. And David Bliss, your dear father, is longing with all his heart to see you.

I hope one day, you and your good husband will come home to England so all the family can meet you.

Pray God I will live long enough to see that happen.

Your loving grandmother
Phoebe Yellering

Amy held the handkerchief to her heart. She didn't want to wet it on her tears.

'Perhaps we can go back to England and visit them,' she said.

'I'll make enquiries about a passage in the morning.'

'Oh, Harold,' she said, resting her head against him. 'Just imagine, I will be going home to meet my father. What a wonderful thing that is to look forward to.'

'You have waited a long time for it,' he said.

Amy closed her eyes to the tears and smiled.

We do hope that you have enjoyed reading this large print book.

Did you know that all of our titles are available for purchase?

We publish a wide range of high quality large print books including:
Romances, Mysteries, Classics
General Fiction
Non Fiction and Westerns

Special interest titles available in large print are:
The Little Oxford Dictionary
Music Book
Song Book
Hymn Book
Service Book

Also available from us courtesy of Oxford University Press:
Young Readers' Dictionary
(large print edition)
Young Readers' Thesaurus
(large print edition)

For further information or a free brochure, please contact us at:
Ulverscroft Large Print Books Ltd.,
The Green, Bradgate Road, Anstey,
Leicester, LE7 7FU, England.
Tel: (00 44) **0116 236 4325**
Fax: (00 44) **0116 234 0205**

Other titles published by
The House of Ulverscroft:

THE TWISTING VINE

Margaret Muir

In Yorkshire, Lucy Oldfield works as a maid at Heaton Hall. But when Lord Farnley's daughter dies, a shadow is cast over its future . . . Feeling insecure and unable to overcome temptation, Lucy steals an expensive French doll from her dead mistress. When the Hall is put up for sale and the staff dismissed, Lucy returns to Leeds. There, she falls victim to the deceit of an admirer, finding herself with a child to support. And then a chance meeting with a gentleman on a train leads to an offer that appears to be too good to be true . . . But will Lucy find herself subjected to even more heartache?

SEA DUST

Margaret Muir

After the death of her youngest child, Emma's life is in ruins. To survive she must escape from her abusive husband and bury the guilt from her past. And then an encounter with a French seaman on the Whitby cliff top provides the opportunity. She can sail to Australia, but must risk being a stowaway on the *Morning Star* . . . Following a vicious attack by one of the crew, Emma is nursed back to health by Charles Witton. As the turbulent sea around them mirrors Emma's emotional conflicts, the ship reaches Cape Town Bay — where disaster lies in wait.

SARAH'S FORTUNE

Mary Street

Coming from a large family and under-standing the virtues of economy, Sarah had no opinion of marrying just for love. But living with her rich relations at Kilburn Hall, she came to appreciate the comforts money could buy. James Foster was crippled, and not handsome, but Sarah was quick to accept his marriage proposal: it promised a life of wealth and consequence. Sarah never believed herself to be of any importance to her wealthy cousin Thomas. So why was he unwilling to accept the situation? And what would happen if James himself came to resent her motives for accepting him?

THE GENTLE WIND'S CARESS

Anne Whitfield

After the deaths of her mother and sister, Isabelle Gibson and her brother are left to fend for themselves in a workhouse. However, when the matron's son attempts to rape her, Isabelle escapes him by marrying Farrell, a moorland farmer. But he's a drunkard and in a constant feud with his landlord, Ethan Harrington. When Farrell bungles a robbery and deserts her, Isabelle and Ethan are thrown together, but both are married and must hide their growing love. Meanwhile, when faces from the past return to haunt her, a tragedy is set to strike that will change their lives forever.

THE COUNTESS AND THE MINER

Olga Sinclair

Countess Anastasia and Irena, a peasant girl, were worlds apart, but when Duncan MacRaith learned that Lord Eveson had raped Irena, he rushed to the big house intent on revenge. Now, with Eveson's departure, the Countess finds him a welcome diversion in her unhappy marriage, and the pair talk, drink vodka and lose all inhibitions. The Countess and Irena both become pregnant, but Irena fears that Eveson had fathered her baby. And then war breaks out in Russia and Duncan disappears whilst serving on the front lines. Irena must battle to find him and a future for herself.